Edward S. Ellis

The Life of Colonel David Crockett

comprising his adventures as backwoodsman and hunter

Edward S. Ellis

The Life of Colonel David Crockett
comprising his adventures as backwoodsman and hunter

ISBN/EAN: 9783337339869

Printed in Europe, USA, Canada, Australia, Japan

Cover: Foto ©Andreas Hilbeck / pixelio.de

More available books at **www.hansebooks.com**

COLONEL DAVID CROCKETT:

COMPRISING

HIS ADVENTURES AS BACKWOODSMAN AND HUNTER; HIS
SERVICES AS SOLDIER AND SCOUT IN THE CREEK
WAR ; HIS ELECTIONEERING CANVASSES ; HIS
CAREER AS CONGRESSMAN ; HIS TOUR
THROUGH THE NORTHERN STATES;
AND HIS SERVICES AND DEATH
IN THE TEXAN WAR OF
INDEPENDENCE.

TO WHICH ARE ADDED

SKETCHES OF GENERAL SAM HOUSTON, GENERAL SANTA
ANNA, REZIN P. AND COLONEL JAMES BOWIE.

By EDWARD S. ELLIS,

AUTHOR OF "THE LIFE OF COLONEL DANIEL BOONE," "NED IN THE BLOCK-
HOUSE," "NED IN THE WOODS." ETC.

PHILADELPHIA:

PORTER & COATES.

PREFACE.

"MAKE room for Colonel Crockett!" said the usher at the White House, one evening, when the famous Congressman from the backwoods presented himself with a number of other callers.

"Colonel Crockett makes room for himself!" was the exclamation of the Member as he strode into the room.

The incident is typical of the man. Gifted by nature with an exhaustless fund of humor, born to privation, hardship and labor, trained, not in the school of books, but in the severer one of experience, he exhibited true manliness, honesty and bravery in all his words and actions.

Colonel Crockett lacked the refinements which a truer education would have given him: he said and did things which cannot be held up as models for the youth of to-day; but a profound sense of justice and of devotion to right permeated his entire life. Rough and uncultured though he was, his career contains much that is commendable and worthy of imitation. His moral heroism was displayed in his defiance of the vast powers of President Jackson when political ruin was the almost inevitable consequence. Of no man can it more truly be said that he preferred being right to being President. His personal daring was shown on many a battle-field; in the dim woods, when, single-handed, he encountered the savage bear; in the swamps, when struggling against malaria, starvation, and the wily Creek warrior; when coursing on his mustang over the Texan prairie and pursued by the fierce Comanche; and when, day after day and night after night, he loaded and fired his deadly rifle from within the sulphurous walls of the Alamo, while Santa Anna and his hosts closed about him and his fellow-patriots in a circle of flame and fire, and when, panting, begrimed and bloody, he stood with the handful of survivors until he saw, like a lightning-flash, the treachery of the Mexican dictator, and, making a last desperate rush, with his drawn bowie-knife, he perished when within a pace of the traitor. Not a defender lived to tell the story of the sublime defence of the Alamo. Neither ancient nor modern history affords a grander exhibition of heroism than was shown on that crimson day when the blood of the Spartan band became the seed from which sprang Texan independence.

Who has ever stood with bared head, and read without a quicker heart-throb, those words chiseled in the cenotaph in the Texan capital, and since destroyed by fire?—

"THERMOPYLÆ HAD ITS MESSENGER OF DEFEAT: THE ALAMO HAD NONE!"

CONTENTS.

CHAPTER I.

CHAPTER XIX.

CHAPTER XX.

CHAPTER XXI.

CHAPTER XXII.

CHAPTER XXIII.

CHAPTER XXIV.

CHAPTER XXV.

THE LIFE

OF

COLONEL DAVID CROCKETT.

CHAPTER I.

Birth of David Crockett—His Parents—Engages to a German
Drover—His Return—Difficulties at School—Runs Away—
Return of the Prodigal—Devotion to his Father.

DAVID CROCKETT was born August 17, 1786, in
Rogersville, the county-seat of Hawkins County,
Tennessee. His grandparents were Irish, who settled at first in Pennsylvania, afterward removed
to North Carolina, and then to East Tennessee,
where both were killed by Indians.   ·

John Crockett, the son, was born either in Ireland or on the passage across the ocean. He
served through the Revolutionary war, and after its
close married Miss Mary Hawkins, a native of
Maryland, who lived between Baltimore and York.
David was the fifth child in a family of six sons
and three daughters. At the time of his birth the
father of David lived at the mouth of the Lime-
stone, on the Nolachucky River. He was in poor

circumstances, and his children received little advantages in the way of school education.

While the subject of our sketch was still a boy his parents settled at a point ten miles above Greenville, in the same county. They remained there a short time, and then, as may be said, they were literally washed out.

When David was about eight years of age, his father opened a tavern on the road from Abingdon to Knoxville. The house of entertainment was a third-rate one, and David says by the time he was twelve years old he learned very well the meaning of "hard times, and plenty of them."

One evening a German who was moving his earthly possessions from Knox County to Rockbridge, Virginia, stopped at the little inn by the wayside with his herd of cattle, and he and the landlord had quite a long talk together. The result was the boy was hired out to accompany the German to help take care of his kine.

David set out with a heavy heart, but the German treated him kindly, gave him good wages and tried to persuade him not to go back home at all. The boy had been so trained in obedience at home that he thought his employer had made some such an agreement with his father and it would not do to refuse. He therefore gave his assent, and stayed with the German several weeks.

One day he recognized several wagons that were going by as belonging to his neighborhood in Tennessee, and the homesick boy applied to one of the teamsters to take him home. The man told him that he was going to stay overnight at a tavern seven miles farther on, but, if he should reach that point before daylight, he would give him permis-sion to ride with him.

The boy cautiously gathered his clothing. in a bundle, put it under his bed, and was so fearful of being late at the appointed place that he rose when it was shortly past midnight. As he stole out-doors he found it had been snowing hard for sev-eral hours. With nothing to guide him but the glimpses of the timber, he pushed forward with that resolution which was such a marked feature of his character in after-life.

The snow continued falling rapidly, and by and by the boy found it to his knees; but he trudged steadily forward through the whirling flakes and blinding darkness, with no thought of turning back. The highway was shut in by timber on each side, and this was the only means of guidance the homesick lad could have, for the road itself was covered with snow to such a depth that not the slightest trace of it could be seen. The only consolation he had was the thought that his tracks would be covered too deeply for his German em-ployer, from whom he was running away, to follow him.

Seven miles of such traveling is severe enough in the dead of night over a lonely road, but the boy kept it up, until finally, through the eddying flakes and darkness, he caught the starlight twinkle of a light. It seemed to him that he had gone three times as far as the distance named by his friend ; so he gave a great sigh, sure he was at his destination at last.

It still lacked an hour of daylight when he reached the inn, but the wagoner was stirring and making ready to start. The half-frozen lad was taken in by the fire, thoroughly warmed, given a good breakfast, and the long journey of four hundred miles began. David kept with him until his impatience became too great over the slowness of his horses, when he started ahead on foot. With some assistance from other friends, he reached home in safety. Parents, brothers and sisters were delighted to see the loved one, who had been gone long enough to make it seem as if he had reappeared from another world.

At this time David Crockett had no knowledge of his letters, and little prospect of ever gaining any. The educational facilities in the backwoods three-quarters of a century ago were not calculated to make very profound scholars. However, there was a small school in the neighborhood, to which he was sent by his father. He attended faithfully for four days, and was just beginning to learn something of the mysteries of the alphabet, when he got into a difficulty with a large boy. After school-hours David hid in the bushes and waited for him. He was considerably older than our hero, but the latter soon compelled him to cry for mercy.

Knowing that the teacher would be sure to adjust the matter on the first opportunity, David, instead of going to school the next day, hid in the woods. He repeated his truancy, until the teacher sent a note to his father inquiring the cause of the boy's absence. This brought out the truth, and the parent started his son to school; and, to make certain he would be there promptly, he kept at his heels with a stout hickory swinging in his hand. David got beyond sight of his angry parent, and hid in the bushes until all danger was past. He was now afraid to go to school or to return home, for he knew that severe punishment awaited him at each place. In his dilemma, he made his way to the house of a neighbor who was on the point of starting for Virginia with a drove of cattle. An elder brother had already hired out to him, and David himself easily secured an engagement. He accompanied the drove through Abingdon, Lynchburg, Orange Court-House, and Charlottesville to Front Royal, where his employer sold out his drove to a man who was not so indulgent to the lad.

David started home with a brother of the original owner, there being one horse between them. The man kept the horse continually, while the boy did all the walking. He tired of this after a while, and they parted company.

David hired himself to another wagoner, and was moving farther away from home when he met his brother, who tried hard to persuade him to go back to his relatives. David shed tears, for he was deeply attached to them all, but his terror of the whipping awaiting him at the hands of his master and father was too great to face, and he refused. He now drifted aimlessly about for months. He hired out at Gerardstown, while his employer went to Alex-

andria for a "back-load," as it is called.   The boy
stayed there until the succeeding spring, when he
decided to go to Baltimore to see whether there
was not some opening for him.

On the way thither he engaged himself to a
wagoner, and, naturally enough, when in the Mon-
umental city drifted to the wharves, where he wandered among the ships lying in the dock.   He was
a ruddy, powerful boy with a bright, pleasing face,
though disposed to be wild in his ways.   One of
the captains made such a flattering proposal that
he agreed to go to sea with him, and started back
for his clothes.

The wagoner, however, was very angry when he
heard of the boy's intention, threatened to lock him
up, and kept such a close watch upon him that he
could get no chance to leave.

Had the wagoner consented, how different might
have been the life and career of David Crockett!

He experienced the usual rough usage of boys in
his situation for the succeeding months, until again
the longing for home came over him.   He determined to go back at all hazards.   He toiled hard;
and when he had gathered a little money, he
hastened impatiently forward, until he came to the
stream known as New River, where the water was
so rough that no one was willing to put him across.
He did his best to persuade some of the more skilful watermen to make the attempt, but no one would
agree to do it; and, with that same energy and resolution which ever distinguished him, he sprang into
the canoe and headed for the other shore.

The voyage was a difficult and a dangerous one. Brave as was the lad, he confessed that more than once he would have given the world, had it been his, to place his foot on dry land. Try his utmost, he could not keep the water out of the boat, and it seemed at times that he could not advance a foot. But at last, wet to the skin, shivering with cold, and thoroughly exhausted, he ran the boat ashore and sprang out. He had been carried full two miles out of his course, but he was overjoyed to find that the difficult passage was made at last.

The wearied boy was now nearing his home, and his heart was stirred as never before. He remembered the severe whipping from which he ran away, but his love for his parents, brothers and sisters overweighed everything else, and he was resolved to meet them with the least possible delay.

It was late at night when he came in sight of the little tavern where his folks lived, and the heart of the young runaway beat high with emotion at the prospect of seeing them again.

Were they all there? Were they alive and well? Had they given him up for dead? What would they say when he should appear among them? Would his father forgive the disobedience of his terrified child? Did they believe he had become such a wanderer over the earth that he himself would forget them, and never show his face among them again? These were some of the questions which presented themselves to the mind of the

boy as he timidly approached his old home, specu-
lating as to what his reception would be.

There is something touching in the action of the
runaway boy, as told by himself. He noticed that
several wagons were standing outside, showing that
the old-fashioned inn was not without its quota of
guests. The lad was fearful of venturing in until
he saw through the window his brothers and sisters
taking their places at the table; then he insinuated
himself among them, and, without being noticed—
for it will be remembered that the Crockett family
was a large one—he began handling knife and
fork as in the olden times. Suddenly the elder
sister recognized her long-lost brother in the large,
muscular, blushing boy at the table. She sprang
up, and, rushing to where he was seated, threw her
arms about his neck, exclaiming—

"It is Davy! It is Davy!"

Everything was confusion. There was a scram-
ble to get at the prodigal son who was lost, but was
found—who was dead, but was alive again. The
runaway felt as though he was an ungrateful dog
to have remained away so long, and that, had he
to go through the same trial again, he would brave
a hundred whippings rather than offend such loving
parents.

There was nothing said of the punishment from
which he had fled, and which was due him, but the
shameful truth remained that David Crockett was
fifteen years old, was growing fast, and yet did not
know a half-dozen letters of the alphabet. He
found his father very much burdened with debt,

for his income was small, and his family large.   To
one neighbor he owed thirty-six dollars, and saw
no prospect of being able to pay it.   In his strait
he applied to Davy, telling him that if he would
work out the note, he would give up all claim himself to his services.

It was characteristic of young Crockett's nature
that he was sincerely attached to his relatives, for
he instantly accepted the proposal, and, going to the
house of the neighbor, began work, and kept it up
for six months without losing a day.   All this time
the place itself was disagreeable to the boy, for it
was the resort of gamblers and drinking men ; and
when his employer made a proposition to hire him
upon the expiration of his term, he refused.   He
went to the house of a Quaker, fifteen miles distant,
where he experienced no trouble in effecting an
engagement, for the lad was strong and skilful.
The Quaker agreed to give him quite liberal wages,
but David had been to work only a short time,
when he showed him a note of his father for forty
dollars, proposing to surrender it to the boy if he
would work six months.   David might well have
asked how long this kind of business was to be continued, but he accepted the proposal, and, as before, he toiled early and late for half a year, at the
end of which time the Quaker surrendered the evidence of indebtedness to him.

During all this time the youth had purposely
kept away from his home; but, with the note in
his possession, he now rode over to the inn one
Sunday evening; and when all the family were

gathered together in the little dining-room, the son took out the note and handed it to his father.

The latter supposed it was presented for collection, and was quite depressed, saying he had no money, and he could see no earthly probability of ever being able to pay it.

Then it was that David, with his heart swelling with happiness, told him the truth. The father was so delighted that he could not keep back the tears, and the son himself felt he had been more than repaid for all his toil and self-sacrifice.

CHAPTER II.

Crockett's School Education—Disappointment in Love—His
Marriage and Removal to Lincoln County—Breaking out of
the War of 1812—Weatherford, the noted War Chief of the
Creeks—Massacre of Fort Mimms—Weatherford's Surrender
to General Jackson—His Famous Speech—Crockett becomes
a Soldier.

DAVID CROCKETT showed his good sense by
making a determined effort to acquire the rudiments of a common school education, for he was
fast approaching manhood, and was still ignorant
of his letters.

He continued to work for the Quaker, who had a
son teaching a mile or so distant, and the boy proposed that he should attend his school four days in
the week, and work the other two to pay for his
board. The Quaker agreed to the proposition, and
David Crockett bent all his energies to study
during the time he could secure for the succeeding
six months.

He possessed much natural ability, and learned
to read and write, and acquired a knowledge of the
elements of arithmetic. These six months com-
prehended all the schooling he ever received in his
life.

Thus matters progressed until Crockett was
eighteen years old, when his next notable proceeding was that of falling in love. The lady of his

choice accepted him, and everything went well, until a few days before the one appointed for the wedding, when Crockett received the astounding information that his affianced was only trifling with him, and that she had completed arrangements for marrying another on the succeeding day.

This was a staggering blow to Crockett, but it was fortunate for him. Such a woman could never have made a good wife; beside which, he was too young to take the care of a family on his hands.

It should be stated that during these years, Crockett was laying the foundation of one phase of his education, to which in after years he owed a great deal of his fame. He was fond of wandering through the woods with his rifle, and became known as one of the most successful of contestants at the various shooting matches. He spent a great deal of his time in hunting for game, and with great success.

Thus the months passed, and it was not long before Crockett forgot his love disappointment in the fascination found in the company of a vivacious young Irish girl, living with her parents some miles away. He became very attentive to her, and though the mother was strongly opposed to the match, she finally gave in, and the young couple were married.*

* Davy Crockett's marriage is on record in Weakley County, Tennessee, as follows: "Davy Crockett, with Thomas Dogett, security, binds himself in a bond of twelve hundred and fifty dollars to Gov. John Sevier, Aug. 1, 1806, to marry Polly Finlay."

The marriage of a young person marks an era in his or her life, and Crockett realized that he had taken a serious step.

He was poor, and his wife's dowry amounted to little; but both were young, strong, hopeful, and industrious. She owned a wheel and was a skillful weaver, while he was capable and glad to work with the sturdy arms which nature gave him. Further, his skill with his rifle occasionally brought something substantial; and, after all, it may be doubted whether Davy Crockett, amid all the honors which came to him in after years, enjoyed life more than when he began keeping house in his little log-cabin in Tennessee, with his pretty, young Irish wife.

Several years passed with hard toil and much happiness, for the two were devoted to each other, and worked hard. But they were obliged to pay high rents, and were unable to lay by anything for the proverbial rainy day. Crockett plainly saw that a change must be made, if he meant to rise to any station above the very low one he then occupied. Two sons had been born to him, and he was as poor in worldly possessions as when he began housekeeping.

In looking around for some more suitable place to live, Crockett's attention was drawn to the duck and elk country. When he decided to try it, his father-in-law agreed to go with him, and the two families emigrated across the mountains, and settled in Lincoln County on the head of the Mulberry Fork of Elk River.

One most pleasing discovery was speedily made

by Crockett—the country was especially rich in game, and he found enjoyable sport in ranging through the wood for bears, deer, wild turkeys, and smaller targets for his unerring rifle.

It was while living in this place, and when some twenty-three or four years of age, that Crockett became still more noted for his great skill with the rifle. He was what is called a "dead-shot," and there were none of his neighbors—many of whom were famous marksmen—who could hold their own in a trial with him.

Many of his famous bear adventures befell him while living in this section; and a certain abrupt, uneducated wit, and readiness of speech—natural to him—rendered him popular with his neighbors, who were of that class best qualified to appreciate such qualities.

Here Crockett lived, spending his time in hunting and working for his growing family, until the breaking out of the war of 1812. The reader is well aware of the powerful efforts which the great Tecumseh, one of the most eloquent geniuses and remarkable men ever produced by the American race, made to unite the Indians of the South against the settlers who were so rapidly occupying their lands. The fire of Tecumseh's oratory set the Southern tribes aflame, and his bursts of eloquence were as thrilling as any of those of the world-famed Demosthenes or Cicero.

Among those who were won over by the wonderful power of Tecumseh was Weatherford, one of the leading Creek chiefs. There is reason to believe that if he had entered upon Tecumseh's plans at once, he would have been able to overrun the entire Mississippi Territory; but his hesitation allowed the favorable opportunity to pass forever from him.

The most noted and lamentable incident connected with the Creek War was what is known as the Massacre at Fort Mimms by Weatherford at the head of a large body of Creek warriors. General Claiborne was so confident that Fort Mimms was the objective point of Weatherford, that he ordered the construction of two additional blockhouses, and cautioned the garrison very impressively of the danger which threatened them.

Shortly after, General Claiborne set out with his command for Fort Early, the most advanced post in the Indian country. On the way, he again wrote Major Beasley, commandant at Fort Mimms, warning him of the certainty of an attack.

The general named the dangerous and merciless Weatherford as the chief who was most likely to assault them. On the next day, after this letter was received, the dreaded sachem appeared before the fort at the head of fifteen hundred Creek warriors.

As was usually the case along the frontier, the appearance of this formidable body was much in the nature of a surprise, despite the warning received the day previous.

It is said that the first notice was brought into the fort by a small negro boy who reported that the "woods were full of them," that is, of Indians.

He would have been whipped to break him of the habit of telling shameful falsehoods, had not his words proven true a very few minutes afterwards.

The gate, in accordance with the law of the border, was open and unguarded; and, in an instant, the Indians began swarming through it. Major Beasley was a brave man, and he quickly rallied his garrison to repel them.

The garrison consisted of two hundred and seventy-five, of whom only one hundred and sixty were soldiers; the rest being old men, women, and children. Instantly began and raged for a quarter of an hour one of the most fearful hand-to-hand encounters that it is possible for the human mind to conceive. Tomahawks, swords, knives, bayonets, pistols—these were the weapons used by the infuriated combatants, as with shout and yell and panting countenances, they fought like so many tigers, striving to get at the throat of each other.

Where the Indians were nearly ten to one, and where they had gained the usual advantage over the whites by outwitting them, the result could not be doubtful.

The garrison fought like Spartans ; one officer fell badly wounded, and was carried by two women to the nearest block-house. In a few minutes he revived, and insisted on being carried back to the gate where the struggle was going on, for he knew that every arm was needed there.

The same heroines carried him back, and he died at his post of duty shortly afterward.

Every officer of the garrison was killed fighting at the gate.

By this time nearly all the soldiers were dead or dying, and the survivors, with the women and children, hurried into one of the block-houses, which they determined to defend to the last. But the Indians succeeded in setting fire to it, and then, ranging themselves outside, they shot down the frantic defenders who preferred such a fate to that of being burned to death.

Of the entire garrison, only seventeen escaped; and most of them were badly wounded. It is estimated that the Creek chief lost more than one-fourth of his entire band. Major Beasley was one of the wounded who was burned to death in the block-house.

It was this dreadful massacre which gave rise to the Creek war. It took place August 30, 1813, and aroused such indignation and such imperative calls for punishment throughout the country, that two powerful armies were organized and sent into the hostile territory to break forever the Indian power.

The savages, appreciating fully these formidable preparations, saw that their conquest was inevitable, and hastened to propose terms of peace. To test their sincerity, General Jackson ordered them to bring in their great war chief Weatherford, bound, and a prisoner.

Shortly after the demand was made, an Indian strode into the tent of General Jackson, and with a proud, defiant air, said—

"I am Weatherford, the chief who commanded at the capture of Fort Mimms; I desire peace for my people, and have come to ask it."

General Jackson was amazed, for it was his intention to execute the sachem when he should be brought in a prisoner, but he was taken aback when the savage ventured into his presence in this bold manner.

"I am surprised that you should come here," said the officer, "for I know your inhuman conduct at Fort Mimms. You deserve death."

In answer to this, Weatherford made his famous reply:

"I am in your power; do with me as you please; I am a soldier; I have done the whites all the harm I could; I have fought them, and fought them bravely; if I had an army I would yet fight; I would contend to the last; my people are all gone; I can only weep over the misfortunes of my nation."

No man could appreciate true bravery more than did "Old Hickory," the hero of New Orleans. He was so struck with the words and manner of his noted visitor, that he said:

"I expected you to be brought bound into my presence, and you deserve death, but I will take no advantage over you; you are at liberty to depart unmolested; you may place yourself at the head of your war party again, and fight us as hard as you please, but if you fall into our hands, you will receive no mercy. The only safety for you and your people is in unconditional submission."

With the dignity and indignation of Tecumseh himself, the talented half-breed chief made answer, "You can safely address me in such terms now. There was a time, when I could have answered you—there was a time, when I had a choice—I have none now. I have not even a hope. I could once animate my warriors to battle; but I cannot animate the dead! My warriors can no longer hear my voice; their bones are at Talladega, Tallushatchie, Emuckfaw and Tohopeka. I have not surrendered myself without thought. While there was a single chance of success I never left my post, nor supplicated for peace. But my people are now gone, and I ask it for my nation and not for myself. I look back with deep sorrow, and wish to avert still greater calamities. If I had been left to contend with the Georgia army, I would have raised my corn on one bank of the river, and fought them on the other. But your people have destroyed my nation; you are a brave man; I rely upon your generosity; you will exact no terms of a conquered people that it would shame them to submit to. Whatever they may be, it would be madness and folly for me to oppose them. If they are opposed, you shall find me among the sternest enforcers of obedience. Those who would still hold out can only be influenced by a mean spirit of revenge. To do this, they would need to sacrifice the last remnant of their country, but they shall not. You have told our nation where they may go and be safe. Your talk is good talk, and they shall listen to it."

Weatherford was allowed to withdraw unmolested, for the circumstances were such, that General Jackson would have scorned to take any advantage over him; but the war was not ended by any means, for however sincere the great chief may have been in his professions, his brother leaders were too revengeful to obey his counsels.

At the time of the breaking out of the Creek War, David Crockett was living ten miles below Winchester, and was about twenty-five years of age, with a sturdy, brave wife, and a growing family of children. When the news of the massacre at Fort Mimms came, it roused such a general war feeling, that Crockett determined to volunteer, though his wife begged him not to leave her.

He sought to convince her that it was his duty to go, for unless the Indians were summarily punished, they would soon overrun the country and murder her and the little ones in their homes. Still further, if every married man waited until his wife gave consent, he would never go to war at all.

Crockett's wife, seeing he was resolved on going, and knowing his determined nature, said no more, but shed a few bitter tears and went about her work.

Crockett made his way to Winchester, where the muster was called, and found there was great excitement among the people, the war fever running high.

The men were paraded and addressed by Lawyer Jones, who was afterwards a member of Congress

from Tennessee.   Crockett was one of the very
first to step out, and a company was quickly raised.
The term of enlistment was for sixty days, it being
the general belief that their services would not be
needed for a longer period.

Crockett went home, bade his wife and children
good-by, and mounting his horse, rode past Huntsville, and camped at a large spring called Beatty's
Spring.   There they stayed several days, while volunteers came in from every direction.

When the number reached thirteen hundred,
they were full of fight, and impatient to be led forward to the scene of hostilities.

CHAPTER III.

Major Gibson and Crockett on a Scout in the Creek Country—
Battle of Tallushatchie—Before Fort Taladega.

WHILE the volunteers were at the Spring, Major Gibson came to them, asking for some trustworthy scouts to accompany him across the Tennessee River into the Creek country, for the purpose of learning something definite of the movements of the Indians.

He wished two of the best woodsmen and rifle-men. Crockett was immediately pointed out as one who would follow the major as far as he dare lead, and possibly would then take the lead himself.

Major Gibson was pleased with Crockett, who was a splendid picture of physical manhood, and asked him to select his companion. This was done, and the major directed both to be ready to leave on the following morning.

The start was made at an early hour, the party consisting of thirteen, all mounted, and with their camp equipage. Each was aware he was going upon a dangerous expedition, but all were resolute men, who were glad of the prospect of something exciting in their experience, and they rode along in high spirits.

Striking the river at a point known as Ditto's Landing, they crossed and penetrated about seven miles, where they went into camp for the night. They had scarcely done so, when a well-known Indian trader who was familiar with that section joined them, and agreed to act as their guide.   .

It was decided in the morning by Major Gibson to divide the party, as they were more likely to gain the information they were seeking by this course than by keeping together. The separation was made, the major's party numbering seven, and that of Crockett six. The understanding was, that Gibson was to take a route leading him by the house of a friendly Cherokee known as Dick Brown, while Crockett, making a circuit, was to pass by the dwelling-place of the Indian's father. After the whites had picked up all the information they could, they were to meet at the junction of two roads, fifteen miles beyond.

The scouts were now in a most dangerous section, for the powerful Creek tribe was on the war-path, and their braves were roaming hither and thither, as fierce as so many tigers. Major Gibson and Crockett were close to their hunting-grounds, and, unless the utmost precaution was used, they were likely to be massacred to a man.

As yet, there was no reason to suspect the savages knew of the expedition, though the Indians were swarming so thickly about them it would seem there was scarcely a possibility that discovery would be long postponed.

When Crockett reached the house of the old Indian, he found a half-breed known as Jack Thompson, who promised to go with him. He was not ready to start at once, and the agreement was made that Crockett was to push his reconnoissance to the junction of the roads, where he would meet Major Gibson, and the half-breed would follow. As it was too dangerous to camp in the highway, Crockett told Thompson to give the hoot of an owl when he reached the fork, and he would answer him with the same signal, so as not to awaken the suspicion of any roving Creeks in the vicinity.

The point of meeting fixed upon was so far away, and it was so necessary to proceed with caution, that Crockett knew it would be dark before the two parties could meet.

The horsemen rode along at a guarded pace, seeing nothing of Indians; and, just as night was closing in, they reached the forks of the road, where Major Gibson promised to join them.

But the major and his men were invisible, nor did they show themselves during the hour Crockett waited for them. As it was too perilous to remain so near the road, the little party turned into a hollow, where they went into camp.

Everything was quiet and the scouts took care not to make any unnecessary noise that might reach hostile ears. The night was far advanced, and Crockett was half reclining upon the ground, when, through the stillness of the night, he heard what seemed to be the hooting of an owl.

"That's Thompson," he thought, as he answered the signal.

In a moment, the call sounded closer, and shortly after, the figure of the half-breed loomed to view

through the darkness. He had kept his appoint-
ment to pilot them as best he could through the
dangerous neighborhood.

Crockett wondered where Major Gibson could'
be: according to his own proposal the officer ought
to have reached the forks of the road before dusk;
but nothing was seen or heard of him, and when
morning dawned, he was still absent.

Crockett now told his men that he had come
over into the Creek country on purpose to hunt a
fight with the Indians, and he did not mean to go
back until he obtained it. Their ostensible purpose was to gain information of the movements of
the Creeks, and it would not do to return until
they should succeed.

His comrades agreed with him, and the little
party pushed to a Cherokee town about twenty
miles distant. Nothing was learned of any account, and Crockett rode to the home of a white
man who had married a Creek woman, and who
lived on the edge of the Creek nation.

There they found plenty of provisions for themselves and horses, but the man was very much agi-
tated over something. When Crockett asked him
to explain the trouble, he said, in accents of terror,
that within the preceding hour ten painted Creek
warriors had left his house, and they were likely to
return at any minute. If they should find the
white men there, they would kill every one of them
as well as the members of the family.

Crockett coolly informed his host that he had
come a long distance on purpose to hunt such par-

ties; and nothing would give him greater pleasure than to receive a call from those ten warriors, for there were just enough to insure an interesting skirmish.

The horrified white man said no more, and the dinner being finished, the party remounted and galloped toward the camp of some friendly Creeks, eight miles distant. It soon became dark, but the moon was at its full and the sky was clear. Should it become necessary to retreat, the horsemen, therefore, could travel as well at night as in the day-time.

They were pursuing their way in this fashion, when they encountered two negroes, who had been stolen by the Creeks, and were now riding away from them. They were able to talk the Indian tongue, and one was sent back to Ditto's Landing, while Crockett took the other with him, as he was likely to prove useful in their visit to the Creek camp.

When the latter was reached, Crockett found about forty warriors, squaws and their children. It was night, and by the light of a pine knot, he engaged in shooting with the bow and arrow, with the younger ones.

While the leader of the little company was thus employed, the negro was talking with the Creeks and picking up such news as he could. He speedily gained that which was anything but pleasant, for hurrying to the side of Crockett, he told him that the Creeks were in momentary expectation of the coming of a large war-party of their countrymen,

in which event the entire company would be killed
without mercy.

Crockett showed no more fear than on the former
occasion, but told the negro to say to the alarmed
Creeks, that if a hostile showed himself, he would
take his skin home to make a pair of moccasins.
The Creeks laughed aloud, and seemed to admire
the audacity of their visitor.

Everything went along peacefully until the night
was well advanced, when they lay down to sleep.
Some of the whites felt uneasy in their situation,
as there was undoubtedly reason for such misgiving, and the horses were kept saddled, so as to be
ready at an instant's call.

The leader was just sinking into a quiet sleep,
when he was roused by the most frightful scream
that ever pierced his ear. He did not comprehend
what it meant, but the negro did, and springing to
his side, he whispered that the war-party were
coming!

Crockett and his men were up in an instant, as
were all the Indians in camp. It proved that the
warrior who had uttered the terrifying scream was
a runner that had just come in with the tidings
that the Creeks had been crossing the Coosa all
day, near the Ten Islands, and they were gathering, or rather, moving forward to give General
Jackson battle.

This was most important tidings indeed, and
Crockett felt it his duty to make known the intelligence with the least possible delay.

The friendly Creeks were so frightened that they

immediately broke up camp, while Crockett and his companions started at a rapid gallop for the river crossing, which was over sixty miles distant.

They passed over most of the ground they had traversed in coming, and when they reached the Cherokee village they found it deserted, but large fires were burning, indicating that the country was full of Indians, and showing Crockett that it would not do to delay his return a single hour.

It was too perilous to stay where the fires were burning, and the party pushed on by moonlight, keeping in the shades of the woods. At daylight, they were within thirty miles of the camp of the army. A brief halt was made, their horses given a few mouthfuls, and they started again, for they carried important information, and the hours were beyond value.

Their steeds were forced to their utmost, and a short while before noon, camp was reached, and Crockett made his report to Colonel Coffee. The latter listened attentively, but his manner showed very plainly that he placed little faith in what was told him. He evidently regarded Crockett as possessing such slight experience and knowledge in these matters that he had been terrified out of his senses, and was telling what was suggested by his imagination, rather than his senses.

Crockett was angered, for, after such prodigious efforts as he had made to carry the news to the colonel, and conscious as he was of its importance, it was exasperating to be discredited. He said nothing, but he admits that he was so indignant that he had hard work to contain himself.

Major Gibson did not return until the next day. When he reported to the colonel, it was precisely to the same effect as was the report of Crockett, who was not appeased when he observed that Colonel Coffee for the first time credited the alarming news.

Extensive breastworks were immediately thrown up, and an express was sent to General Jackson at Fayetteville, urging him to advance at once to prevent the annihilation of Colonel Coffee and his command.

General Jackson responded with his usual energy, and, by making forced marches, reached camp next day. Some eight hundred of the volunteers, among whom was Crockett, were now sent back, crossing the Tennessee river and passing through Huntsville, so as to cross the stream at another place, in the hope of striking the Indians from an unexpected direction.

In fording the river at Melton's Bluff, they met with much difficulty, losing several of their horses, but they pressed vigorously forward, and finally reached Black Warrior's Town, standing upon the present site of Tuscaloosa, at one time the capital of Alabama.

The Indian town was quite extensive, but the warriors, as was expected, were gone, the trails showing that they had departed only in time to escape the approaching army.

The soldiers found an extensive field of corn and

a good supply in the cribs, including a large quantity of beans. All this was taken possession of, and the town burned; after which the soldiers set out to join the main body of troops. A good deal of marching followed, and, as the supplies of meat ran out, Crockett's rifle was called into play, and did much toward procuring supplies of the needed food.

The command marched to Camp Wills, and thence to Ten Islands on the Coosa, where they established a fort, and the spies were sent out to gather all information possible. Learning of an Indian town eight miles away, they proceeded to surround it. The Indians fought with much desperation, but were taken at great disadvantage, and the slaughter was frightful. The white soldiers, in some instances, were guilty of as great atrocities as were the Creeks at Fort Mimms. Crockett states that forty-six warriors, who were driven into one house, were burned to death, while an Indian woman who deliberately drew her bow and shot a lieutenant dead, was riddled by at least twenty bullets.

Crockett himself fought with characteristic intrepidity, being in the fight from the opening to the close.

This battle is generally known as that of Tallushatchee, in which the whites lost five killed, and forty-one wounded; while the Indian warriors were all slain, and the women and children taken prisoners.

The soldiers built Fort Strother, known sometimes as Ten Islands. Returning once more to camp, and joining General Jackson, the army suffered greatly for the want of provisions. All their meat was gone, and there seemed to be no means of obtaining more. This lasted for several days, when an Indian came into camp, late one night,· and asked for "Captain Jackson." He was immediately conducted to his tent, where he must have given important information, for within the succeeding hour, orders to march were issued. The Coosa river was crossed, and the army proceeded in the direction of Fort Taladega, which was occupied by friendly Creeks.

When near the station, the Americans found themselves confronted by eleven hundred warriors, the very flower of the Creek nation. They were all fully armed and impatient for the fight.

A couple of days before, they had encamped on the spot, and sent word to the Creek garrison that if they did not come out and fight with them, they would take the fort and put all to death. The frightened Indians asked three days in which to consider the matter, and improved the grace by sending a runner with the news to General Jackson, who was now approaching the battle-field.

CHAPTER IV.

The Battle of Taladega—A Narrow Escape from Ambush—
Frightful Slaughter—Want of Food—Mutiny of the Volun-
teers—Crockett returns Home, and Re-enlists—Joins Major
Russell's Spies—Attacked by the Indians at Night—Battle
of Enotochopko—Fife, the friendly Chief—Crockett returns
Home, and again Re-enlists—Before Pensacola—A Scouting
Expedition—Dangerous Ground.

FORT TALADEGA was garrisoned entirely, as we
have stated, by friendly Indians, whose message to
General Jackson was that they would be massacred
by the overwhelming body of Creeks in their front,
unless he sent them instant relief.

The fort stood about thirty miles from Ten
Islands, but General Jackson having encamped a
short way off, came in sight at daybreak. Of
course the spies of the Creeks discovered his advance, and were in communication with those in
the fort. They told the garrison that General
Jackson was approaching with a great many fine
horses, blankets, and guns; and that if they would
come out and join them, they would divide the
plunder between them. The friendly Creeks made
the promise to help them, when the battle was
ready to open.

General Jackson formed his plan of battle in the
same manner as that of the Spanish Armada of
old; but a portion of his command narrowly es-

caped an ambush—those terrible methods of war-
fare, which are always in favor with the Indians.

The Creeks being camped immediately about the
fort, Jackson's forces divided so as to surround
them, with a view of cutting off all escape. The
movement was completed without difficulty, and
Major Russell, with his company of spies, was sent
to open the battle.

As they approached the fort, the top was seen to
be lined with the friendly Indians who kept shouting, with frantic gestures.

" How do, brother? how do, brother?"

The sight was a curious one, for the warriors
were without clothing, and were painted a fiery
red. They kept leaping and saluting, until Major
Russell was past the fort, and moving toward the
Creeks beyond. Here the hostile warriors had
concealed themselves so skillfully that Russell suspected nothing, and was riding directly into the
trap, while his friends of the fort were doing their
utmost to apprise him of his danger.

The officer did not understand their meaning,
and a few minutes later he and his command would
have been cut to pieces, had not two of the garrison leaped down, and, running in front of him,
caught the bridle of his horse, drawn him aside, and
pointing ahead, told him that hundreds of Indians were lying on the ground and waiting for
him.

Major Russell instantly halted, and it was high
time that he did so. At the same moment, the
Creeks opened with a fierce fire, and, springing to

their feet, came rushing down upon the whites in great numbers.

There was no hope of the soldiers withstanding the shock. The company sprang off their horses, and made for the fort, while their riderless steeds galloped with saddles and bridles flying, toward the main line of the army.

The Indians sped straight on after the animals, until they came within gun-shot, when a volley was poured into them. They wheeled about, and made for the line on the other side, where they were received in the same manner. They then charged so desperately against the line that the militia gave way, and the Creeks, seeing no hope of turning the tide of battle, ran pell-mell for the mountains, three miles distant.

The fleeing warriors were hard pressed, and their loss was great. There were 299 bodies found, and many must have been carried away. The whites lost 15 killed, and 85 wounded; some of the latter dying afterward.

This famous battle of Taladega was fought under General Jackson's immediate command, December 7, 1813. It was a crushing blow to the warlike Creeks, though the hostilities on their part were not yet ended.

The expectation was that a supply of provisions would arrive at Camp Strother at Ten Islands for the army; but, when the latter reached the station, there were no tidings of the supplies; and even that which had been left behind of General Jackson's private stores had been distributed. The con-

dition of the army became critical, for its suffering
was great, and it was not long before a mutinous
spirit manifested itself.

One day a half-famished soldier saw General
Jackson seated on a log, and chewing something.
Thinking it an opportune time to make his wants
known, he approached his commander, and told
him he was so nearly starved, that he knew not
what to do. Jackson said he would gladly divide
his food with him, and, taking a handful of acorns
from his pocket, held them out for the private to
help himself. The latter declined the offer with
thanks, and when he rejoined his companions, said
that no complaint should be made, when their
commanding officer was living on acorns.

To add to the discomforts of the soldiers, the
weather became exceedingly cold, and their
clothing was nearly worn out. Their horses were
feeble, and matters were in a deplorable shape.
The militia officers proposed to Jackson that they
should be permitted to go home, get fresh horses
and clothing for another campaign, for the
time of the volunteers had been out for several
weeks.

Jackson refused with his usual emphasis, but the
soldiers were desperate, and they prepared for a
general stampede, Crockett being among the leaders. The commander stationed his cannon so as
to command a bridge which the rebels would have
to cross, and issued orders to fire upon them if
they dared to advance. The soldiers were also
ranged in double lines with guns cocked. The

mutineers were equally determined, and with their guns ready, they pressed forward.

It was a critical moment, and it looked as if a collision was inevitable, but those who were expected to conquer were in sympathy with the suffering soldiers, and, fortunately, not a gun was fired. The disaffection, however, was so great at one time, that the expedition was on the eve of abandonment.

General Jackson pronounced the volunteers the strangest ones he ever saw, inasmuch as they volunteered to fight; and then, when the desire took possession of them, they volunteered to leave.

Crockett with the rest made his way home, and they procured other horses and clothing better suited for the winter season. While there, word was received from General Jackson, demanding that they should return and enlist for six months. As they had already served three instead of two months—the time of their original enlistment—the majority refused. A few, however, rejoined the army, and among them was David Crockett.

Our hero attached himself to Major Russell's company of spies, those that came so near being destroyed at Fort Taladega, and started after Jackson's army, which was on the move. When it was overtaken, a fort was established, and garrisoning it, the rest of the army pushed on to Horse Shoe Bend on the Tallapoosa river.

Signs of Indians were abundant, and the whites went into camp for the night. A couple of hours before daybreak, the sleepers were aroused by the firing of guns, and springing up, found the Indians had attacked them.

Jackson's men immediately drew off into the darkness, expecting the Creeks would follow, in which case they could be shot down by the light of the camp-fires.

But the Creeks were cunning, and kept under the protecting shadows, so that the soldiers could only fire at the points where they saw the flash of their guns. When day broke, the Indians withdrew, having killed four, and wounded several others, but there was no means of knowing whether the assailants had suffered any harm at all.

The army pressed on, and was soon engaged in fording a large creek. About half the soldiers were over, when the concealed Indians opened a destructive fire upon the left wing. Major Russell and his brother had remained behind that morning on breaking camp, in the hope of learning something of the plans of the Creeks. While the attack was going on, the Russells were seen galloping at full speed toward the army, closely pursued by Indians.

The latter immediately opened fire upon the artillerymen, and proved the best of sharpshooters. Hiding themselves behind the fallen trees, they drew careful bead upon the exposed men at the guns, and at nearly every flash a cannonier would fall.

At this trying crisis, Crockett states that a couple of their colonels showed the white feather,

and hastily crossed the creek, so as to place themselves out of range.   Colonel Carroll distinguished
himself by extricating the army from its perilous
position—one-half being on one side the stream,
and one-half on the other.   The whites had a powerful ally in the person of a friendly Indian known
as Fife, who joined them with two hundred of his
warriors at Taladega.   After some hard fighting
the enemy were repulsed, and Crockett admits
that it was a vast relief to him when the firing
stopped, for it seemed during the battle as if every
tree and log concealed a dusky sharpshooter, who
devoted himself entirely to picking off the white
men.

   This battle is known in history as that of Enoto-
choplo, and it was not the end of the struggle in
that section.   Shortly after, the Indians renewed
the attack with greater success than before.   They
drove in a picket, and General (lately promoted
from Colonel) Coffee attacked the left wing of the
assailants, but his men were so few that he was in
imminent danger of being cut off.   General Jackson saw the peril, and sent the friendly chief, Fife,
with his band of warriors to his relief.   The Indians were soon repulsed, but they renewed the
battle with greater fierceness, and in a short time
General Coffee was involved in deeper difficulty
than ever.   Fife went to his relief again, and drove
back his countrymen only by a savage charge with
the bayonet.

   Crockett returned to his family in Tennessee,
where he was most joyfully received, for his wife

naturally enough imagined that all manner of misfortune had befallen him, and his reappearance was
much like that of a dear friend whom we have
given up for lost.

But the daring backwoodsman had not been
with his family long, when calls were made for
volunteers to go to Pensacola. Crockett was so
anxious to fight the British, that he enlisted again,
despite the entreaties of his wife, who had hoped
that he would leave her no more.

One of Crockett's neighbors had been drafted,
and he offered the volunteer a hundred dollars to
go as his substitute. The young man said his
training forbade his hiring out to be shot at, but he
meant to go, and the drafted man should do the
same, so that the government would get the services of both.

Crockett attached himself to his old leader Major
Russell, who followed on after the main army.
There were over a hundred men in the company,
which marched across the river at Muscle Shoals,
where our hero forded it, just before the burning of
Black Warrior's Town. They rode on through the
Choctaw and Chickasaw nations to Fort Stephens,
and thence to the junction of the Tombigbee and
Alabama rivers.

This was close to Fort Mimms, where, as the
reader will recall, the Creeks had committed their
great massacre of the previous year. When the
point was reached, Major Russell found himself
two days behind the main army, who had left their
horses because there was no forage between the.

Point and Pensacola. Major Russell did the same, and started on foot for Pensacola. At noon, the next day, General Jackson's army was overtaken and found encamped on a high eminence, over-looking the famous city of Florida.

But the arrival of Major Russell and his com-pany, although joyfully welcomed by Jackson and his soldiers, was too late to share in the glory of capturing the town, which had been taken by Old Hickory just before.

As there was no need of the soldiers in this place, Major Russell and his company started back the next morning for the point where they had left their horses, with the view of using them in movements against the Indians who were still causing a great deal of trouble.

General Jackson and the main army set out for New Orleans, and Major Russell halted several days at Fort Montgomery, close to Fort Mimms.

A good supply of provisions was secured by shooting the cattle which had formerly belonged at Fort Mimms, but which had run at large so long as to become wild. Leaving for Montgomery, Crockett's company marched some distance toward Pensacola and then, turning to the left, passed through a dismal, piny country, until they reached the Scamby river, near which they encamped. The force numbered about a thousand men, one-fifth of whom were Chickasaw and Choctaw Indians. On the evening of the arrival, a boat came up from Pensacola, bringing a good supply of the much needed provisions.

A little later, the Indians were given permission to cross the river. They were accompanied by sixteen white soldiers, Crockett being one of the number. They stayed all night on the opposite bank, and early in the morning started on a tour of exploration.

Only a short distance was traveled, when they reached the flooded lands, through which they forced their way, the water sometimes reaching to their armpits. At the end of a mile and a half they found higher ground, where they halted to warm themselves, and dry their clothing. They proceeded on up the river for perhaps six miles, when their Choctaw spies, who were in advance, came running back in great alarm, saying that they had discovered a camp of Creek Indians. A conference was held, when it was agreed that the white men should advance and fire into the camp, after which the Indians were to rush forward and scalp the enemies.

With this understanding, the start was made, when it was discovered that the hostiles were on an island, where they were practically inaccessible. While the spies were discussing the matter, they were startled by hearing the discharge of guns. A charge was instantly made for the point whence , came the reports of the rifles, and the two advance spies were encountered, who reported that, while they were moving cautiously forward, they met two Creeks who were out hunting horses. The spies pretended they were Shawanoes, escaping from General Jackson, and asked for something to

3

eat. The Creeks told them that nine miles up the
river was a Creek camp where they could get all
they wished, and that their own camp was on an
island a short distance away. The Choctaws then
attacked and killed the two Creeks and scalped
them.

Shortly afterward the house of a Spaniard was
found where his wife, himself, and four children
had been scalped. Crockett began to feel that he
was upon very dangerous ground, but he continued
forward until he struck the river, down which he
and his friends continued until they came opposite
the Indian camp.

CHAPTER V.

The Creek Indians—Termination of the War—Crockett's Return
Home—Death of his Wife—His Second Marriage—His Tour
of Exploration—Dangerous Illness—Removal to the Tract
purchased by the Government from the Chickasaws—Justice
of the Peace—Solicited to Run for the Position of Major of a
Regiment, and Concludes, for Good and Sufficient Reasons, to
become a Candidate for the Colonelcy.

THE Creek Indians, who figure so prominently
in the preceding pages, were living, when first
known to the whites, on the Flint, Chattahoochie,
Coosa, and Alabama rivers, in Florida. Their tra-
ditions, language, and peculiarities all point to a
common origin with the Choctaws and Chickasaws.
They seem to have emigrated from the northwest
to Florida, whence they returned to the region between the Ocmulgee and Tallapoosa rivers. As
this is one network of creeks and rivulets, the early
settlers gave it the name of the Creek country, and
thus the Indians living there acquired the name.
Those that remained in Florida were called Semi-
noles (or Wanderers). When the settlements began in the Carolinas and Louisiana, the alliance of
the Creeks was sought by the French, English, and
Spaniards. The overthrow of the French power in
North America and the cession of Florida to England, brought the Creeks entirely under English
influence. At that time they numbered 5,860 warriors, and fifty towns.

When the Revolution broke out, the Creeks were hostile to the Americans. A treaty of peace was made with them in 1790. As we have shown, they were our bitter enemies in the war of 1812, emphasizing their position by the massacre at Fort Mimms on the 30th of August, 1813. The subsequent events of the Creek war may be thus summed up:

The Indians were defeated at Tallushatchee, November 3, by General Coffee; at Taladega, on the 7th, by General Jackson; at Hillabee, on the 11th, by General White; at Attassec, on the 29th, by General Floyd; and at Eccanachaca, December 23, by General Claiborne. Jackson defeated them at Emuckfau, January 18, 1814; and on the 24th, at Enotochopco. The final struggle took place at Horse-Shoe Bend on the 27th of March. There it was that the Creeks gathered their warriors for their last decisive stand. They numbered fully a thousand fighting men, among whom were several of their leading prophets, who had harangued them into the belief that it was impossible for the whites to conquer them, and that the prophets themselves could not be killed by a bullet. The earthworks of the Creeks were constructed with such ingenuity that the only way in which they could be carried was by storm.

"Determined to exterminate them," says General Jackson in his report, "I detached General Coffee with the mounted men and nearly the whole of the Indian force, early on the morning of yesterday (March 27, 1814) to cross the river about two

miles below their encampment, and to surround
the Bend in such a manner as that none of them
should escape by attempting to cross the river.

" Beam's company of spies, who had accompanied General Coffee, crossed over in canoes to
the extremity of the Bend, and set fire to a number of the buildings which were there situated ;
they then advanced with great gallantry towards
the breastwork, and commenced a spirited fire
upon the enemy behind it."

This force, however, despite its gallantry, was
unable to effect its purpose, and the regulars, under
Colonel Williams and Major Montgomery joined in
an assault which was irresistible.

The Creeks were utterly routed, scarcely any of
the warriors escaping. Their power was shattered,
and the Creek war ended.

Crockett took no noteworthy part in the hostilities beyond what has already been recorded. He
was engaged on a sort of general scout through
the Indian country with his company, during
which his skill in shooting game saved him and
his comrades more than once from actual starvation.

Finally, however, he considered his mission as a
soldier ended, and he returned home, where he
was most joyfully welcomed by family and neighbors.

Two years of quiet contentment followed. He
worked steadily on his farm with the industry and
perseverance which won success ; but he was visited
by a sad affliction. His young and pretty wife,

who had proven such a true companion to him, was taken sick and died. She left her husband with his two sons and an infant daughter.

The blow was a severe one, and yet it could not have crushed the backwoodsman so utterly as his own words would have us believe; for no great time had elapsed when he married a widow whose husband was killed during the war, and who had a son and daughter. She was a worthy helpmeet, however, for she was good and industrious, and owned a valuable farm—which certainly was no disqualification in the eyes of her second husband.

Crockett settled down at once, and remained at home until the following autumn, when he and three of his neighbors started to explore a portion of the Creek country on the other side of the river. They rode a considerable distance, staying over night at the house of an acquaintance. The following day one of their number went out to hunt, but was bitten by a poisonous snake. He stayed at the house, while Crockett and the other two went on.

Finally the three halted in a rich country, the site of the present city of Tuscaloosa. They went into camp, and as there were no settlers about them, their horses were hobbled; but some two hours before daybreak, the hunters were awakened by the tinkling of the bells placed about the necks of the animals. The sound gradually died out in the distance, and showed that the horses were going home on a rather lively trot.

As soon as it was light, Crockett started in pursuit, carrying his heavy rifle. The chase was an exasperating one, leading him through creeks, swamps, and over mountains and through woods. At every settler's house he heard of them as being only a short distance in advance, and the trail was so fresh that he was confident he was close behind them. Now and then the straining ear fancied it heard the faint tinkle of bells in the distance, and then the indignant hunter would start forward with renewed speed, sure of having them in hand, and being able in a short time to punish them for their dishonorable proceedings.

When night came, and Crockett found he had traveled fully fifty miles, he was forced to the conclusion that he could not overtake the runaways, (and it was perhaps fortunate for them he could not in his savage mood), so he tarried with a settler over night.

In the morning, Crockett was tired out, sore and ill, but he was so anxious to rejoin his friends, that he set out, hoping to get better as he proceeded.

Instead of improving, he steadily grew worse, and finally dropped down beside the trace, hoping that he would shortly rally. While he lay there, a small party of Indians came along and offered him some melons, but the poor fellow was too sick to eat. They then informed him by signs that he would soon die and be buried. Crockett says that he was forced to agree with them in their view of the situation.

The hunter rose to his feet, but was so weak and ill that he staggered from side to side, and could scarcely save himself from falling on his face. One of the Indians proposed to go with him, and carry his gun. The sick man accepted the offer, giving him a half-dollar for doing so.

At last he reached the nearest house, where he was put to bed, so ill that he became delirious, and hovered for days on the very edge of death. His vigorous constitution and the careful nursing finally pulled him through, and at the end of a month he returned home, looking like a walking skeleton.

His wife supposed he was dead, for his neighbors had returned and reported that they met Indians who had helped carry him away to die, and had actually assisted in burying him.

Crockett saw that the section where he lived was sickly, and he determined to leave it. In the succeeding autumn, therefore, he set out to look for the country that had been purchased of the Chickasaw Indians. When eighty miles from home, he was taken sick again, probably from camping out on the way. During his sickness he became so well pleased with the country, that he resolved to settle in it. It was on the verge of the purchased tract, and little law or order existed. But he thought that if other people could get along without law, he could also.

Accordingly, he removed his family to the head of Shoal Creek; but, as is generally the case with new countries, the emigrants that flocked about them were such characters, that the more orderly ones saw the necessity of organizing for self-protection.

There was not much in the way of written law,
for Crockett and his friends thought that each man
could interpret his duty for himself, and where he
was given a conscience, he had only to follow the
light within him.

David Crockett was appointed one of the magis-
trates, and he executed his duties with characteristic energy and promptness. When a man owed
a debt and refused to pay, Crockett ordered his
arrest, and the constable lost no time in bringing
the culprit into court. Crockett would listen to
the case, and if justice prompted, he would give
judgment against him and issue an execution,—
by which time the awful majesty of his manner
generally scared the defendant into a wild eagerness to pay his debts.

If a man was charged with stealing, and it was
proven against him, the magistrate generally ordered him to be whipped, and the work was always
done with thoroughness. The warrants which
Crockett issued were verbal, and consisted of the
words, "Catch that fellow, dead or alive!"

As a rule the fellow was caught.

This state of things continued until the legislature added the settlements to those of Giles County,
when Crockett and others received legal appoint-
ments as "'Squires," and he was notified that his
warrants must be issued in writing.

This was hard work for Crockett, who knew
little about writing and orthography, but he had a
good constable, who helped him. But Crockett
applied himself, and soon acquired such a facility,

that he was able to keep his books and records without assistance.

In this place, the following extract from the Lawrenceburg (Tenn.) correspondence of the *Cincinnati Gazette* of a recent date, is interesting:

DAVY CROCKETT'S HOME.

His Old Log House in Tennessee. Mrs. Crockett as a Miller.

This place is made memorable for having been the old home of Davy Crockett, who once lived about a mile and a half northwest of Lawrenceburg. He built a mill on the crescent branch of Shoal Creek, about half a mile above Simonton's factory, on said branch. Here he lived several years and followed milling and hunting, though it is believed that Mrs. Crockett mostly tended the mill while Davy was off hunting or electioneering. The venerable William Simonton, a respected citizen of the place, says he used to go to the mill there when he was a boy, and Mrs. Crockett was always grinding. She was a woman of great strength and could handle sacks of grain with great ease. The mill itself is gone, but a portion of the dam can yet be seen when the water is low. The house he occupied still remains. It is a hewed log-building, about 20 x 24. Though the roof has been replaced by a new one, the old round log joists remain. We examined with feeling of intense interest, both inside and out, this last memento of the remarkable man whose name has become historical. We have also been so fortunate as to obtain several documents he issued while a justice of the peace, all in his own handwriting. He wrote a better and plainer hand than we had supposed. We here append a verbatim copy of an execution he issued with his own hand, which is now in our possession :

STATE OF TENNESSEE, LAWRENCE COUNTY:

To any lawful officer to execute: You are hereby commanded that of the goods and chattels, lands and tenements of John Palley you Caus to be made the sum of 3.82½ cts. debt; whar as Brown & Nixon obtained a judgment against the Sd Palley, before me given under my hand and seal this 10th day of October, 1818.

DAVID CROCKETT, J. P.

It has this indorsement on the back:

Brown & Nixon vs. Palley, execution.   Debt, $3.82½; Shff's fees, $1; J. P. fees, 37.

Respecting his decisions, while holding this humble but responsible office, Crockett says that his judgments were never appealed from, as he gave them on the principles of common honesty and justice between man and man, and relied on natural born sense instead of law learning to guide him, for he had never read a page of any law book in all his life.

Crockett was discharging the duties of his station in this vigorous and commendable manner, when he was approached by a Captain Matthews, who told him he was a candidate for the office of colonel of a regiment, and that he wished Crockett to run for that of first major. The " 'Squire " wished to decline, but Matthews was urgent, and at last Crockett agreed to stand for the position.

As a matter of course, he counted upon the earnest support of the captain, who was an influential man in the section, being an old settler and the owner of a valuable farm.

With a view of creating or rather extending his popularity, he gave a corn-husking, to which an immense number were invited, among them being Crockett and his family.

During the progress of the merry-making, an acquaintance called Crockett aside and gave him the astonishing information that Captain Matthews was pressing to the utmost the canvass of his son for the very office for which he had solicited and gained the consent of Crockett to run.

Nothing stirred the resentment of the backwoodsman quicker than such double dealing as this; and, taking the old gentleman aside, he informed him that his son need feel no uneasiness, as he had fully made up his mind not to run against him for the majority.

" Instead of running for his office, "added Crockett, " I have resolved to become a candidate against *you* for the colonelcy of the regiment."

CHAPTER VI.

Crockett elected to the Colonelcy—He becomes a Candidate for Legislative Honors, and is Elected—His Financial Misfortunes—His Visit to the Country along the Obion—A Severe Tramp.

CAPTAIN MATTHEWS saw from the manner of Crockett that he was in earnest, though the untrustworthy officer assured him that he was very sorry his son had determined to run for the office, against the judgment and wishes of his father.

The captain then made a speech to the assembled crowd, and told them he was a candidate for the colonelcy of the regiment, and he hoped they would give him their votes. At the same time, he added that his opponent was his neighbor, " 'Squire David Crockett."

All eyes were turned toward the renowned backwoodsman, who, in turn, was compelled to address them. He admitted that it was true he was a candidate, and, inasmuch as he found he had to run against the whole family, he concluded to begin with the head of it. He was humorous and entertaining, and such a speech is more acceptable to the ordinary crowd than is any scholarly effort.

When the election came off, Crockett was elected colonel of the regiment by a large vote, and another friend beat the son of Captain Matthews for the majority—a result which could not but be particularly pleasing to him who had been treated so unfairly.

This incident, unimportant in itself, was the turning-point of David Crockett's life, for it marked his entrance into the political field, wherein he reaped the honors which made him famous throughout the land. It gave him his first taste of the sweets of popular applause, and drew him along the deceptive path which so often leads to preferment and honor, but not infrequently ends in disappointment, moral wreck, and death.

It was David Crockett's first step of a peculiar, though brilliant career, which brought him the keenest of all disappointment, and ended in his death amid the smoking walls of the immortal Alamo.

The election of Crockett to the colonelcy gave him great popularity, and drew public attention to him. It was not long after, that he was asked to become a candidate for the legislature in the counties of Lawrence and Heckman. In the month of February, 1821, he submitted his name to the support of his friends, and the next month started with a drove of horses to North Carolina. He was gone three months, and during that time his ambition grew until, on his return, he threw his whole energies into the canvass, the occupation being altogether a new one to him.

The first fact which strongly impressed Colonel Crockett was, that there was no more ignorant man in the State, concerning the public questions which it was his duty to consider, than was he.

The candidate made a visit into Heckman county, where his constituents told him they wished to move their town nearer the center of the county, and that he must favor it. Crockett said he would give the matter his earnest consideration, and looked wise and favorable to the plan, though he admits that it passed his comprehension how the whole town could be shifted to another location.

Shortly after, there was a famous squirrel hunt on Duck river, at which it was agreed that a large barbecue, and a regular country frolic, should be held. The party which shot the fewest squirrels was to pay for the entertainment of the other. This constituted a species of electioneering in which Crockett was at home. The company to which he was attached, as a matter of course, secured the largest number of the little animals, the candidate himself bringing in a great many. Before the dancing began, there was a demand for a speech from Crockett. His opponent was present and joined in the importunity, for he was sure any attempt at public speaking on his part would expose him to ridicule.

Very few men could have met the ordeal as did Colonel Crockett, for no one was more sensible than he of his ignorance; but his inexhaustible fund of humor was at his command, and he drew plentifully upon it. What so pleasing to an American crowd as an amusing story? The speaker told a number, which set his hearers in a roar, and of course won him many friends.

But he displayed an unerring appreciation of an assemblage in this country, by announcing that he was as dry as a powder-horn, and inviting them all to refresh themselves at the bar. They accepted with ardor, and the invitation went as straight to their hearts as they did to the counter for their supply of stimulants.

Colonel Crockett next proceeded to the town of Vernon, which was the one that asked to be "moved." He assured them he would think about it—as, in fact, he had been doing for a long time, without arriving at a conclusion—but he wished to satisfy himself first that the proposed removal would be right.

This was eminently fair, and it left both parties in a pleasant state of hope.

Our hero's competitor and the candidates for Governor and for Congress attended the commencement of court on the Monday succeeding the bar- · becue, where Crockett made his first speech. It was expected that he would hold forth again, with the others, and he was in a great state of uneasiness, for the ordeal was one of the most trying that can be imagined.

But good fortune attended him, the other speakers occupied most of the time, and when the hour came for the backwoodsman, the audience were just in the mood to appreciate his short, pointed, and humorous stories, which in a few minutes gained him more votes than the labored efforts of his opponents won to themselves.

In one respect the untutored Tennessean showed

good sense by listening carefully to all the speeches, and taxing his memory with the statements of the rival candidates. In this practical manner he gained a knowledge of political affairs, which stood him well through the remainder of his canvasses.

With his natural ability and quickness to grasp the situation, he steadily and rapidly increased his popularity. When election came off, he received nine votes more than double those of his competitor.

A few days after his election Crockett was in Pulaski, where he met Colonel Polk, afterwards President of the United States.

" Well, Colonel," said Polk, " I suppose we shall have a radical change of the judiciary at the next session of the legislature."

Crockett promptly replied that such was his opinion, and instantly moved out of range of hearing.

But when he took his seat in the legislature, he listened attentively to the proceedings, and in a brief time was as well informed as the majority of his associates.

While Colonel Crockett was on the very eve of his political career, he met with a great business misfortune in the washing away of his mill and distillery.

It ruined him for the time, financially; but, on the advice of his honest wife, he turned over every dollar's worth of property he had to his creditors, and with strong, trustful hearts, the two began life over again.

Colonel Crockett, despite his industry and enterprise, seems always to have been of a roving disposition. He had scarcely returned from serving
his term in the legislature, when, accompanied by
his eldest son and a young man named Henry, he
set out to visit the country along the Obion river.
They were not long in selecting the spot whereon
to establish their new home. The nearest house
was seven miles distant, and the next was fifteen
miles away, so there was no fear that Crockett
would not have the elbow-room he declared was
always so agreeable.

Having fixed upon the site of his new cabin, he
and his two companions concluded to make a call
upon Mr. Owens, their next door neighbor, distant
seven miles, as we have already stated. The cabin
stood on the other bank of the Obion, and the
journey to it was a memorable one to all.

Crockett had brought a single horse from home,
upon which to pack their provisions. He was led
to the water-side, and hobbled out to graze, until
they should be ready to return. There was no
boat with which to cross the river, which was very
high, and overflowed a great deal of the surrounding country. The circumstances being such, it is
difficult for us, at this remote day, to appreciate
the resolution they showed in making their call
upon their neighbor. We cannot help believing
that it would have been much more sensible had
Crockett and his friends deferred their visit until a
favorable season.

. But they plunged into the chilling waters, which

frequently rose to their necks, or rather to those of the young man and Crockett, for the son of the latter was so young and small, that he was frequently forced to swim when the others forded their way. The father took the lead, with a long pole in his hands, with which he sounded the water in front, to avoid stepping into any of the numerous sloughs.

When they had toiled forward for a half mile, they reached the channel of the river, where they halted for a few minutes to decide how that was to be crossed. While the colonel stood irresolute, and looking at the deep, swift, turbid current, he observed a tree on the other side, which had fallen over in such a way that its top reached nearly across. Close to the backwoodsman was another tree, which, could it be made to fall properly, would supply the "missing link."

Crockett began cutting with his tomahawk, and when it fell, it descended just as he wished, and the three made their way across the channel and into shallow water again without difficulty. But there was more of the water than was agreeable to the most devoted fisherman, for the three continued picking their way forward, sometimes only to their knees, sometimes to their armpits, and occasionally resting for a minute or two upon a tiny bit of land. They toiled in this fashion, all shivering with cold, and again the wonder comes to us that three human beings should have ventured upon such an expedition, when there was no adequate necessity for doing so.

At last they reached land, and were gratified to catch sight of the cabin of their neighbor Mr. Owens, a short distance off. There they were given the best care imaginable, for the little boy of Crockett was shivering as if with the ague. At the time Crockett reached the place, Owens himself and several men were on the point of leaving, but they turned back to the house with him.

The men with Mr. Owens were the owners of a boat, (which was the first that ever ascended that far up the Obion river,) and a crew that they had hired to carry it a hundred miles further up stream.

A pleasant, social time was spent together, and in the evening Crockett and the young man Henry accepted an invitation to go on board the boat with the owners and crew, and all had a merry time of it. In the morning they proceeded with the boat to a point where a tornado had filled the river with timber, but they found the water so low that they decided to wait for a rise. Accordingly they dropped down stream again to a point opposite the home of Mr. Owens.

It rained pretty hard the next day, but the effect on the waters was not sufficient, and the whole party went with Crockett to the spot where he had decided to build his cabin. With the help of his friends, they quickly put up a building more noticeable for its rugged strength than for its architectural beauty. The boat owners turned over to Crockett four barrels of meal, one of salt, and ten gallons of whiskey—the last being a commodity always highly prized by the eccentric backwoodsman.

In payment for these, Crockett agreed to accompany the party up the river to the landing-place. He shot a deer and procured some fine bacon, which he left at the cabin with his son and the young man, who were to stay there until his return. He expected to be gone about a week.

The boat reached the point where the tornado had filled the Obion with so much timber, and it was tied up for the night. Crockett saw no prospect of getting the craft through that day, so he set out to shoot a deer for his friends.

It was a fine country for game, and he had not gone far when he brought down a large buck, with which he started back for the boat. On the way, he struck the trail of a company of elks, and immediately started after them. Before he came in sight of the game, he saw two large bucks, which he shot. Hanging them up, he resumed his pursuit of the elk, but it was noon before he caught sight of them, and they were so timid that they kept beyond rifle-shot.

Crockett found he was several miles from the boat and in a ravenous condition, for he had not eaten a mouthful since morning, and his exercise was of the kind calculated to give a man the most vigorous appetite.

He concluded to forego his pursuit of the elks, and started down the edge of the river. He had gone a very short distance only, when he caught sight of two more plump-looking elks, which were brought down by his unerring rifle. Both were hung up, and he pushed forward. Just at sunset, he descried three more, and shot one, but the other two made off before he could reload. This being hung up, made six which he had shot during the day, and, as night was close at hand, he set out for the point where he had left the boat early in the morning.

But the craft was invisible, and wondering what it could mean, Crockett shouted at the top of his voice. Receiving no reply, he fired his gun, and an answering report came from a point two miles up the river. This showed that, contrary to the expectation of the Tennessean, the boat had been forced through the fallen timber.

It was now dark, and the tramp through the vines and briers and over fallen trees was of the severest nature. He reached his friends at last, thoroughly worn out and exhausted.

CHAPTER VII.

End of the Voyage—The Cabin in the Woods—Removal of Crockett's Family—A Memorable Trip after Gunpowder—Crockett sets out upon a Bear Hunt.

IT proved harder work to get the boat up the river than any of the crew expected, and instead of accomplishing it in three or four days, it was nearly two weeks before the voyage terminated. When it ended, the owners gave Crockett a small skiff, and, accompanied by a young man named Harris, who had concluded to live with him, they set out for the lonely cabin in the wilds of Tennessee.

Crockett's son and his companion were found well and hard at work, and the four wasted no time in idleness. They planted corn, but the spring was quite advanced, so that no fence was erected. Crockett, as opportunity presented, roamed the woods, and during the spring, shot a large number of deer and ten bears. The section proved one of the best for game that the great hunter had ever visited.

During the months spent here, the four persons never saw the face of any other white person, excepting that of their neighbor Owens, seven miles away. There were plenty of Indians scattered here and there through the woods. When Colonel Crockett climbed to the top of some eminence,

and, like Daniel Boone under similar circumstances, looked off over the vast area of forest
stretched out before him, he could catch sight here
and there of the thin blue column of smoke rising
in the clear air, which showed where the half savage
Indian had built his rude lodge, and where he led
a lazy, vagabond life, while his squaw did all the
work and drudgery that was done about him.

The wife and family of Crockett were a hundred
and fifty miles distant, and he set out to bring
them to his new home. When he reached them,
he was obliged to attend an extra session of the
legislature. Then he made the removal that he
had decided on long before, and kept hard at work
until autumn. Then, as was his custom, he took
to the woods with his rifle and dogs, and kept his
family well supplied with meat.

As Christmas approached, Crockett found his
supply of ammunition was running low. His
brother-in-law had moved to a point on the other
side of a tributary of the Obion, and had brought
out a keg of powder for Colonel Crockett, but
it was still at the cabin of the more recent
settler.

Despite a freshet, the coldness of the weather,
and the distance and difficulties in the way, Crockett determined to make the twelve-mile journey
for the ammunition. His wife protested, assuring
him that he would certainly freeze or drown, but
opposition never affected Colonel Crockett, who
saw no meat in the larder, and no means of obtaining more, without first securing the powder.

In face of dangers that would have deterred the most daring ranger of the woods, he set out for the home of his brother-in-law, and there is no one of the extraordinary experiences of Colonel Davy Crockett which more strikingly illustrates the indomitable resolution and pluck of the eccentric Tennessean than this hunt for gunpowder. When he set his mind upon doing anything, nothing less than Providence himself could turn him aside from its accomplishment.

To begin with, the weather was not only bitterly cold, but it was steadily growing colder. To reach his relative, six miles away, it was necessary for Crockett to cross a tract a mile wide, which was overflowed with the chilling, swift-running current, and which in some places was too deep to ford, and there was nothing in the nature of a boat at his command. All the preparation that he made was to take along a dry suit to don, after passing the river.

The snow lay several inches on the ground when he started, and never, says the backwoodsman, until then, did he suspect how much suffering a man can undergo, and not die.

The river flowed within a quarter of a mile of his cabin, and, when he reached its margin and looked out over its surface, it seemed to him that he was standing on the edge of the ocean. As far away as the eye could reach, was the one vast expanse of turbid yellow water, sweeping forward toward the greater stream. Hundreds of trees forced their nodding tops through the splashing current, while limbs, leaves, and debris were continually spinning past, or whirling about in the numerous eddies.

A skillful waterman with a strong skiff or canoe at his command, would have hesitated a long time before venturing into a rapid current where he was sure to encounter so many dangerous obstructions, but the only cause for Crockett's hesitation was that he might take his bearings—rendered the more difficult, on account of the submergence of the surrounding country.

It did not require long to locate himself, when he stepped into the icy water and moved toward the other shore. The depth was not very great, and he proceeded with little difficulty until he reached the channel which was spanned by a fallen tree. That still held its place, and he crossed over upon it. Some distance further on was a deep slough, which was also bridged by a log, and which was wider than the channel.

But Crockett could see nothing of the log, because it was under the water, though he knew there was a small island in the slough, and that a sapling stood close beside the submerged tree.

He concluded that there was all of eight feet of water beneath this log and three feet above it. It was a very difficult and dangerous task to get across, and he stood some time debating as to the best means of reaching the other side, for he never entertained the thought of turning back.

At last he cut a sapling near him, and succeeded in lodging it against the one standing on the island.

He then cut a pole, and crept along on the small tree, till he reached the one against which it was lodged, which was several feet above the water.

Groping about with his pole, he found the log, three feet below the surface, as he had supposed. Having taken his bearings, so to speak, he crawled back, and got his gun that he had left at the stump of the sapling. He then made his way to the place of lodgment, and moved down the other sapling, so as to reach the log. The rushing current reached his waist, and it was a most difficult task to pick his way across the unsteady support. If he lost his foothold, he would be instantly thrown into water where he would be forced to swim desperately for life.

Feeling his way along, inch by inch, he finally got across the more dangerous portion, and had waded but a short distance, when he found himself on the edge of another slough, where the tree upon which he was usually accustomed to cross, was bobbing about on the surface, instead of holding its position as did the other.

The colonel thought the best way to manage this was by walking over it, and he set out to do so. Moving carefully, he reached the middle, when, like a flash of lightning, it turned beneath him, and he dropped into the water to his neck.

This was terribly discomforting, with the water close upon the freezing-point, but Crockett pressed on with the same determination which characterized him through life, and without any more misadventures, he reached dry land.

He stopped and changed his clothes, but he was so nearly frozen that there was scarcely any feeling in his limbs. He had managed to keep his extra clothing dry by holding them aloft on his gun, when he fell into the deep water; but he was nearly perishing with cold.

The only means that suggested itself to prevent his freezing to death was to stir his blood by some rapid exercise. He set out to run, but could scarcely walk, he was so benumbed. By perseverance, however, he rallied somewhat, and was able to keep moving.

Night was closing over the forest, but the sturdy backwoodsman never gave up, and by and by caught the glimmer of a light among the trees. He kept on, and shortly after was with his relatives.

As may be supposed, they were astonished to see him, and he was soon made comfortable.

In the morning it was piercingly cold, and his friends persuaded him not to attempt to reach home. He consented to stay, and killed two deer for them. But the weather grew still colder, the temperature steadily sinking until the third morning, when there was a half inch of ice wherever the water was stationary.

His relatives insisted that it was more dangerous than ever to return, for while the river was as deep, and was colder than ever, there could not be enough ice to support his weight.

But Crockett could not forget that his family were without meat, and he could stay away from them no longer.   He would reach home, or perish in the effort.

Taking up his keg of powder and bundle of clothes, he set out with that grim tenacity of purpose which was the most distinguishing feature of Colonel Davy Crockett's life.

When he reached the edge of the water, he could not see that it had subsided any, but the whole surface was one smooth sheet of ice.

"Ah, if that were only strong enough to bear me," was the thought of the hunter, as he peered toward the dark line among the trees, which showed the limit of the stream on the other side.

Another night of such weather doubtless would have made it as firm as a board floor, and so given him the best possible road to his home, but he could not be persuaded to turn back.

He stepped cautiously on the ice, and it cracked beneath his heavy tread in a way which showed it was on the point of yielding.   Sure enough, he had gone but a few paces, when he went through in water above his knees.   Immediately he drew his tomahawk, and began cutting a passage through the ice in front of him.

After awhile, the frozen surface looked firmer, and he mounted upon it again.   It splintered beneath him, but did not give way, and he walked forward, quite hopeful of getting over without much difficulty, but a moment later, it broke, and he sank above his knees again.   As before, he broke his way until he reached the place where the slough was crossed by the floating log, which gave him his fall a short time before.

This time, however, the ice held it quiet, and he passed over without any mishap.

Arriving at the second difficult place, where, as will be remembered, the log was a long distance under water, he found the current so swift, that it was not frozen at all. Accordingly he waded just as he did before. When he reached the sapling, he left his gun and climbed out with his powder-keg first, and then went back after his gun.

By this time Crockett was nearly frozen to death, for no man not possessing a prodigious vitality, could have withstood such exposure as he had undergone for several hours. He was wet from head to foot, and the water was frozen upon him, so that his heavy garments bore him down like a coat of mail.

But, while struggling bravely forward, he noticed that the ice was broken in front of him, and he thought it must have been done by a bear. Desperate as was the condition of the hunter, he determined to shoot the animal, if the opportunity presented. He therefore primed his gun, and started upon the trail.

The latter, however, led toward his home, and finally, to his door. It had been made by the young man at his house, who had been sent out by the distressed wife to look for her husband. When Harris came back with the report that no trace could be found of him, the poor woman was sure he had perished.

He came very near it, but quickly rallied, and

felt no regret for the dangerous journey, inasmuch as he had secured the indispensable ammunition, and was prepared to procure food for his family so long as the woods contained their royal game for his unerring rifle.

As may be supposed, the Tennessean did not remain at home, now that he was supplied with ammunition. It rained hard at night, and before morning turned to sleet. All hands set out for a hunt, but Crockett went off alone in search of his favorite game—bears. He was led to the belief by a dream of an encounter with a gigantic African—a sign which he says he never knew to fail, when in a bear country.

Crockett had two good dogs and an old hound, which he took with him. He traversed six miles up the river, and was then about two-thirds of that distance from the Obion itself, to which he concluded to go, as he had not yet seen anything of the game he was hunting.

Reaching the main stream, he turned down it, but the weather, which was so bad when he started, grew worse. The sleet descended fiercely, and the bushes were so loaded and bent down with ice, that it was almost impossible to force his way through the undergrowth. In a short time, however, the dogs scared up a drove of wild turkeys. As the game was too valuable to pass by, Crockett shot two of the largest gobblers. Slinging them over his shoulder, he tramped until he became so wearied that he threw them on the ground, and sat down to rest a few minutes.

The oldest hound, who was investigating on his own account, approached a fallen tree, around which he snuffed a few minutes, and then, elevating his nose toward the sky, gave utterance to a howl which, to the ears of the hunter, "meant business."

The next instant, the hound was skurrying through the wood, with the dogs after him. Crockett threw his turkeys over his shoulder, and set off as rapidly as he could travel in the same direction.

In a few minutes, he heard them baying again, and making haste, he soon came up to them.

The backwoodsman was hopeful of finding game in the tree, but a careful search failed to show anything of the sort. He concluded that the dogs had chased a turkey, which had flown away. Before he reached the hounds, they scampered off, and it was not long before they raised another alarm. But, as before, they were barking up the wrong tree.

They repeated the performance several times, until Crockett lost all patience, and determined that, as soon as he could approach nigh enough, he would shoot the old hound for repeating his false alarms.

CHAPTER VIII.

Colonel Crockett as Bear Hunter—Becomes a Candidate and is elected twice to the Legislature—Votes against General Jackson for U. S. Senator—Crockett defeated for Congress.

COLONEL CROCKETT did his hounds injustice. They were on the trail of a bear, as he discovered shortly afterward.

As the hunter advanced, the dogs galloped ahead, occasionally stopping to look back and see how well he was traveling, and then they were off again, barking louder than ever.

The hunter had been deceived so often, that he was exasperated, as we have said, to a destructive point. He grasped his rifle with the resolve to end such work on the part of his dogs, when they reached the edge of a clearing or prairie, where the astonished Tennessean caught sight of one of the largest black bears upon which he had ever looked.

He was of such enormous size and strength, that the dogs were afraid to close in with him. They had seen the game from the first, but the hunter was too far in the rear to catch sight of him until that moment.

The scene was of that nature that it sent the blood tingling through the veins of the hunter. He hung his two turkeys on the limb of a tree and then, gun in hand, ran out upon the prairie, panting with eagerness to overtake the animal; for, if

there was any sport in the world which Colonel
Crockett rated above all other amusements known
to man, it was that of bear-hunting.

Before he could overtake the dogs, the bear entered a dense thicket, and it was hard work following him.   But it was not necessary to go far, when
the huge animal was descried climbing a large
black oak.   Reaching a thick limb, he turned awk-
wardly around, and sat facing the hunter, who, at
a distance of eighty yards, put fresh priming in his
gun and fired at him.   The bear gave a start and
uttered a snort ; and, standing where he was,
Crockett hastily. reloaded and fired at him again.

This shot brought the bear scratching and tumbling to the ground.   At the same instant, one of
the dogs uttered a howl of pain, and Crockett, with
his hunting knife in one hand and his tomahawk in
the other, advanced upon the enraged animal.   The
latter instantly released the hound which he was
hugging with altogether too much emphasis for his
comfort, and fixed his eyes upon the hunter.   The
latter retreated with even greater precipitancy than
he had advanced, for he knew that if the wounded
animal gave him one embrace, it would be likely to
crush the life from him.

Running back to where his rifle lay on the
ground, Crockett reloaded it, carefully sighted and
lodged a bullet in the bear with such good aim,
that it died with scarcely a struggle.

The killing of the brute was an important step
in the enterprise, but it was scarcely less necessary
to get the animal home.   In the excitement of the

pursuit, Crockett had lost his bearings, and he now blazed the saplings at short distances, as he started to find his cabin. When he reached it, he took his friends and four horses, with which he made his way back to where the carcase of the bear lay.

It was growing dark, but they set to work .and dressed the game. It was of great size, and Crockett says he is positive it weighed fully six hundred pounds. He never in all his life, except- ing on one occasion, saw it excelled : that was when he slew a bear which was found to weigh six hun- dred and seventeen pounds.

The backwoodsman had every reason to be grati- fied with his success, for his family was* now sup- plied with the best kind of meat, sufficient to last many weeks. He continued hunting more from a love of the sport than from necessity, and when February came, he had so many peltries that he packed a horse with them, and started for the little town of Jackson, some forty miles distant. He disposed of them for a fair price, and bought such provisions as his family needed, including ammu- nition for himself.

Crockett was well known, and he met a number of old acquaintances in Jackson. The good nature and humor of the backwoodsman made him popu- lar everywhere, and he spent several hours in pleasant social converse.

Among those encountered were three candidates for legislative honors, one of whom was a relative of General Jackson, while Crockett liked all three of them. As they were taking a drink together, some one present remarked to Crockett that he would have to offer himself as a candidate. He said that he lived forty miles back in the woods, and he had no thought of any such thing. With a hearty good-bye, he and his little boy started on their long journey homeward through the wilderness.

Any one who understands the character of Colonel Davy Crockett, can tell the inevitable consequence of this apparently unimportant incident. He was known as a daring soldier who had proven his courage in the Creek war; he was a wonderfully accurate rifle shot, as he had shown in many a shooting match, and in his extraordinary hunting exploits; he was free-hearted, abounding with quaint amusing stories, and with a natural readiness of wit and fun, which never deserted him. In fact he was one of the people, with natural qualities which led them to look upon him as their especial champion.

Besides, he had already served one term with credit in the Legislature, and there was never a whisper uttered against his honesty.

When the people, at the merrymakings, or at the old-fashioned inn, or in the village stores, or on the corners, gathered to discuss politics, it was inevitable that the sturdy figure of the gallant Crockett— the embodiment of fun, wit, bravery, and integrity, should be referred to in admiring terms by the majority of these men, many of whom had gone through similar experiences, and all of whom could appreciate the sterling qualities of the famous Tennessean.

It was something more than a week after this trip of Crockett to Jackson, that a man stopped in front of his cabin and told him he was a candidate for the Legislature. The backwoodsman was certain there was some mistake about it, but his informant drew a newspaper from his pocket, and showed him where he was announced in large type as one anxious for legislative honors.

Crockett was angered, for with all his roughness of speech and manner, he was sensitive. He believed this was intended as a burlesque, and many were seeking to hold him up to ridicule. He told his wife that he would make the joke a dear one to them. He hired a young man to run the farm while he started out to electioneer for himself. He had acquired the art in his previous experience, and his opponents might well look with apprehension upon his candidacy.

It was not long before he began to make himself well known through the county. He made a good impression everywhere he went, and people soon began talking about the bear-hunter—the backwoodsman and the Tennessean from the cane-brakes. This continued and increased until the three opposing candidates were compelled to see that he was looming up so prominently that he was already stronger than any single one of them.

They consulted together, therefore, and it was agreed that at the Spring Term of Court to be held in March, they would have a conference or caucus, and two were to withdraw in favor of the strongest.

As may be supposed, each of the three exerted himself to the utmost to secure the nomination, but it fell to Dr. Butler, the relative of General Jackson, who was talented and popular, and for whom Crockett entertained a strong personal liking. It followed now, as a matter of course, that all united in opposition to Crockett's candidacy.

It required just such a situation to bring out the mettle of the backwoodsman, and he threw himself into the canvass with a heartiness which threatened to carry everything before him. Dr. Butler's relationship with General Jackson helped him greatly, for the star of Old Hickory never shone brighter than in those days, more than half a century ago.

The meeting at which the candidate was to be selected was held in Madison County, which was the strongest in the representative district that was composed of eleven counties.

Crockett's account of his canvass for himself is very entertaining. At the time, Colonel Alexander was a candidate for Congress. He was a warm friend of Crockett, and introduced him to many. At a public meeting, while Crockett was talking with a number of new acquaintances made in this manner, Dr. Butler, his competitor, walked briskly by, nodding to a number of his friends, but failing to salute Crockett. The latter was sure the Doctor did not recognize him, and he called out to him demanding what he meant by sailing by at that rate. As the astonished gentleman faced about, the backwoodsman, in his laughing, hearty manner, said:

" Well, Doctor, I suppose they have weighed you out to me, but I should like to know why they fixed your election in *March*, instead of *August*. That's a new style of doing business—taking it out of the people's hands and settling it by caucus."

By this time, Dr. Butler recognized the man before him, and offering his hand called out,

" Why, Crockett, is that you?"

" Of course it is," was the answer, " but I want you to understand that I havn't come out here to electioneer for myself. I've just crawled out of the cane to take a look at the white folks and see what I can see. When I do start in the electioneering business, I will make it a point to leave every man in as good circumstances as I found him."

" How is that?"

" I will have a large buck-skin hunting-shirt made, with two pockets, each holding about a peck. In one I will place a bottle of whiskey, and in the other a big twist of tobacco."

" Where is the particular advantage of that?"

" When I ask a man to take a drink, he will throw away his quid. After his drink, I will give him a fresh chew, and so you see he will be no poorer than when I first met him."

The bystanders laughed at this idea, and Butler said, " Colonel, you can beat me electioneering. I fear I wouldn't have much chance if you should start in against me."

"You'll have better evidence of that before August, for when I start in I will make things lively. You've got many advantages over me; you've plenty of money, and are a relative of Old Hickory, but I'm going in on the products of the country. I've got industrious children, and the best of coon dogs, and they will hunt all day and night, to help my election. When coon fur is'nt worth anything, I'll take to the woods for wolves, for each one's scalp is good for three dollars."

Crockett went on in this strain for several minutes, while the bystanders laughed and Dr. Butler seemed as much amused and astonished as any of them. He could not begin to hold his own with such a voluble talker as Crockett, and he did little but listen and laugh with the rest, who broke into a regular roar when the backwoodsman had finished.

It was such work as this that told in favor of Crockett, who gave his whole energies to prosecuting his own canvass.

As the canvass progressed, two other candidates entered the field, and politics absorbed the exclusive attention of the entire district for the time being.

How well Colonel Crockett did his work, may be gathered from the simple statement that he beat all the candidates by two hundred and forty-seven votes. Not only that, but he served the succeeding term from his district. This was in the years 1823 and 1824.

He served for four successive years in the Legislature, notwithstanding he moved during the time more than one hundred and fifty miles, and was, consequently, dependent upon strangers for his second election.   This is a forcible truth of the great power of his talent for electioneering.

While in the Legislature, there was a bill before it for the creation of a county.   The author of it wished to run the boundary line, so as to support his popularity; to this the Colonel was opposed, because his interest was affected by it.   They were hammering at it for some time; whatever the author of the bill would effect by speaking, the Colonel would undo by log-rolling; until the matter was drawing to a close, when he rose and made the following speech :

" Mr. Speaker,—Do you know what that man's bill reminds me of?   Well, I 'spose you don't, so I'll tell you.   Well, Mr. Speaker, when I first come to this country, a blacksmith was a rare thing; but there happened to be one in my neighborhood; he had no striker, and whenever one of the neighbors wanted any work done, he had to go over and strike till his work was finished.   These were hard times, Mr. Speaker, but we had to do the best we could.   It happened that one of my neighbors wanted an axe, so he took along with him a piece of iron, and went over to the blacksmith's to strike till his axe was done.   The iron was heated, and my neighbor fell to work, and was striking there nearly all day; when the blacksmith concluded the iron would n't make an axe, but 'twould make a fine mattock; so my neighbor, wanting a mattock,

concluded he would go over and strike till his mattock was done; accordingly, he went over the next
day, and worked faithfully; but towards night the
blacksmith concluded his iron wouldn't make a
mattock, but 'twould make a fine ploughshare; so
my neighbor, wanting a ploughshare, agreed that he
would go over the next day and strike till that was
done; accordingly, he again went over, and fell
hard to work; but towards night the blacksmith
concluded his iron wouldn't make a ploughshare,
but 'twould make a fine *skow;* so my neighbor,
tired of working, cried, a skow let it be—and the
blacksmith, taking up the red-hot iron, threw it
into a trough of water near him, and as it fell in,
it sung out '*skow.*' And this, Mr. Speaker, will be
the way with that man's bill for a county; he'll
keep you all here doing nothing, and finally his bill
will turn out a *skow,*—now mind if it don't."

It was during the first session of Crockett's representation from his new district that he showed his
independence in political, as well as in personal
matters.

The term of Colonel John Williams, as United
States Senator from Tennessee had expired, and
he was a candidate for re-election. He had done
his duty acceptably, and Colonel Crockett sympathized with him, for, in his judgment, there was no
reason why he should be defeated. Several candidates were proposed, but the popularity of the
Colonel was so great that it was finally admitted
that there was but one man in the country who
could beat him, and that was General Andrew

Jackson. Although the General was in nomination for the Presidency, he did not hesitate to "take the responsibility," and he became a candidate.

He received ten more votes than Williams, and was elected. But Colonel Crockett, who was then warmly attached to his old chief, voted against him because he saw no reason for doing otherwise.

It was an unpopular and dangerous thing to vote against General Jackson, as Crockett found to his cost, not many years afterward; but nothing could induce the honest Tennessean to record his vote in favor of a measure or movement which was contrary to his convictions of justice.

He was taken to task by many of his constituents for his vote against the "Gineral," but he notified them he had acted in accordance with his convictions, that he would never wear a collar around his neck, and Colonel Crockett never did.

The confidence in the integrity of the gentleman from the backwoods was shown by his re-election with scarcely any opposition at the next session of the Legislature. ·

Indeed, it is proven still more emphatically by the request of the district that Crockett would run for Congress. Colonel Alexander, their representative, had given great offence by his vote on the tariff law, and there was a general turning toward the honest backwoodsman, who could be relied upon at all times, and under all circumstances, to do that which he believed to be right.

But, when the proposition was made to Crockett, he shrank back in dismay. The thought of going to Congress fairly took away his breath, and he assured his friends that he could not consent to it. But, when a politician talks in that fashion, he is close upon the point of yielding. Colonel Crockett became a candidate.

But the stars in their courses fought against him on this occasion. It was the year when cotton brought twenty-five dollars a hundred. Colonel Alexander explained that it was due entirely to the tariff law which he supported so ardently when in Congress, and that the line of policy laid out by himself would result in bringing a much higher price for all their products.

No species of argument is more convincing than this, no matter how baseless it may be. Colonel Crockett made the most gallant fight possible, but he was placed at an exceptional disadvantage.

When the election came off, Colonel Alexander was elected to Congress by just two votes majority above Crockett.

CHAPTER IX.

The Exploits of Colonel Crockett as a Bear Hunter.

THE two years served by Colonel Crockett's successful opponent in Congress were passed by the backwoodsman without any noteworthy events, so far as the public career of the man is concerned, and yet, in another respect, they were, to many, probably the most interesting period of his life, for he has left on record an account of some of the most astonishing bear hunts in which any hunter was ever engaged.

Colonel Crockett, like many a man in his circumstances, was blind to his own unfitness for anything like a business transaction of any moment. He was simply a humorous and brave bear-hunter, who was personally pure and honest, and yet who ought never to have been a member of Congress. No thoughtful man can help feeling that his presence among the lawmakers of the nation was in the nature of a farce, though it must be admitted that in many respects he was the superior of some of his colleagues.

In the autumn of 1825, Crockett entered into a lumber speculation, his plan being to build two large boats, and load them with pipe-staves for the market. The lake was some twenty-five miles distant. Thither he went, and hired a number of men to build the boats, and get out the staves. Crockett himself worked until he knew the bears in the woods were fat, and in prime condition.

It did not take him a great while to procure all the meat his family needed for a long time; and, when one of his neighbors asked him to lend a hand in the same business, or rather amusement, the Tennessean was only too glad to comply.

The hunt was an extensive one, for Crockett was engaged for two weeks, accompanied by his eight trained hounds. He averaged a bear a day, and having supplied his friend with far more than he expected, he returned to his boat-building and stave-making.

He wrought steadily, until the old yearning became irresistible. Accompanied by his young son, he started across the lake, with a view of hunting in that section. When night came, the hunt was begun in earnest, and in a short time Crockett killed three bears. Wolves were plenty, and in the morning the Colonel erected a strong scaffold, upon which the carcases were placed, after being salted. This was done with a view of keeping them beyond the reach of the wolves, who were always hungry and on the lookout for such choice delicacies.

The morning meal was hardly concluded, when he and his son were visited by a party of hunters, with a large pack of dogs, so emaciated and woebegone in appearance that Crockett broke into laughter, and asked whether any of them could bark without leaning up against a tree to rest. He suggested that they should stay at the camp and feed the poor curs on some of the bones which he had thrown away.

The suggestion seemed to strike the callers as a good one, and they remained behind, while Crockett and his boy set out to continue their hunt.

They were in an excellent region, and had not gone far when the hounds started up a large he-bear, which made directly for the camp just left by the man and boy. They followed hard after him, but he ran into the arms, so to speak, of the other party, who shot him before Crockett could get within range. The Tennessean willingly resigned all claim upon him, and headed for Big Clover Creek, not far away.

Just as the hunter reached the stream and was about entering a cane-brake, his dogs all broke and went ahead, their short sharp yelps speedily announcing they had struck the trail of some kind of game. These sounds speedily told Crockett that the hounds had divided into two parties, and both had their "hands full."

He sent his little boy to look after one, while the father hurried toward the other. Reaching the spot where his dogs were making such a rumpus, he found they had a two-year old bear upon the ground, with the five canines furiously attacking him. Deeming the game scarcely worth expending a shot upon, Crockett stepped quickly forward and dispatched him with his knife.

Just then, the report of the boy's gun was heard, and when the father reached the spot, the lad had also killed his animal. The elder hunter had scarcely time to compliment the pluck of his son, or rather his skill, for Crockett took such things as a matter of course, when one of the dogs was heard barking a short distance away.

Immediately the rest of the hounds broke for him, while Crockett and his boy were close in the rear. The single dog had treed a bear which was very large and ready for fight; but his position placed him at the mercy of the backwoodsman, who speedily sent a bullet through his heart, and brought him tumbling to the ground.

Thus they had killed three bears within a half-hour, an exploit which few of the most successful hunters of the present day have equaled, or can equal.

As was his rule, Crockett proceeded to dress the prizes at once. Then he set out to find some water and a good place to camp for the night. He had taken a dozen steps perhaps, when the dogs suddenly scented something again, and were off like so many meteors. Crockett forgot his thirst on the instant, and dashed after them. But the trail proved such a long one, that he gave it up and started back.

Proceeding in this leisurely fashion, Crockett came upon a poor, sickly looking man, languidly grubbing in the woods. When asked why he was thus employed, he said he was working for a person who intended to settle there. He added that he had no meat for his family, and was seeking to earn some from his employer.

The woe-begone appearance of the poor fellow excited the sympathy of Crockett, who told him that if he would go with him, he would speedily secure more meat than he could earn in a month grubbing. The fellow looked wonderingly at the hunter, and then, saying he had never seen a bear killed, he went to his cabin a short distance away in the wood, and told his wife of the proposition. She was anxious to have him accept it, and he did so.

Accompanied by the grateful stranger, the hunter led the way back to where the three bears had been killed, and started a fire. The carcasses were then salted and scaffolded, but the dogs continued invisible. They had followed the scent they struck to such a distance, that their cries could not be heard. Crockett afterwards ascertained that they had treed a bear near a settler's cabin, and kept barking at it all night, doubtless wondering what kept their master away so long.

At daylight, the settler living near, went out and shot the bear. Crockett and his forlorn-looking friend set out on another hunt. When the former entered upon such amusement, it became very serious for the bears in the neighborhood. Before nightfall he had shot four more, and at the end of the week, he had killed seventeen. The grateful stranger was absolutely astounded at the extraordinary success of Crockett, who seemed to have no difficulty at all in bringing down a bear whenever he started to do so.

At the termination of the hunt, the man was

given a thousand pounds of good, fat bear-meat, and he was scarcely able to express his gratitude. Crockett met him a year later, when he looked plump and in good spirits, saying that the meat secured on that single hunt lasted his family the entire year.

For the time being, it seemed as if the fates intended Colonel Crockett to be a bear-hunter and nothing more. He had scarcely reached home, when one of his neighbors said he was entirely out of meat, and asked the Colonel to take him upon a bear-hunt. If there was any request in the world which it was hard for the Tennessean to refuse, it was of that nature, and he agreed to do as his friend wished.

He told him, however, that it was so late in the season, they were likely to find the bears had gone into winter quarters. A curious fact connected with these creatures is, that they hibernate for something like three months in each year. Those in the latitude of Tennessee generally take this long sleep from the first of January until April. At the beginning they are generally fat from the abundance of food secured in the autumn. They crawl into hollow trees or caves, where they sink into a somnolent state, and the only sustenance received during the long period is from sucking the bottom of their paw,—if indeed it can be said they receive any sort of nourishment from that source.

During their hibernation, of course, they are living upon their surplus fat. When they venture forth in spring they are lean, hungry, and fierce; and if the reader is not a very experienced hunter, we suggest that it is just as well to let bruin alone at that season. He doesn't take any interference or molestation in good part.

Crockett set out on this hunt accompanied by his neighbor and his own little boy, who promised to become as great a hunter as his father. The lad was already a skillful shot, and he was gaining an experience which was of inestimable value to him.

They went to the section where the seventeen bears had been killed, and the three began business in earnest. They toiled hard and patiently the entire day, but never started one. It looked indeed as if the great inroad made the week before, had frightened off the few survivors left behind.

The provisions taken along with them soon gave out, and Crockett sent his boy to a settler's cabin some three miles away, to procure meat. The people who were scattered through the west and southwest were always hospitable, and abundant food was furnished the lad. At the same time, the settler expressed his pleasure to learn that the two hunters were after bears. He told the lad they had been very troublesome, and had killed a good many of his hogs. He urged Crockett's son to bring his father and his friend to his house that evening, promising to give them good accommodations, and furnish his dogs all the meat they could want.

But when the boy got back, his father and

friend were after a bear, which was found to have taken refuge in a large cane, where, as is their custom, he had constructed a sort of cabin in which to take his long, winter sleep.

The dogs were afraid to venture in until their master urged them, when they made a rush, and the sleepy monster the next minute came scrambling out.   Crockett's neighbor was so eager to kill a bear, that he was given the shot, which was fatal at once.

The carcase was dragged back to camp, where the hunter found his boy awaiting him.   They spent the night with a friend who lived near, and, having salted their meat, the next morning continued their hunt.

The section selected lay between Obion river and Red Foot Lake.   There was a large lot of timber that had been leveled and strewn about by a recent tornado, and it was among this that Crockett expected to find the royal game for which he was searching.

Five miles were ridden without detecting the least sign, and the hunters were beginning to doubt the success of their enterprise, when they entered some high ridges where the cane was abundant. Crockett's eye rested upon a huge black oak, with a big hole in the upper portion.   It was just the place that would attract the favorable view of a bear seeking winter quarters, and the Tennessean made an investigation.

The bark was clawed and scratched in a way which proved that one of the beasts had ascended the trunk. But there were no marks to show he had come down again. The inference was plain : the bear was within the tree.

A bear in climbing a tree does not slip, his long sharp nails holding firmly ; but in coming down he slips continually, so that it is easy to tell whether he has descended the tree or not.

The friend had gone ahead some distance, but the leader called him back, saying they had found a tree with a bear within, and it would never do to allow such a golden opportunity to pass unimproved.

Crockett's plan was to cut another tree, so it would fall against the oak. The one selected was so slight that it could be easily climbed, and the boy was to go up and take a look in the hole to make sure the bear was within.

Accordingly Crockett began chopping down the smaller tree, but was not half through, when the savage barking of the dogs near at hand convinced their master that they had come upon the winter quarters of another bruin.

Crockett was so certain upon this point, that the two abandoned the cutting of the tree and hastened away to where the dogs were making such an ado. Sure enough, when they reached the spot, a large bear was seen up a tree, just in the position for shooting. Yielding to his friend's earnest request, Crockett allowed him to fire, and the huge unwieldy mass came tumbling heavily to the ground.

At this juncture the Colonel noticed that his best dog was missing, and believing he would not be absent at such a time unless he was engaged in important business, his owner went to a piece of high ground to listen. He heard him barking at no great distance, and instantly pushed his way through the wood toward him.

When he reached the spot, the other dogs were ahead of him, and sure enough, another bear was seen up the tree. A single shot from Crockett's rifle ended his career, and he then went back to his friends to finish butchering the first bear killed.

They next proceeded to where the boy had been left chopping the tree. It had fallen, but in the wrong direction, and the lad then attacked the oak itself with his axe. To his surprise, he found it to consist only of a thin shell, through which it was easy to cut. Leaving his boy and friend to continue cutting, Crockett moved off about a hundred yards with the hounds, so as to keep them from being injured by the falling tree.

By this time the noise and racket aroused the bear from his slumbers, and, climbing up the interior of his house, he thrust his nose and head out of the door, and looked inquiringly down at the people cutting away at the foundation, as if seeking to learn what their purpose could be.

The poor fellow soon learned. Growing suspicious, he carefully crawled out from his quarters and was descending, when a single ball brought him tumbling like a log to the ground, where the dogs instantly flew at him like so many tigers. Wounded as the brute was, he would have made havoc among the canines, had not Crockett, at the critical moment, sent another bullet into him which ended his struggles at once.

The three bears were salted and placed on scaffolds to keep them out of the reach of wolves, and the little party went into camp.

In the morning the boy was left behind, and the two men started in the direction of the fallen timbers, which were some three miles away. When the section was reached, it was impassable for their horses, and the hunters, therefore, dismounted and began picking their way through the "harricane," as Crockett called it.

They were thus engaged, when they came directly face to face with a bear. The latter concluded it was his place to turn out of the road, and immediately made off. Crockett's friend, with several of the dogs, followed him, while the leader himself started in another direction, his dogs' cries showing they had treed some kind of an animal.

At about the middle of the fallen timbers, the hounds brought the bear to bay upon the top of a broken tree, perhaps twenty feet high. Crockett was so tired and trembling from his severe exertions, that when he fired, he only broke the shoulder of the brute. It brought him to the ground, however, where a second shot finished him.

The neighbor appeared a few minutes later, and leaving him to dress the bear, Crockett set out for their horses, with a view to bring them as closely as possible to the spot. The animals were loaded with all they could carry, and the two started back, reaching camp at sunset, where the boy was found patiently awaiting them.

It would be supposed that by this time, Colonel Crockett had had enough hunting for one day, and would be glad to obtain rest, but he was always ready for such royal amusement—amusement in fact that could never lose its charm to him.

But when almost within camp, the dogs' cries fired him again, and leaping off his horse, he started after them as eagerly as he had done in the invigorating hours of the morning. He was thus engaged, when night came on. The woods were rough and hilly, and the fallen timbers and cracks in the earth—caused by something like an earthquake shock—compelled him to use the utmost care and caution to prevent himself from falling so violently over some obstruction as to break his gun.

We cannot believe that one professional hunter in a thousand, after spending the entire day in the most arduous pursuit, and when close to the welcome camp as night was closing in, would have turned about and tramped through fallen timber, dense cane and undergrowth, being compelled frequently to crawl for long distances on his hands and knees—while the air was freezingly cold—and all for the sake of gaining another shot at a bear— such prospect being very slight indeed.

But Colonel Davy Crockett was just the hunter to do this, and the reader will join with us in saying that it was not the first time he had proven that he possessed an indomitable determination in the execution of any plan, such as was never surpassed, and is very seldom equalled.

The pluck, resolution, and tenacity of purpose of Crockett were nothing less than marvelous.

For fully three miles he picked his way in this difficult manner, and then suddenly found himself on the edge of an unknown stream of water. Its width and depth being conjectural, it will be taken for granted that he turned back.

Such a thought we are warranted in supposing never entered his head. He scarcely hesitated, but stepped into the creek, and began wading across. The water was like ice, and rose to his knees, but he was so warm and perspiring from his recent severe exertion, that the sensation was not specially discomforting; but one shudders to think of the risk to his health thus run—a risk which would be certain to produce serious results with most people.

The barking of the dogs continued from one point—showing they had treed their game, and the hunter pushed on until he found himself part way up a hill, which became so steep, that he was forced to stop. He groped along the creek till he found a depression, by whose aid he was able to flank the hill, so to speak; but in the darkness he passed the dogs, and spent considerable more time before he could reach them.

There was no moon or stars, and the night, consequently, was very dark; but when Crockett at last found his way to the spot, he saw the hounds were barking at the base of a huge, forked poplar.

Casting his experienced eye to the fork above, the hunter could dimly discern a dark mass which he knew was a bear. It did not move, but was evidently looking down upon the man and dogs below. The view being so indistinct, Crockett could not make his aim sure, and he set about to gather fuel with which to start a fire.

Even this could not be obtained, and, as there was no other course left to him, he decided to shoot by guess. The best he could do was to fire at the dark mass, which he did. The result was that bruin, instead of falling, climbed higher, and made his way out on a limb. This was a good thing for the hunter below, as it brought the game in partial relief against the sky, and his aim was thereby assisted.

But a second shot did not move him, and Crockett began loading for a third shot. While thus engaged, there was a thunderous thump at his side, and he saw that his game had landed, and was fighting savagely with the dogs that were furiously assailing him.

It was not the occasion for another shot, and Crockett drew his knife, and held himself ready to use it the instant the bear should assault him. One of his hounds was white in color, and was the only object the owner could perceive: all the rest was a black, struggling mass.

The ground was intersected in many places by

the large seams which the earthquake shock had left, and it was not long before the bear rolled into one of them; but he still kept up his defence with such fury that the hunter shoved the muzzle of his rifle against him, and pulled the trigger. It produced no tangible result, however, except to induce him to struggle out of the gap to the surface. He soon dropped back, however, and the fight continued until Crockett lost all patience, and, springing down in the crack, stooped beneath the beast, felt along his shaggy body until he found the right spot, and then drove his knife to his heart.

The weather was intensely cold, and the hunter's leathern breeches, wetted in crossing the creek, were frozen stiff. But putting forth his great strength, he succeeded in drawing the bear from the gap in the earth, by which time he was suffering so much, that he felt he must build a fire to keep from freezing.

But, strive as much as he might, his material was so poor, he could not get enough flame to warm him, so he resorted to exercise. Springing to his feet, he yelled and danced several jigs, more noticeable for their vigor than their grace. This might have answered under ordinary circumstances, but his limbs were so thoroughly tired from his severe exertions of the day, that he suffered more, while putting forth his efforts in that direction, than from cold.

When he paused, he found he was becoming so benumbed, that he was in imminent danger of freezing to death. He threw wood on the fire, but it was so green that the little heat served only as a distressing aggravation.

Despite his furious efforts in the way of exercise, he was becoming chilled through and through. Colonel Crockett possessed an iron constitution, but the intensely cold weather was too much for him, and he saw as never before, that he was close to death.

Something desperate must be done at once, and he did it. Stumbling to a tall tree of narrow girth, he climbed vigorously to the top, and then, hugging it as tightly as was prudent, allowed himself to slip to the ground again.

This violent friction of his limbs warmed them, and helped to keep the spark of life from leaving his body.

Incredible as it may seem, he continued this strange exercise all through the night. The warmth thus gained would last only a few minutes, when up the tree he would go, and, when he had labored to the branches near the top, down he would slide, with a rough swiftness which stirred the blood all through his system. It might be termed a species of coasting, though there was little enjoyment in it.

It served, however, to preserve the life of the Tennessean, when it is more than probable that otherwise he would have perished.

When daylight came at last, Crockett managed to get his game hung up safely, and then set out for camp. His friend and boy were found there, glad enough to see him, for they had concluded he had gone astray. The bears' in the vicinity were scaffolded, and the three then started for the one last killed by Crockett.

When the neighbor saw the fight made for the animal, and especially the descent of the hunter into the yawn in the earth, where he forced himself directly beneath the savage brute, he declared that he would not have run such a risk for all the bears in the Tennessee woods.

The day was principally spent in salting the game already shot, the intention being to resume the hunt on the following morning. When night came again, Crockett found himself in such sore need of rest that he stretched out upon the earth by the camp fire, feeling as though he could sleep a week.

But his slumbers were disturbed by a most startling cause—being nothing less than an earthquake. The earth was violently shaken ; and, as may well be supposed, the hunters were terrified. They were in the region where occurred the remarkable earthquake of 1811, and there could be no mistake about the second shock. The sensation of the ground swaying back and forth beneath them was of that nature that it would jar the nerves of the bravest man. The violence subsided after awhile, and they slept undisturbed through the rest of the night.

In the morning the hunters assumed the offensive again, and in the course of a few hours had killed two more bears, making ten altogether.

As they had but five horses with them, they had

now secured all the meat they could carry to their homes, distant full thirty miles, and they loaded up and started on their return.

Up to that period, Colonel Crockett had killed fifty-eight bears, during the fall and winter. In the spring, as soon as the fierce creatures ventured forth again, he resumed hunting. In the course of a month, he shot forty-seven more, which brings the sum total of the bears killed by the great back-woodsman in less than a year, to the astounding figures—105.

And with this statement, we feel it is appropriate to close the record of Colonel Davy Crockett as a bear-hunter.

CHAPTER X.

Crockett's Lumber Speculation—On the Mississippi—An Overwhelming Disaster and Narrow Escape from Drowning.

IT will be remembered that Colonel Crockett
was engaged in a lumber speculation at the time of
beginning his remarkable bear-hunts, described in
the previous chapter.

The labors of the famous backwoodsman with
his men did not amount to a great deal, and when
he returned to them, they were about ready for
the voyage. Two boats were loaded with 30,000
staves, and they started down the river to New
Orleans with them.

There was little difficulty in getting out of the
Obion, but when they entered the Mississippi, they
found good cause for alarm. It is well known that
the most skillful pilots in the world are needed to
conduct a craft through the dangerous windings
and turnings of the Father of Waters—with the innumerable snags, sawyers, shifting bars, and treacherous currents; and it did not take Crockett long
to discover that the man whom he engaged as a
pilot, and who professed to know all about the
channel, was absolutely ignorant of his duties.

All were excessively frightened, and Crockett
states that the most scared one among them was
himself. Thinking it best they should all meet

their fate together, he lashed the two boats side by side.

But this only made matters worse, for the crafts became practically unmanageable. The terrified lumbermen toiled and trembled, and did the best they could until nightfall, when they fell in with some Ohio boats. ·

As it grew dark, Crockett thought it was a good time to land, and the crews made a desperate effort to do so. But they were utterly unable to check their boats, which were swinging down the Mississippi with alarming momentum. At the critical moment, the Ohio men shouted to Crockett to keep running all night, and he concluded to adopt the suggestion, for the good reason that no choice was left to him.

At no great distance below, they were caught in the "Devil's Elbow," and Crockett was sure he never knew of a more appropriate name in all his life. He and his men tugged and panted until they were ready to drop from exhaustion, but they were in the most extreme peril all the while. More than once, each concluded that his only chance for life was a fierce struggle in the water, where the prospect of their getting out was but one in a thousand.

At last they swung through the horrible "Elbow," and, believing that any place was preferable to the Mississippi—that is, when verdant backwoodsmen were situated as were they—they made another effort to effect a landing. They failed, and then they tried again. Failing as before, they gave over the attempt, and with a grim sort of despair, concluded to let things drift, and to be prepared, as best they could, for the general smash up which all believed was close at hand.

So it proved.

The worn out Crockett after awhile went down into the cabin of his boat, and sat by the fire to meditate how much superior hunting bears in the Tennessee canebrakes was to this aimless floating on a treacherous river. His craft was speeding sideways swiftly down stream, the one in which Crockett himself was seated being in the rear.

There was too much danger impending to sleep, and, no matter how tired the men might be, there was no opportunity given them.

Crockett was in this disgusted mood when, all at once, he heard the men running hurriedly over the deck, and pulling with might and main. A few seconds later, the boat went broadside against an island where a large raft of timber had lodged.

A more alarming situation cannot be imagined. The tendency of the current was to draw both boats under the rafts, where there would be no possible escape for the inmates. Crockett understood his danger like a flash, and, springing to his feet, found the craft was going under, sure enough. He leaped to the hatchway, but a mass of water was pouring in, and it was impossible to force his way through it.

Remembering a large aperture in the side which had been used to dip water through before the boats were lashed together, he made for that. But the craft was turned so that it was only with the greatest difficulty he was enabled to reach it. When he did so, it was found too small for him to force his body through, but it was his only hope, for the water was rushing in like a millstream behind him.

Thrusting his hands through, he yelled for his friends to help him. Several caught hold of his arms and began pulling with might and main, but his body caught fast.

"Harder! harder!" commanded Crockett, "and be quick about it, for the water is rising to my neck; pull my arms off if necessary!"

Thus urged, they made a tremendous effort, and he was drawn through. Nearly all his clothing was torn from his body, but he was thankful enough to escape with his life from the awful fate that impended but a few seconds before.

Crockett's rescue was scarcely accomplished, when his boat was sucked under the raft, as if caught in a maelstrom. The men leaped aboard the raft, where they sat all night, within a mile of land. Most of the company were bareheaded, and three were without any covering for their feet. Among the latter was the future member of Congress.

And yet, despite his pitiable predicament, Crockett said he never felt happier, for his delivery from an appalling death was so wonderful that it kept his heart continually warmed with gratitude.

The crew were sturdy characters, who had lived in the backwoods, and were accustomed to privation and suffering. So they gathered in a group and cheered each other as best they could, with jest and story, while they waited for the long night to end.

Colonel Crockett would have been required to pay a large premium to secure an insurance on his cargo at that moment; and when he looked ruefully at the head of the raft, where the gurgling waters gave no sign of the two boats that had sunk forever from his sight, he was forced to admit that his first venture in sending staves to the New Orleans market was not of a nature to encourage him to continue in the business.

At sunrise they descried a boat coming down the river, and hailed it. A skiff was sent out to the shipwrecked lumbermen, and they were all taken aboard and carried down to Memphis, in which city a good Samaritan was found in the person of a Major Winchester, who furnished all with clothing and necessary funds.

Crockett and one of his crew went to Natchez to make inquiries concerning the larger boat, which they supposed had floated from under the raft. He was told that it had been seen about fifty miles below Memphis. An attempt had been made to land it, but without success.

This ended the career of Colonel Crockett as a lumber merchant.

CHAPTER XI.

Colonel Crockett's Successful Candidacy for Congress—Serves Two Terms—His Opposition to General Jackson defeats another Re-election—Unfair and Desperate Means used to prevent his Success—He is elected for a Third Term.

COLONEL DAVID CROCKETT now enters upon the career which, a half century ago, made him one of the most famous men in the entire country. His previous life had been mainly spent in hunting bears, fighting Indians, with an occasional interval of manual labor, and he now assumes a part which should receive (alas, how rarely it does!) the profoundest study and efforts of statesmen.

In the month of August succeeding the adventures described in the preceding chapter, the Congressional election came off in Tennessee. The backwoodsman, while hunting and toiling, had meditated upon the honors which he so narrowly escaped, and having had a taste, as may be said, of the intoxication of public office, he determined to enter the political fight against not only his old opponent, Colonel Alexander, but also General Arnold.

The fight upon which Crockett entered was a formidable one; for, in the first place, he had no funds, and in this free country of ours, a political candidate in that plight, is like a shipwrecked mariner in mid-ocean, without boat or plank to cling to.

However, a good friend turned up at the right moment, and voluntarily proffered the backwoodsman all the money he was likely to need, while he put in a good word for him whenever the opportunity presented.

The peculiar results of this canvass may be understood, when it is remembered that Colonel Alexander had served a number of years in Congress, and that Arnold was a major-general of militia and a successful lawyer, so that, as Crockett said, he had the law and military prestige to work against.

But these two gentlemen virtually conducted themselves as though they were the only candidates in the field : Crockett was not considered of any account, but all the time he and his tried friends were doing the most effective kind of work.

It is no difficult problem to discover the reasons of Crockett's success.   Humor, wit, good nature, and readiness in the way of anecdote will always win, when pitted against learning, ability, and capacity, unweighted by the other qualities.

Crockett prosecuted his canvass in his own peculiar manner.   He looked exceedingly wise when asked difficult questions, and was very careful to be non-committal upon matters in which the sentiment of the community was pretty evenly divided.

Once, when in the eastern counties of the State, the three candidates met at the same town, and were announced to speak from the same platform.

Much to Crockett's disgust, he was compelled to lead off. He did so in one of his characteristic speeches, abounding with humor and anecdote, and of a nature to set the groundlings in a roar.

He did not talk long—which was certainly a virtue in him, as it is in the generality of orators. It was during this occasion that an incident occurred, and the manner in which the Tennessean turned it to his advantage shows his readiness of resource in that direction—a readiness which is rarely equaled.

Colonel Alexander followed Crockett, and General Arnold came last. The final speaker devoted himself to answering the arguments of Alexander, but studiously ignored the existence of the backwoodsman. It is not probable that Crockett said anything worth serious attention, for he was not capable of doing so, but the total obliviousness to his personality by both speakers was a mistake. It cut Crockett, and stirred him to renewed vigor, at the same time giving him the curious weapon which he turned to his own account with such wonderful quickness.

General Arnold was pretty well through his speech, demolishing Alexander with his sledge-hammer arguments, when a flock of guinea-fowls passed near the platform, making such a deafening racket that the speaker was forced to stop until they were driven away.

He then finished his speech, when Crockett stepped up to him, and said loud enough for all to hear:

"Colonel, you're the first man I ever saw who understood the language of guinea-fowls. You made no reference to me in your speech, but when *they* began to call out '*Crockett! Crockett!*' you ordered them driven away.

There is a similarity between the cry of this noisy domestic fowl and the name of the renowned Tennessean backwoodsman, and he displayed genuine wit by the way in which he turned it to account.

The audience caught the point instantly, and set up a shout of laughter, while Colonel Alexander looked nonplussed. Such an incident, it is fair to believe, gained of itself a large number of supporters for the illiterate candidate.

It was observed by those with whom Crockett came in contact, that he was plentifully supplied with funds, but no one knew where he got them. A great deal of this money was expended in "treating" those whom he encountered in his tours through his district, for such an occupation was a congenial one to him, and he could have made little progress without resorting to it.

There was no man who could tell a joke or humorous story with better effect than Crockett; there was no one who was so quick of repartee as he, and his quaint expressions were of the kind to delight the voters of the state.

Then it was known that he was personally brave; that he had served creditably through the Creek war; that he was the greatest bear-hunter in the whole country; that he was an unerring shot with his rifle, and he was kind-hearted and sympathetic. These qualities when thrown in the scales against learning, eloquence, experience, ability and fitness, will outweigh them with the generality of mankind, nine times out of ten.

It mattered not that Crockett was ignorant on the important questions discussed, and that it was beyond his power to comprehend many of the important measures likely to come before Congress; the people felt he was "one of them." They took personal pride in his skill with the rifle, and his inimitable powers as a humorist and funny story-teller. The consequence was they "rallied" at the polls with such enthusiasm that he beat his competitors by the astounding majority of 2,748 votes, —a result which exceeded his most enthusiastic expectations.

Colonel David Crockett was elected a member of Congress at last, and, as a matter of course, he was in exuberant spirits, as was perfectly proper that he should be. He was congratulated from every quarter, and though his opponents were chagrined over their defeat, yet there was a certain open-handed generosity about the backwoodsman which won their good will, and neither entertained any resentment toward him who had made such a gallant fight in his own behalf.

The first thing Crockett did on going to Washington was to draw two hundred and fifty dollars, which he sent to his friend in Tennessee, who had so opportunely advanced him the necessary funds with which to prosecute his canvass. Nothing afforded the backwoodsman more pleasure than to reciprocate a favor of that nature.

It is difficult at this remote day to appreciate the experience of Colonel David Crockett in Washington. His peculiarities of manner and dress, his native humor and eccentricities, soon drew attention to him, and he became famous throughout the country. Hundreds visited the Capitol for no other purpose than to see the member from the wilds of Tennessee, who had slain such a fabulous number of bears and Indians. The most absurd stories were told of his prowess with gun and knife, and there was scarcely anything too wildly improbable to be believed.

"Davy Crockett Almanacs," lives of "Colonel Davy Crockett" were sold broadcast over the land, and speeches and sayings were put in his mouth of which he never dreamed. Such a man was *sui generis*, and he attained a prodigious popularity—such a popularity as is often seen in our country, but which is never of long duration.

There are very few who can reach such a point as did Crockett in the public eye, and maintain their natural simplicity of character. The reputation of a wit and humorist is dangerous and difficult to sustain. It involves draughts upon the fancy which cannot always be met, for it is the nature of true wit that it is killed by premeditation. The humor which bubbles unbidden to the surface, and the wit which flashes like the lightning-drawn scimeter, are those which please and astonish.

David Crockett uttered many things which would

have done credit to " Poor Richard" himself; his jollity and inevitable good nature were contagious, and gave a glow to some of his expressions which they lost when placed in cold type. A great many of his utterances were simply coarse, without wit, and his humor often was of that nature as only to excite a laugh among the low and vulgar.

But withal, he possessed a natural readiness which frequently made itself manifest. Above everything else, it must be conceded that he was personally honest, during his career in Congress, and indeed through life.

It may be, that no higher meed of praise can be given a public officer.

When Crockett entered Congress, he was a great friend and supporter of what was known as the Jackson party. John Quincy Adams was President, and Crockett had no sympathy with his principles.

He was elected a second time by an immense majority, but during this term he began to feel a dissatisfaction with the dictatorial methods of General Jackson. It seemed to the backwoodsman as though Old Hickory expected a blind obedience from all his friends without regard to any compunctions of conscience.

In those days, about the most popular thing a man could do, especially in Tennessee, was to support General Jackson, without turning to the right or left.

Colonel Crockett could not deliberately do that which he believed to be wrong, no matter what rewards and punisments loomed up before him. While a great admirer—as who is not?—of the stern old hero of New Orleans, it was impossible for the backwoodsman to be a blind supporter of him. There were some of his measures which came before Congress that he could not vote for nor advocate.

One of these was General Jackson's famous Indian Bill, which Crockett opposed from principle, though his friends assured him it would be his political death. It was a favorite measure of the President, and he would never forgive opposition from *that* quarter. Unless Crockett became its supporter, he would never be permitted to be elected to Congress again.

The reply of the Tennessear was what might have been expected.

"I believe the measure is unjust and wicked, and I shall fight it, let the consequences be what they may. I am willing to go with General Jackson in everything I believe right and honest, but beyond that I wont go for any man in creation. I would sooner be honest and politically d——d, than hypocritically immortalized."

After this little speech, there was no trouble in finding out where the member from Tennessee stood.

But it was politically a dangerous step for Crockett, for when his term ended and he went home, he found great excitement prevailing. The report was spread that he had turned against General Jackson—the especial idol of the State. He was assailed by all the newspapers, and scores of public speakers seized the occasion when the lion had the festering thorn in his paw to flout him to his face.

The accounts of the political struggles of those days vividly remind us of those which occurred since, and are occurring to-day, and will probably continue to the end of time.

General Jackson caused all the ammunition possible to be sent to Crockett's district to be used against him. The editors examined the records, and found that he had missed something like seventy votes during his membership. Computing these at eight dollars apiece, it followed that he had swindled the government out of $560.

This was but a specimen of the numerous unjust charges brought against Crockett, who had certainly done what he conceived to be his duty.

Still more unfair means were resorted to. The most dishonest was that of announcing him to speak in different portions of the district, on which occasions it was promised that he would explain the whole unfortunate Jackson business.

Crockett was unaware of these engagements, and of course was not present. His enemies were sure to be represented on the ground, and they took pains to spread the report that Crockett had shown the white feather, and dare not face an indignant constituency.

The backwoodsman knew nothing of this dishonorable business until it was too late to explain it to a people whose sense of fair-mindedness would ·

have caused them to rally about him in overwhelming force. When the result of the election became
known, it was found that Crockett had a majority
in seventeen counties, but the eighteenth beat him.

The Tennessean was therefore compelled to stay
in the backwoods for a couple of years, but he had
become thoroughly imbued with the fever for office,
and he spent most of the time in "laying his pipes"
for the next election.

His experience and natural ability enabled him
to do this so successfully that he created a revolution of sentiment in many quarters. While the
Tennesseans believed General Andrew Jackson to
be the greatest man that ever was or would be
born, yet they liked fair play, and they saw the injustice that had been done the honest Congressman.

The enemies felt that something desperate must
be done to defeat him, and the Legislature resorted
to the popular method of "gerrymandering" the
district, so as to insure a majority against the out-
spoken Crockett.

It was cut up and divided with as much skill as
is displayed in these later days, and the war-horses
of the opposition threw their energies into the canvass to defeat the candidate who would not stay
defeated. Every possible means was used, and the
fight was one of the hottest ever fought in the State.

When the summing up took place, it was found
that Colonel David Crockett was elected by a majority of 202 votes.

CHAPTER XII.

Colonel Crockett at Home.

THE following interesting account of Crockett at home was written by an old acquaintance of the backwoodsman.

"Some time in the month of ——, in the year ——, while traveling through the Western District, I heard Colonel Crockett, or the great bear-hunter, so frequently mentioned—and with his name were associated so many humorous anecdotes—that I determined to visit him. Obtaining directions, I left the high road and sought his residence. My route, for many miles, lay through a country uninteresting from its sameness; and I found myself on the morning of the third day within eight miles of Colonel Crockett's. Having refreshed myself and horse, I set out to spend the remainder of the day with him—pursuing a small blazed trail, which bore no marks of being often traveled, and jogged on, wondering what sort of a reception I should meet with from a man who, by quirky humors unequalled, had obtained for himself a never-dying reputation.

"The character which had been given of the Colonel, both by his friends and foes, induced me to hope for a kind welcome; but doubting,—for I still believed him a bear in appearance,—I pursued my journey until a small opening brought me in sight of a cabin which, from description, I identified as the home of the celebrated hunter of the West.

"It was in appearance rude and uninviting, situated in a small field of eight or ten acres, which had been cleared in the wild woods; no yard surrounded it, and it seemed to have been lately settled. In the passage of the house were seated two men in their shirt sleeves, cleaning rifles. I strained my eyes as I rode up to see if I could identify in either of them the great bear-hunter; but before I could decide, my horse had stopped at the bars, and there walked out, in plain homespun attire, with a black fur cap on, a finely proportioned man, about six feet high, aged, from appearance, forty-five. His countenance was frank and manly, and a smile played over it as he approached me. He brought with him a rifle, and from his right shoulder hung a bag made of a raccoon skin, to which, by means of a sheath, was appended a huge butcher's knife.

"'This is Colonel Crockett's residence, I presume?'

"'Yes, sir.'

"'Have I the pleasure of seeing that gentleman before me?'

"'If it be a pleasure, you have, sir.'

"'Well, Colonel, I have rode much out of my way to spend a day or two with you, and take a hunt.'

"'Get down, sir; I am delighted to see you; I

like to see strangers : and the only care I have is, that I cannot accommodate them as well as I could wish. I have no corn; you see I've but lately moved here; but I'll make my little boy take your horse over to my son-in-law's; he is a good fellow, and will take care of him.' Walking in,—' My brother, let me make you acquainted with Mr. —— of ——; my wife, Mr. ——; my daughters, Mr. ——. You see, we are mighty rough here. I am afraid you will think it hard times, but we have to do the best we can. I started mighty poor, and have been *rooting 'long ever since;* but d—n apologies, I hate 'em; what I live upon always, I think a friend can for a day or two. I have but little, but that little is as free as the water that runs—so make yourself at home. Here are newspapers and some books.'

" His free mode of conversation made me feel quite easy; and a few moments gave me leisure to look around. His cabin within was clean and neat, and bore about it many marks of comfort. The many trophies of wild animals spread over his house and yard—his dogs, in appearance war-worn veterans, lying about sunning themselves—all told truly that I was at the home of the celebrated hunter.

" His family were dressed by the work of their own hands; and there was a neatness and simplicity in their appearance very becoming. His wife was rather grave and quiet, but attentive and kind to strangers; his daughters diffident and retiring, perhaps too much so, but uncommonly beautiful,

and are fine specimens of the native worth of the
female character—for, entirely uneducated, they
are not only agreeable but fascinating.   There are
no schools near them, yet they converse well—and
if they did not one would be apt to think so, for
they are extremely pretty, and tender to a stranger
with so much kindness the comforts of their little
cabin.   The Colonel has no slaves; his daughters
attend to the dairy and kitchen, while he performs
the more laborious duties of his farm.   He has but
lately moved where he now resides, and consequently had to fix anew.   He took me over his
little field of corn, which he himself had cleared
and grubbed, talked of the quantity he should
make, his peas, pumpkins, etc., with the same
pleasure that a Mississippi planter would have
shown me his cotton estate, or a James River Virginia planter have carried me over his wide inheritance.

" The newspapers being before us, called up the
subject of politics.   I held in high estimation the
present administration of our country.   To this he
was opposed.   His views, however, delighted me;
and, were they more generally adopted, we should
be none the loser.   He was opposed to the administration, and yet conceded that many of its acts
were wise and efficient, and would have received his
cordial support.   He admired Mr. Clay, but had
objections to him.   He was opposed to the tariff,
yet, I think, a supporter of the bank.   He seemed
to have the most horrible objection to binding himself to any man, or set of men.   He said he would

as lieve be an old 'coon dog, as obliged to do what any man, or set of men, would tell him was right. The present administration he would support as far as he would any other; and that was, as far as he believed its views to be correct. He would pledge himself to support no administration—when the will of his constituents was known to him, it was his law; when unknown, his judgment was his guide.

" I remarked to him, that his district was so thorough-going for Jackson, I thought he would never be elected.

" He said, 'he didn't care ; he believed his being left out was of service to him, for it had given him time to go to work; he had cleared his corn-field, dug a well, built his cabins,' etc., and says he, 'if they won't elect me with my opinions, I can't help it. *I had rather be politically damned than hypocritically immortalized.*'

" He spoke very highly of Benton, and was delighted with P. P. Barbour, whom he would have preferred for President to Jackson or Clay; and of whom he remarked, 'I'll be d—d if Barbour ain't as quick as Dupont's treble.'

" He spoke with much pleasure of his former acquaintances at Washington, and assigned, at my instance, the reasons why he was beaten at the last election ; but they were better summed up by an Irish gentleman, with whom I had the pleasure of conversing while in the District. He said, ' 'twas a poor *bate* that, to be *baten* only three or four hundred votes in seventeen counties ; and he would

not have been *baten* at all, but that he carried on
his back Jackson, and every lawyer and printer in
the district.'

"His rifle next came upon the tapis, and from
him I learned that he was cleaning her up for a
shooting match, to which I was invited. To gratify
me, he, with his brother, went out and shot several
times. One who is little accustomed to shooting,
can form no idea of the skill of the backwoods
marksmen. Even the fiction of Cooper, in the skill
of his far-famed Hawk-eye, I have seen surpassed.
And were the deeds of La Longue Carabine and
old Betsy brought into comparison, an impartial
judge would have to decide in favor of the latter.
Not only does the Colonel shoot well, who has indeed been a splendid shot, but the finest corps of
riflemen in the world might be selected from the
north-western part of Tennessee.

Forty yards off-hand, or sixty with a rest, is the
distance generally chosen for a shooting-match.
These are considered equivalent distances; that is,
either may be selected—if no distance be specified,
this is implied.

Off-hand shooting is always preferred by a good
marksman, and is generally the closest. In shooting with a rest, the rifle rebounds, and consequently throws its ball with much less accuracy.
To prove this, take two rifle or gun-barrels, which,
by placing them together, will touch only at each
end, and you will find no difficulty in springing
them together by means of your two fingers. In
speaking of the accuracy of the Western riflemen,

I can conceive of nothing that I could say which would amount to fiction. I have known them, at the distance of one hundred yards, to shoot six balls out of eleven within less than half an inch of the centre ; and in all their shooting matches, no ball is allowed to count which is not found within an inch. They use for patching, cotton cloth, and wipe their rifles after every discharge. I think they would even shoot with more accuracy than they do, did they use percussion locks, which possess many advantages over the flint-lock.

"The time having arrived, on we went to the shooting-match. The place selected was a grove, near which stood a tippling house. We found many persons already assembled, and they continued to flock in until several hundred were collected. They disposed of themselves in different groups about the grove, some lying down, others standing, and indulged pretty much in the same topic of conversation—that is, each man wanted his neighbor to put up something to be shot for. There was something very striking in their appearance. Almost every man was clad in the garb of a hunter,—with a 'coon skin bag, from which was suspended a large knife and an alligator's tooth for a charger,—than which nothing can be more beautiful. Many articles were brought to the gathering for sale ; yet no person, though he might want them ever so badly, thought of buying. They must all go through the process of being shot for, before any man would consent to own them. This was literally the case with every article. Whenever anything very pretty

was exhibited, you would hear many persons telling the vender not to sell it, but to put it up—that
is, make up chances, and have a shooting-match.

"There is no country in the world which can
beat the Western District in originality of names.
I once overheard two men bargaining for a horse:
said one to the other, 'I will give you two hundred
dollars worth of dogs for him.' Two hundred dollars worth of dogs! said I to myself—two hundred
dollars worth of dogs!!—What can that mean?
Upon asking for an explanation, I found out that
bonds, or promissory notes, were termed dogs—
and that they were said to be of a good or bad
breed, according to the ability and punctuality of
the obligor.

"But to my tale. The crowd, to brighten their
ideas, or rather to increase their propensity to
shoot, which, by the bye, needed no stimulus, occasionally took a little—and when they were sum-
moned to the field, where an ox or two was to be
awarded to the victor, I could see many a man who
was 'how come you so?' Each man who was to
shoot, carried with him his target: this consisted
of a small board which had been burned black, and
rubbed smooth, on which a small piece of white
paper had been pinned. The judges took possession of all the boards; and, from the centre spot
on each, described four concentric circles, commencing with a radius of one-fourth of an inch,
then half an inch, three-fourths of an inch, and
one inch.

"The judges having measured the distance at

which they were to shoot, from a tree against which their targets were to be placed—and having marked out on the ground a circle, to prevent their being intruded upon under penalty of a *quart*, all was ready.   There was no regularity in shooting; each marksman called for his target when it suited him.   One, taking his position, cried out, ' Put up my board '—it was done : and the crowd flocked together, on either side, from the target to the marksman, forming a lane of living people about four feet wide, with their heads inclining inwards, to see the effect of the shot.   The marksman stood for a moment as if sculptured from marble, the muzzle of his gun pointing to the earth—then raising it gradually, it became horizontal, poised for an instant, and there burst forth a sheet of living flame —the ball was buried in the paper, and at the annunciation of it, a wild shout rent the air.

   "' D—n it, clear the track, and put up my board,' was shouted from the lips of Crockett, and I discovered old Betsy poised aloft in the air.   The lane was again formed, and Crockett lounged idly at his stand, with his gun upon his shoulder, which was carelessly thrown off, and discharged the moment it became horizontal.   The same effect ensued— the ball was buried in the paper, and another wild shout rent the air.

   I never have witnessed more excitement; the scene was kept up for several hours by various marksmen—and the welkin did not ring with louder applause, when on Long Island the far-famed Eclipse passed Henry, one of Virginia's favorite sons, than did the backwoods of Tennessee at each successful shot.

" I observed that many a marksman, after shooting two or three times, would hide his rifle in the woods, as he said, to allow it rest, and the idea at first seemed to me superstitious, but there were two objects in doing so—it was hid to prevent any person from playing a trick upon it ; and allowed to cool, that its barrel might not glimmer. A heated barrel always glimmers, and a good marksman never shoots when the rays of the sun may warp his vision, but, if practicable, seeks a shade.

" Evening came on, and the crowd showed no disposition to disperse. A thousand shooting matches were in embryo : this man wanted a pair of shoes, another a hat, a third some cakes for his children—not one of which things would they dare to carry home, until it had gone through the regular process of being shot for. Whether this practice proceeds from a natural fondness for adventure, or from a spirit of economy, I know not—for I saw several men pay two or three prices for an article, before they were fortunate enough to get it. But, methought, when one went home where, perhaps, sat some

" ' —————————————— sulky, sullen dame,
Gathering her brows, like gathering storm,
Nursing her wrath to keep it warm,'

it would appease her but little to state that their joint earnings had been spent for ginger-cakes, but that it would act like a sedative, when it was

announced that they cost but a thimble of powder,
with a leaden-ball.

"The evening passed off amid a continual ringing of rifles, and night came on, and yet there was
no disposition to disperse—it was damp and foggy,
and consequently very dark, and, to my utter as-
tonishment, candles were called for, to enable them
to shoot. The distance was diminished; and though
their heads must have spun round like whirligigs, I
think they rather improved in shooting. There
was a candle held near each sight of the rifle, and
one also on each side of the target; and in this
manner did they continue through the night to dis-
pose of the merchandise, which had been brought
for sale during the day. I sat up very late; candles were continually called for, and new parties
formed. Weary of the scene, I retired to bed.

"In the morning I arose with the first dawn of
day, and mounted my horse. The noise had somewhat abated, though the candles were burning, and
the rifles ringing, and they continued to do so
while I was in hearing."

CHAPTER XIII.

A Sensible and Timely View of a Certain Constitutional
Question.

FROM time to time, Congress has appropriated
money for charitable purposes. The following account of Crockett's experience, while in Washington, is in that line, and is therefore timely and
instructive. The narrator says :

" While Crockett was in Congress I had business
which required me to spend several weeks in Washington city. Waiting upon one of the departments,
or rather one of the chief clerks, for my turn, I had
much leisure upon my hands; for, though my
business might have been dispatched as well in
two hours as in two months, yet I had to wait. I
had made up my mind that I would not leave until
my business was settled. My only regular employment was to go every day to the office to learn
that it could not be attended to that day.

" Crockett was then the lion of Washington. I
was a great admirer of his character, and, having
several friends who were intimate with him, I found
no difficulty in making his acquaintance. I was
fascinated with him, and he seemed to take a fancy
to me.

" I was one day in the lobby of the House of
Representatives when a bill was taken up appro-

priating money for the benefit of a widow of a distinguished naval officer. Several beautiful speeches had been made in its support, rather, as I thought, ,because it afforded the speakers a fine opportunity for display than from the necessity of convincing anybody, for it seemed to me that everybody favored it. The Speaker was just about to put the question, when Crockett arose. Everybody expected, of course, that he was going to make one of his characteristic speeches in support of the bill. He commenced:

"'Mr. Speaker—I have as much respect for the memory of the deceased, and as much sympathy for the sufferings of the living, if suffering there be, as any man in this House, but we must not permit our respect for the dead or our sympathy for a part of the living to lead us into an act of injustice to the balance of the living. I will not go into an argument to prove that Congress has no power to appropriate this money as an act of charity. Every member upon this floor knows it. We have the right, as individuals, to give away as much of our own money as we please in charity; but as members of Congress we have no right so to appropriate a dollar of the public money. Some eloquent appeals have been made to us upon the ground that it is a debt due the deceased. Mr. Speaker, the deceased lived long after the close of the war; he was in office to the day of his death, and I have never heard that the Government was in arrears to him. This Government can owe no debts but for services rendered, and at a stipulated price. If it is a debt, how much is it? Has it been audited, and the amount due ascertained? If it is a debt, this is not the place to present it for payment, or to have its merits examined. If it is a debt, we owe more than we can ever hope to pay, for we owe the widow of every soldier who fought in the war of 1812 precisely the same amount. There is a woman in my neighborhood, the widow of as gallant a man as ever shouldered a musket. He fell in battle. She is as good in every respect as this lady, and is as poor. She is earning her daily bread by her daily labor, and if I were to introduce a bill to appropriate five or ten thousand dollars for her benefit, I should be laughed at, and my bill would not get five votes in this House. There are thousands of widows in the country just such as the one I have spoken of; but we never hear of any of these large debts to them. Sir, this is no debt. The Government did not owe it to the deceased when he was alive ; it could not contract it after he died. I do not wish to be rude, but I must be plain. Every man in this House knows it is not a debt. We cannot, without the grossest corruption, appropriate this money as the payment of a debt. We have not the semblance of authority to appropriate it as a charity. Mr. Speaker, I have said we have the right to give as much money of our own as we please. I am the poorest man on this floor. I cannot vote for this bill, but I will give one week's pay to the object, and if every member of Congress will do the same, it will amount to more than the bill asks.'

"He took his seat. Nobody replied. The bill was put upon its passage, and, instead of passing unanimously, as was generally supposed, and as, no doubt, it would, but for that speech, it received but few votes, and, of course, was lost.

"Like many other young men, and old ones too, for that matter, who had not thought upon the subject, I desired the passage of the bill, and felt outraged at its defeat. I determined that I would persuade my friend Crockett to move a reconsideration the next day.

"Previous engagements preventing me from seeing Crockett that night, I went early to his room the next morning, and found him engaged in addressing and franking letters, a large pile of which lay upon his table.

"I broke in upon him rather abruptly, by asking him what devil had possessed him to make that speech and defeat that bill yesterday. Without turning his head or looking up from his work, he replied:

"'You see that I am very busy now; take a seat and cool yourself. I will be through in a few minutes, and then I will tell you all about it.'

"He continued his employment for about ten minutes, and when he had finished it turned to me and said:

"'Now, sir, I will answer your question. But thereby hangs a tale, and one of considerable length, to which you will have to listen.'

"I listened, and this is the tale which I heard:

"'Several years ago I was one evening standing

on the steps of the Capitol with some other members of Congress, when our attention was attracted
by a great light over in Georgetown. It was evidently a large fire. We jumped into a hack and
drove over as fast as we could. When we got
there I went to work, and I never worked as hard
in my life as I did there for several hours. But, in
spite of all that could be done, many houses were
burned and many families made houseless, and,
besides, some of them had lost all but the clothes
they had on. The weather was very cold, and
when I saw so many women and children suffering,
I felt that something ought to be done for them,
and everybody else seemed to feel the same way.

" ' The next morning a bill was introduced appropriating $20,000 for their relief. We put aside
all other business, and rushed it through as soon as
it could be done. I said everybody felt as I did.
That was not quite so; for, though they perhaps
sympathized as deeply with the sufferers as I did,
there were a few of the members who did not think
we had the right to indulge our sympathy or excite
our charity at the expense of anybody but ourselves. They opposed the bill, and upon its passage demanded the yeas and nays. There were
not enough of them to sustain the call, but many
of us wanted our names to appear in favor of what
we considered a praiseworthy measure, and we
voted with them to sustain it. So the yeas and
nays were recorded, and my name appeared on the
journals in favor of the bill.

" ' The next summer, when it began to be time

to think about the election, I concluded I would take a scout around among the boys of my district. I had no opposition there, but, as the election was some time off, I did not know what might turn up, and I thought it was best to let the boys know that I had not forgot them, and that going to Congress had not made me too proud to go to see them.

"'So I put a couple of shirts and a few twists of tobacco into my saddle-bags, and put out. I had been out about a week, and had found things going very smoothly, when, riding one day in a part of my district in which I was more of a stranger than any other, I saw a man in a field plowing and coming toward the road. I gauged my gait so that we should meet as he came to the fence. As he came up I spoke to the man. He replied politely, but, as I thought, rather coldly, and was about turning his horse for another furrow, when I asked him if he could give me a chew of tobacco.'

"'Yes,' said he, 'such as we make and use in this part of the country; but it may not suit your taste, as you are probably in the habit of using better.'

"'With that he pulled out of his pocket part of a twist in its natural state, and handed it to me. I took a chew, and handed it back to him. He turned to his plow, and was about to start off. I said to him : 'Don't be in such a hurry, my friend; I want to have a little talk with you, and get better acquainted.' He replied:

"'I am very busy, and have but little time to talk, but if it does not take too long, I will listen to what you have to say.'

"'I began: "Well, friend, I am one of those unfortunate beings called candidates, and——"

"'Yes, I know you; you are Colonel Crockett. I have seen you once before, and voted for you the last time you were elected. I suppose you are out electioneering now, but you had better not waste your time or mine. I shall not vote for you again.'

"'This was a sockdologer. I had been making up my mind that he was one of those churlish fellows who care for nobody but themselves, and take bluntness for independence. I had seen enough of them to know there is a way to reach them, and was satisfied that if I could get him to talk to me I would soon have him straight. But this was entirely a different bundle of sticks. He knew me, had voted for me before, and did not intend to do it again. Something must be the matter; I could not imagine what it was. I had heard of no complaints against me, except that some of the dandies about the village ridiculed some of the wild and foolish things that I too often say and do, and said that I was not enough of a gentleman to go to Congress. I begged him to tell me what was the matter.

"'Well, Colonel, it is hardly worth while to waste time or words upon it. I do not see how it can be mended, but you gave a vote last winter which shows that either you have not capacity to understand the Constitution, or that you are wanting in the honesty and firmness to be guided by it. In either case you are not the man to represent me. But I beg your pardon for expressing it in that way. I did not intend to avail myself of the privilege of the constituent to speak plainly to a candidate for the purpose of insulting or wounding you. I intend by it only to say that your understanding of the Constitution is very different from mine; and I will say to you what, but for my rudeness, I should not have said, that I believe you to be · honest.'

"'Thank you for that, but you find fault with only one vote. You know the story of Henry Clay, the old huntsman and the rifle ; you wouldn't break your gun for one snap.'

"'No, nor for a dozen. As the story goes, that tack served Mr. Clay's purpose admirably, though it really had nothing to do with the case. I would not break the gun, nor would I discard an honest representative for a mistake in judgment as a mere matter of policy. But an understanding of the Constitution different from mine I cannot overlook, because the Constitution, to be worth anything, must be held sacred, and rigidly observed in all its provisions. The man who wields power and misinterprets it is the more dangerous the more honest he is.'

"'I admit the truth of all you say, but there must be some mistake about it, for I do not ·remember that I gave any vote last winter upon any constitutional question.'

" ' No, Colonel, there's no mistake. Though I live here in the backwoods and seldom go from home, I take the papers from Washington and read very carefully all the proceedings of Congress. My papers say that last winter you voted for a bill to appropriate $20,000 to some sufferers by a fire in Georgetown. Is that true ? '

" ' Certainly it is, and I thought that was the last vote for which anybody in the world would have found fault with.'

" ' Well, Colonel, where do you find in the Constitution any authority to give away the public money in charity ? '

" Here was another sockdologer ; for, when I began to think about it, I could not remember a thing in the Constitution that authorized it. I found I must take another tack, so I said :

" ' Well, my friend ; I may as well own up. You have got me there. But certainly nobody will complain that a great and rich country like ours should give the insignificant sum of $20,000 to relieve its suffering women and children, particularly with a full and overflowing Treasury, and I am sure, if you had been there, you would have done just as I did.'

" ' It is not the amount, Colonel, that I complain of ; it is the principle. In the first place, the Government ought to have in the Treasury no more than enough for its legitimate purposes. But that has nothing to do with the question. The power of collecting and disbursing money at pleasure is the most dangerous power that can be intrusted to

man, particularly under our system of collecting
revenue by a tariff, which reaches every man in the
country, no matter how poor he may be, and the
poorer he is the more he pays in proportion to his
means. What is worse, it presses upon him without his knowledge where the weight centres, for
there is not a man in the United States who can
ever guess how much he pays to the Government.
So you see, that while you are contributing to re-
lieve one, you are drawing it from thousands who
are even worse off than he. If you had the right to
give anything, the amount was simply a matter of
discretion with you, and you had as much right to
give $20,000,000 as $20,000.   If you have the right
to give to one, you have the right to give to all;
and, as the Constitution neither defines charity nor
stipulates the amount, you are at liberty to give to
any and everything which you may believe, or pro-
fess to believe, is a charity, and to any amount you
may think proper. You will very easily perceive
what a wide door this would open for fraud and
corruption and favoritism, on the one hand, and for
robbing the people on the other. No, Colonel,
Congress has no right to give charity. Individual
members may give as much of their own money as
they please, but they have no right to touch a dollar of the public money for that purpose. If twice
as many houses had been burned in this county as
in Georgetown, neither you nor any other member
of Congress would have thought of appropriating a
dollar for our relief. There are about two hundred
and forty members of Congress. If they had shown

their sympathy for the sufferers by contributing
each one week's pay, it would have made over
$13,000.   There are plenty of wealthy men in and
around Washington who could have given $20,000
without depriving themselves of even a luxury of
life.   The Congressmen chose to keep their own
money, which, if reports be true, some of them
spend not very creditably; and the people about
Washington, no doubt, applauded you for relieving
them from the necessity of giving by giving what
was not yours to give.   The people have delegated
to Congress, by the Constitution, the power to do
certain things.   To do these, it is authorized to
collect and pay moneys, and for nothing else.
Everything beyond this is usurpation, and a viola-
tion of the Constitution.'

"'I have given you,' continued Crockett, 'an im-
perfect account of what he said.   Long before he
was through, I was convinced that I had done
wrong.   He wound up by saying:'

"'So you see, Colonel, you have violated the
Constitution in what I consider a vital point.   It is
a precedent fraught with danger to the country,
for when Congress once begins to stretch its power
beyond the limits of the Constitution, there is no
limit to it, and no security for the people.   I have
no doubt you acted honestly, but that does not
make it any better, except as far as you are personally concerned, and you see that I cannot vote
for you.'

"'I tell you I felt streaked.   I saw if I should
have opposition, and this man should go to talking,

he would set others to talking, and in that district I was a gone fawn-skin. I could not answer him, and the fact is I was so fully convinced that he was right, I did not want to. But I must satisfy him, and I said to him :

"'Well, my friend, you hit the nail upon the head when you said I had not sense enough to understand the Constitution. I intended to be guided by it, and thought I had studied it fully. I have heard many speeches in Congress about the powers of Congress, but what you have said here at your plow has got more hard, sound sense in it, than all the fine speeches I ever heard. If I had ever taken the view of it that you have, I would have put my head into the fire before I would have given that vote, and if you will forgive me and vote for me again, if I ever vote for another unconstitutional law I wish I may be shot.'

"He laughingly replied: 'Yes, Colonel, you have sworn to that once before, but I will trust you again upon one condition. You say that you are convinced that your vote was wrong. Your acknowledgment of it will do more good than beating you for it. If, as you go round the district, you will tell the people about this vote, and that you are satisfied it was wrong, I will not only vote for you, but will do what I can to keep down opposition, and, perhaps, I may exert some little influence in that way.'

"'If I don't,' said I, 'I wish I may be shot; and to convince you that I am in earnest in what I say I will come back this way in a week or ten days, and if you will get up a gathering of the people, I will make a speech to them. Get up a barbecue, and I will pay for it.'

"'No, Colonel, we are not rich people in this section, but we have plenty of provisions to contribute for a barbecue, and some to spare for those who have none! The push of crops will be over in a few days, and we can then afford a day for a barbecue. This is Thursday; I will see to getting it up on Saturday week. Come to my house on Friday, and we will go together, and I promise you a very respectable crowd to see and hear you.'

"'Well, I will be here. But one thing more before I say good-by. I must know your name.'

"'My name is Bunce.'

"'Not Horatio Bunce?'

"'Yes.'

"'Well, Mr. Bunce, I never saw you before, though you say you have seen me, but I know you very well. I am glad that I have met you, and very proud that I may hope to have you for my friend. You must let me shake your hand before I go.'

"'We shook hands and parted.

"'It was one of the luckiest hits of my life that I met him. He mingled but little with the public, but was widely known for his remarkable intelligence and incorruptible integrity, and for a heart brimful and running over with kindness and benevolence, which showed themselves not only in words but in acts. He was the oracle of the whole country around him, and his fame had extended

far beyond the circle of his immediate acquaintance. Though I had never met him before, I had
heard much of him, and but for this meeting it is
very likely I should have had opposition, and been
beaten. One thing is very certain, no man could
now stand up in that district under such a vote.

" 'At the appointed time I was at his house,
having told our conversation to every crowd I had
met, and to every man I stayed all night with, and
I found that it gave the people an interest and a
confidence in me stronger than I had ever seen
manifested before.

" 'Though I was considerably fatigued when I
reached his house, and, under ordinary circumstances, should have gone early to bed, I kept him
up until midnight, talking about the principles and
affairs of government, and got more real, true
knowledge of them than I had got all my life before.

" 'It is not exactly pertinent to my story, but I
must tell you more about him. When I saw him
with his family around him, I was not surprised
that he loved to stay at home. I have never in
any other family seen a manifestation of so much
confidence, familiarity and freedom of manner of
children toward their parents mingled with such
unbounded love and respect.

" 'He was not at the house when I arrived, but .
his wife received and welcomed me with all the
ease and cordiality of an old friend. She told me
that her husband was engaged in some out-door
business, but would be in shortly. She is a woman

of fine person; her face is not what the world
would at first sight esteem beautiful. In a state of
rest there was too much strength and character in
it for that, but when she engaged in conversation,
and especially when she smiled, it softened into an
expression of mingled kindness, goodness, and
strength that was beautiful beyond anything I
have ever seen.

" ' Pretty soon her husband came in, and she left
us and went about her household affairs. Toward
night the children—he had about seven of them—
began to drop in; some from work, some from
school, and the little ones from play. They were
introduced to me, and met me with the same ease
and grace that marked the manner of their mother.
Supper came on, and then was exhibited the love-
liness of the family circle in all its glow. The
father turned the conversation to the matters in
which the children had been interested during the
day, and all, from the oldest to the youngest, took
part in it. They spoke to their parents with as
much familiarity and confidence as if they had been
friends of their own age, yet every word and every
look manifested as much respect as the humblest
courtier could manifest for a king; aye, more, for
it was all sincere, and strengthened by love. Verily
it was the Happy Family.

" ' I have told you Mr. Bunce converted me politically. He came nearer converting me religiously
than I had ever been before. When supper was
over, one of the children brought him a Bible and
hymn-book. He turned to me and said :

"'Colonel, I have for many years been in the habit of family worship night and morning. I adopt this time for it that all may be present. If I postpone it some of us get engaged in one thing and some in another, and the little ones drop off to sleep, so that it is often difficult to get all together.'

"'He then opened the Bible, and read the Twenty-third Psalm, commencing: 'The Lord is my Shepherd; I shall not want.' It is a beautiful composition, and his manner of reading it gave it new beauties. We then sang a hymn, and we all knelt down. He commenced his prayer 'Our Father who art in Heaven.' No one who has not heard him pronounce those words can conceive how they thrilled through me, for I do not believe that they were ever pronounced by human lips as by him. I had heard them a thousand times from the lips of preachers of every grade and denomination, and by all sorts of professing Christians, until they had become words of course with me, but his enunciation of them gave them an import and a power of which I had never conceived. There was a grandeur of reverence, a depth of humility, a fullness of confidence and an overflowing of love which told that his spirit was communing face to face with its God. An overwhelming feeling of awe came over me, for I felt that I was in the invisible presence of Jehovah. The whole prayer was grand—grand in its simplicity, in the purity of the spirit it breathed, in its faith, its truth, and its love. I have told you he came nearer converting me religiously than I had ever been before. He did not make a very good Christian of me, as you know; but he has wrought upon my mind a conviction of the truth of Christianity, and upon my feelings a reverence for its purifying and elevating power such as I had never felt before.

"'I have known and seen much of him since, for I respect him—no, that is not the word—I reverence and love him more than any living man, and I go to see him two or three times every year; and I will tell you, sir, if every one who professes to be a Christian lived and acted and enjoyed it as he does, the religion of Christ would take the world by storm.

"'But to return to my story. The next morning we went to the barbecue, and, to my surprise, found about a thousand men there. I met a good many whom I had not known before, and they and my friend introduced me around until I had got pretty well acquainted—at least, they all knew me.

"'In due time notice was given that I would speak to them. They gathered up around a stand that had been erected. I opened my speech by saying:

"'Fellow-citizens—I present myself before you to-day feeling like a new man. My eyes have lately been opened to truths which ignorance or prejudice, or both, had heretofore hidden from my view. I feel that I can to-day offer you the ability to render you more valuable service than I have ever been able to render before. I am here to-day more for the purpose of acknowledging my error than to seek your votes.   That I should make this acknowledgment is due to myself as well as to you. Whether you will vote for me is a matter for your consideration only.'

" ' I went on to tell them about the fire and my vote for the appropriation as I have told it to you, and then told them why I was satisfied it was wrong.   I closed by saying:

" ' And now, fellow-citizens, it remains only for me to tell you that the most of the speech you have listened to with so much interest was simply a repetition of the arguments by which your neighbor, Mr. Bunce, convinced me of my error.

" ' It is the best speech I ever made in my life, but he is entitled to the credit of it.   And now I hope he is satisfied with his convert and that he will get up here and tell you so.'

" ' He came upon the stand and said :

" ' Fellow-citizens—It affords me great pleasure to comply with the request of Colonel Crockett. I have always considered him a thoroughly honest man, and I am satisfied that he will faithfully perform all that he has promised you to-day.'

" ' He went down, and there went up from that crowd such a shout for Davy Crockett as his name never called forth before.

" ' I am not much given to tears, but I was taken with a choking then and felt some big drops rolling down my cheeks.   And I tell you now that the remembrance of those few words spoken by such a man, and the honest, hearty shout they produced, is worth more to me than all the honors I have received and all the reputation I have ever made, or ever shall make, as a member of Congress.

" ' Now, sir,' concluded Crockett, 'you know why I made that speech yesterday. I have had several thousand copies of it printed, and was directing them to my constituents when you came in.

" ' There is one thing now to which I will call your attention. You remember that I proposed to give a week's pay. There are in that House many very wealthy men—men who think nothing of spending a week's pay, or a dozen of them, for a dinner or a wine party when they have something to accomplish by it. Some of those same men made beautiful speeches upon the great debt of gratitude which the country owed the deceased—a debt which could not be paid by money—and the insignificance and worthlessness of money, particularly so insignificant a sum as $10,000, when weighed against the honor of the nation. Yet not one of them responded to my proposition. Money with them is nothing but trash when it is to come out of the people. But it is the one great thing for which most of them are striving, and many of them sacrifice honor, integrity, and justice to obtain it.'

" The hour for the meeting of the House had by this time arrived. We walked up to the Capitol together, but I said not a word to him about moving a reconsideration. I would as soon have asked a sincere Christian to abjure his religion.

" I had listened to his story with an interest which was greatly increased by his manner of telling it, for, no matter what we may say of the merits of a story, a speech, or a sermon, it is a very rare production which does not derive its interest more from the manner than the matter, as some of my readers have doubtless, like the writer, proved to their cost.

"By Crockett's aid I succeeded in having my business settled in three or four days afterward, and left Washington. I never saw him again."

CHAPTER XIV.

Colonel Crockett's Visit to Baltimore, Philadelphia, and
New York.

NATURALLY enough Colonel Crockett's ideas ex-
panded, after he had occupied a seat in Congress
for a couple of sessions. He had never been north
of the capital, and he felt a strong curiosity to
make a tour through the principal cities.

He had formed many friends among the members from the North and East, who strongly urged
him to make such a visit. At the opportune
moment, his physician recommended " Travel,"
and he decided to undertake the journey. He left
Washington April 25, 1834.

The same evening he reached Barnum's Hotel,
Baltimore, where he was most genially entertained,
and the following morning started for Philadelphia,
feeling somewhat timid and apprehensive about
going to such a large city, where every man, woman and child was a total stranger to him.

As the steamer approached Philadelphia, Crockett
observed the captain hoisting three flags. When
asked what it meant, he said it was a signal which
he had promised to give, if he had Colonel Crockett
on board. When the latter observed an immense
crowd standing on the dock, he began to suspect
the truth—his proposed visit had become known

through the North, and had aroused a great curiosity to see him.

As the boat came close to the wharf, the captain
pointed to the backwoodsman, who was standing
near him, and the crowd broke into hurrahing and
swinging their hats.

"That's for *you*," said the pleased captain, and
Crockett saw he had suddenly became famous.
No wonder, as he expresses it, he felt "queer" at
the sight.

The instant he stepped upon the wharf, and
came within reach of the multitude, they began
crowding around him and extending their hands
with eager enthusiasm. "Let me shake hands with
an honest man!"

This expression was heard from hundreds, and
Colonel Crockett was fully justified in feeling great
pride and satisfaction with the compliment.

Several got hold of the visitor, and, taking him
in charge, placed him in an elegant barouche,
drawn by four fine horses. The repeated cheering
of the people kept the delighted but bewildered
Crockett bowing all the way to the old United
States Hotel in Chestnut Street.

There was no diminution in the crowd, and
Crockett was conducted up-stairs and out to the
balcony. His appearance set the crowd cheering
again, and in answer to the calls for a speech, he said:

"Gentlemen of Philadelphia—My visit to your
city is rather accidental. I had no expectation of
attracting any uncommon attention. I am traveling for my health, and have no wish to add to the

excitement while there is such high political feeling. I am unable to find language with which to
express my gratitude to the citizens of Philadelphia. It seems like a burlesque—it is so new and
strange to me. But I see nothing but friendship
in your faces, though you are all strangers to me.
If your curiosity is to hear the backwoodsman, I
assure you I am ill prepared to address such enlightened people. But, if you will meet me to-
morrow at one o'clock, at the Exchange, I will try
to address you in my plain, blunt manner."

Then, amid cheers, he bowed and withdrew from
view.

When it became dark, and the backwoods member of Congress thought he would not be recognized, he ventured upon Chestnut Street. He was
like a country school-boy let out for a little vaca-
tion in a new and wonderful city, where the sights
were like those of fairy-land. He sauntered gaping
along, taking pains to avoid turning off the main
street, through fear of losing his way. He was not
long in discovering that the Quaker City is one of
the best laid-out cities in the world, and that no
man of intelligence need ever go astray amid the
windings of its almost innumerable streets.

When he laid his head on his pillow that evening, his brain was in such a whirl he could hardly
sleep. He was especially apprehensive from the
promise he had made to address the people the following day, but as he had extricated himself from
many a worse dilemma, he was hopeful he would
be equally fortunate on the morrow.

The next morning he was gratified to receive cordial calls from his old acquaintances—Judge Bald-
win, Judge Hemphill, John Sergeant, and others.

It followed in due course that Crockett was
struck with wonder at the sights shown him. He
was taken to the Water Works, the Mint, and to
the Asylum for the Insane. At the last place he
was deeply impressed, for the sight was one calculated to stir the heart of any thoughtful person.
Crockett was grateful that he was spared such a
sad affliction, and his heart was stirred to see the
care and kindness exercised toward the unfortunates.

It was near time for him to make his promised
speech at the Exchange Buildings, and when he
went there, he found fully five thousand people
impatiently awaiting him. He started out on a
rambling talk with considerable misgiving; but he
gathered confidence, as he proceeded, from the
continuous cheering and good will shown him. He
spoke for about a half-hour, and received three
rounds when he was through.

In the evening the famous visitor was taken to
the Walnut Street Theatre. He enjoyed the performance of " Jim Crow," but he has recorded his
regrets that these places of public amusement so
frequently admit words and actions in their plays
which are not fit for a modest woman to hear.

The following morning he was waited upon by a
committee, who presented him with a splendid seal
for his watch chain. It contained an engraving of
a horse-race, with the appropriate words, "*Go
ahead.*"

A deputation from the Young Whigs then called and asked for some information as to the proper size and weight of a good rifle, as it was their intention to present him with such a weapon. Crockett gave his views on this important question, for no one can deny his authority to do so, and he was then conducted to the Naval Hospital.

It is hardly necessary to give the round of his visits, which took him to the Navy Yard, over the Schuylkill Bridge, and past Girard College. His last night was marked by a grand supper, given him by a number of his admirers.

Wednesday morning, April 29th, Crockett started for New York, having accepted an invitation from Captain Jenkins of the steamboat New Philadelphia.' The ride up the Delaware was a delightful one, as it is to-day, and he enjoyed it to its full. At Bordentown they took the cars for Amboy, and when told they ran twenty-five miles an hour he could scarcely believe it. What convinced him that the speed was fearful, was the fact that when he thrust his head out of the window and ejected some spittle, he overtook and received it all in his own face before he could get his head out of the way.

It required a high rate of speed to do that.

At Amboy they took the steamboat again, and another delightful ride awaited Crockett up the bay. When he arrived at New York, he was especially struck with the immense number of vessels, which reminded him of a vast forest denuded of its vegetation.

As before, the wharf was crowded, and the same enthusiastic reception was accorded the honest congressman from Tennessee. Before he could land he was taken in charge of by a committee of Young Whigs, who drove him in a carriage to the American Hotel, where he held a numerously attended reception. He visited a new and elegant fire engine which had just been completed, and took lunch with the managers. In the evening he visited Park Theatre, and saw Fanny Kemble play, expressing great pleasure with the performance.

The famous visitor had returned to his hotel, and sat talking with some of his friends, when he caught the alarming cry:

"*Fire! Fire!*"

He sprang up like a flash, caught his hat, and started to rush out.

"Hold on, Colonel," said one of his friends, with a laugh; "it isn't near us."

"But ain't you going to help put it out?" asked the astonished Crockett.

"No, our help isn't needed," was the reply; "we have fire companies, and we leave the entire business to them."

"Well, that's mighty queer," was the bewildered remark of the visitor, as he resumed his seat; "if that had been in my neighborhood, I would have jumped on the first horse at hand and ridden like a streak of lightning for the fire, and scarcely ever taken breath till it was put out."

Crockett was so curious to see how they managed a conflagration in the metropolis, that his friends went out with him.

The hour was late, and when the fire was reached the engines were just ready for work. When the stream began playing, however, they quickly extinguished the flames that were raging in a four story dwelling.

Crockett thought this was wonderful work, and so it was; but had he visited New York to-day, he would have seen a fire-engine made ready to start for a fire in precisely two seconds from the sounding of the alarm!

Incredible as this seems, the feat had been performed again and again by the fire-engines of that city.

Furthermore, the speed of the railroad train, which so amazed the rural congressman, is now frequently surpassed threefold. There are cars which run more than a mile a minute between New York and Philadelphia every day of the week. We have ridden on the engine of a regular train, and, watch in hand, found that at certain sections of the road it was making fully seventy-two miles an hour. When will the maximum of speed be attained?

Colonel Crockett "saw the sights" in the great city, calling at the newspaper offices, making a speech at the Exchange, and visiting Peale's Museum, so popular as an entertaining resort a half century ago. He was cordially received by the mayor, who, like another great man, had been a tanner in his youth, and the two famous "products of American soil," mutually congratulated each other on their success.

He dined with Colonel Draper in the evening, where he met the famous humorist of the day, Major Jack Downing. The contact of these two wits around the dinner table afforded rare amusement to those who were present.

Although little appetite was left him, Crockett was compelled to attend a supper later in the evening, with the Young Whigs. He there met the accomplished Augustus S. Clayton, of Georgia, whose powers as a speaker took a great deal of the burden from Crockett's shoulders.

CHAPTER XV.

In the Metropolis—Visit to Boston—Honors given him every-where—Return to Washington—Adjournment of Congress—Goes Home by way of Philadelphia—Memorable Incidents on the Route.

COLONEL CROCKETT was toasted as the "un-deviating supporter of the constitution and laws." When he arose, he was received with great cheer-ing, and made one of his best speeches, concluding with a story illustrating his own disposition to fol-low the lead of General Jackson, so long as he went straight; but when his paths became devious, Crockett declared his self-respect forbade his fol-lowing him.

His story was of the farmer, who directed his boy to plow straight toward the red cow, who just then occupied the right position. The lad obeyed to the letter, and all would have been well had not the cow wandered all about the field, taking the lad after her.

The next morning ushered in moving day in New York, and the sight was one which amazed Crockett, as well it might. It seemed to him as if the entire city was fleeing panic-stricken before the approach of some pestilence.

The visitor was fairly terrified by a tour he made through Five Points, which at that day was perhaps one of the most woeful spots on the globe. When the brave Crockett saw the bleared-eyed drunkards and leering desperadoes, whose faces were stamped with the most hideous imprint of crime, he declared he would rather risk himself in the thick of the worst kind of an Indian fight, than to venture into the neighborhood after dark. At this day the record of Colonel Crockett's visit to Philadelphia, New York, and Boston reads curiously enough. He tells his experiences with such simplicity that they are more attractive than the most finished disquisitions of foreign visitors who have been right royally entertained by us, and then have gone back home and done their most to hold us up to ridicule.

While Crockett was taking his walk on this annual moving day, he was introduced to Honorable Albert Gallatin, who was also engaged in transferring his worldly goods and who apologized that he had no more time at his command. It may be mentioned as an interesting fact that Gallatin pointed to the house which he was vacating, and said it was to be torn down to make room for a large "tavern." This building, which Crockett saw begun while he was in New York, was the famous Astor House.

When the visitor returned to his hotel he found the bill of the Bowery Theatre, on which it was announced in large letters that he would be present at that evening's entertainment. As Crockett had given no authority for any such announcement, he was offended, and decided not to go.

When he was sent for he refused, and the manager came for the famous backwoodsman member of Congress, who told him very distinctly that he had not gone to New York to make an exhibition of himself. The manager plead so hard, however, that Crockett finally consented, and went to the place of amusement for a short while. As a matter of course, he attracted a great deal of attention, and was received with due honors.

In the morning he accepted an invitation to go over to Jersey City to witness some rifle-shooting. Crockett looked on awhile, when one of the participants asked him to take his gun and give them an exhibition of what he could do.

The distance was a hundred yards with a rest. The Tennessean fired off-hand, and came within two inches of the centre. He said his distance was forty-five yards. Colonel Mapes placed a quarter of a dollar as a target, and Crockett ruined it on the first fire.

At three o'clock on the succeeding day the famous visitor took the steamboat for Boston, having accepted the invitation of Captain Comstock made some time before. A splendid state-room was placed at the service of the Tennessean, and an immense crowd was at the wharf to cheer him as he departed.

His journey was one continued delight to Colonel Crockett until he was taken in charge at the Tremont House, which he pronounced one of the finest "taverns" he had ever inspected. He was treated with the greatest hospitality, and Ches-

ter Harding, the famous painter, who went to Mis-
souri fourteen years before to paint the portrait
of Colonel Daniel Boone, secured several sittings
from the backwoodsman member of Congress.

There are no end to the entertaining and wonderful sights in a city like New York, Philadelphia,
or Boston—especially to one who visits it for the
first time. Among those that were inspected by
Crockett, were Faneuil Hall, the Public Market,
the India Rubber Works at Roxborough, at which
place he was presented with a rubber coat, the car-
pet factories, the Navy Yard at Charlestown, the
historic battle-ground of Bunker Hill, where he
was so impressed by the sacred memories cluster-
ing about the spot, that he swore to defend his
country at all times and in all places, so long as
Heaven gave him the power to use tongue or
hand.

It was inevitable that the famous Crockett should
be urged to dinner in ten times as many places as
was possible. In the evening, he was taken in a
coach and four to dine with a club of one hundred
young Whigs. The feast was a right royal one,
and the backwoodsman made one of his witty and
appropriate responses to a toast to himself.

His stay in the city was one continued round of
sight-seeing, dining out, speech-making and jollifi-
cation. The following morning he strolled through
the city, and when he came back to the Tremont
House, a gentleman asked him to take a walk with
him to the Old State House. Crockett did so, and
ran into a good-natured trap that was set for him.

An immense multitude were present. He was conducted up-stairs, and out on a platform, where he bowed to the shouting people. But they were not content, and he was forced to make a speech to them.

Perhaps the most genuine pleasure the visitor received was in the Institution for the Blind. One of the students, whose sight was totally wanting, called at the hotel for Crockett to conduct him to the institution. When the congressman expressed his wonder at the idea of being led about the city by one without eyesight, he was told that the boy could traverse every portion of it without losing himself for an instant.

Crockett therefore placed himself in his care, and in the institution he saw the boys and girls read books, cipher, play the piano and other musical instruments. He was filled with wonder and pleasure, and records a tasteful tribute to the humanity of Colonel Thomas Handaside Perkins, who gave fifty thousand dollars to the blind asylum.

On his return to the hotel he found an urgent invitation to visit Harvard University awaiting him. But Crockett shrank from entering the famous institution of learning, giving as his reason that he was afraid they would bestow upon him the title of " LL. D.," to which he had no more claim than had General Andrew Jackson, who received it some time before.

A visit was made shortly afterward to Lowell, with its famous cotton mills, and Mr. Lawrence, one of the mill owners, presented Crockett with a suit of broadcloth, made out of wool brought from Mississippi. In the evening the congressman was dined again by a company of young Whigs, and made one of his best speeches in response to the toast to himself.

The hospitality shown Davy Crockett was of that kind for which Boston is proverbial. He was scarcely given time to sleep, but was taken everywhere by his enthusiastic friends, dined and wined, and presented with many tokens of the respect which his sturdy and rugged honesty awakened among the New Englanders.

He was deeply touched by the generous kindness shown him, and urged his Southern associates to follow his example of visiting their Northern friends, assuring them that their mutual good-will would be greatly strengthened when they should come to meet and know each other better. There can be no question that the Tennessean was sound in his philosophy.

The Colonel returned to New York by way of Providence. In the latter city he was invited to dine at two different hotels, but he declined both invitations, as he needed rest. Besides, he was anxious to get back to Washington, now that his face was turned in that direction. He made scarcely any halt until he reached Camden, where he called upon a friend, and while he and others were being entertained, several had their pockets picked of a considerable sum of money.

At Baltimore he was met at the wharf and escorted to Barnum's Hotel, where a large crowd

was assembled. They would not permit him to
withdraw until he had given them a speech. He
reached Washington and walked into the House
of Representatives just in time to give his vote on
the question of adjournment. There was considerable surprise shown at his turning up so unex-
pectedly. Adjournment took place shortly afterward, and Crockett started for home by way of
Philadelphia.

He sojourned at the United States, where he
felt entirely at home. The committee who had
purchased the rifle, notified him that it would be
presented in the evening, and he was conducted to
a hall to receive the splendid weapon.

Accompanying it were a fine knife and tomahawk. John M. Sanderson passed the gun over to
Crockett, with an appropriate speech, and the
backwoodsman thanked them cordially for the
kindness. He said that no present could have been
selected that would have pleased him so much, and
that it was the finest rifle upon which he had ever
looked.

He added, that when he held such a weapon in
his hands, he always felt independent. If it should
become necessary he would gladly use it in the
defence of his country; and should the struggle
come after he was laid in the dust, his sons would
do their best to take his place in the ranks of their
country's defenders.

Little did Davy Crockett imagine that within
two years from the time he uttered these brave
words, he would be called upon to give up his life

fighting for the liberty of the Lone Star State against the hordes of Mexican invaders.

The next day Crockett accepted an invitation and spent the day at the " Fish House," as it was called on the Schuylkill, where he amused himself, with scores of others, shooting, fishing, eating and drinking. This was the third of July, and, as a matter of course, the Tennessean was used to the fullest advantage on the glorious anniversary immediately succeeding.

At an early hour he went to Musical Fund Hall, where a number of distinguished orators enter- · tained the audience for a long time. But Colonel Crockett was speedily recognized, and the demands for a speech were so uproarious that he was forced to comply. He was greatly embarrassed, for he knew that some of the orators were the first in the city, and there were a great many ladies in the audience.

In the afternoon he delivered a speech at the " Hermitage," after a fine dinner, where he was entertained most bountifully. This was unquestionably the most delightful national anniversary spent by Davy Crockett. A visit to the Chestnut Street Theatre, where he was compelled to speak a few words to the audience, concluded the celebration of this most memorable day.

Mr. Dupont, the famous powder manufacturer, asked Crockett's permission to present him with a half dozen canisters of his best sportsman's powder ; and having received such permission, sent him a dozen canisters.

The morning succeeding this, saw Crockett on his way to Pittsburgh. The journey over the mountains was very pleasant, and the renowned Colonel attracted a great deal of attention in passing through the country, for it may be said that at that time he was in the very culminating days of his glory.

Pittsburgh was reached in the night. When the backwoodsman went down to the wharf to look for a steamboat, he found Captain Stone, who told him he had waited a day on purpose to take him along with him. Of course, the delighted Crockett accepted passage with him. The Captain was a man after his own heart, and the two spent many enjoyable hours on the river. Captain Stone was never tired of listening to Crockett's accounts of his tour through the North and East, and he in turn was equally prolific with his own experiences on the river, during his eventful career as a boatman.

At Wheeling, the Colonel walked ashore to stretch his limbs and look about him. But he was almost immediately recognized, and a crowd followed him eager to get a look at the "honest man." He was invited by a committee to dine with them at three o'clock, but he could not accept, as the steamboat was to leave before that hour. Accordingly they gathered on the shore in large numbers, and cheered Crockett as he slowly passed out of sight on the steamboat, he waving his hat in return for their salutes.

In Cincinnati, the demands were so clamorous,

he could not resist them. He took a lunch with his admirers, and delivered one of his short incisive speeches, greatly to the delight of his listeners.

With as little delay as possible, he proceeded to Louisville, where his friends had arranged quarters for him at the finest hotel in the city. As he was obliged to stay there several days, he could not escape another speech. The fact was, the bustling experience of the Colonel for the last few years had made quite a popular stump orator of him. While on his tour through the North, the demands in this respect were due, of course, more to curiosity than anything else.

But he was popular, beyond any other speaker, in his own home, amid the sparse settlements and the wilds of Tennessee, where the hunters and backwoodsmen rode scores of miles through the "blazed" trails to hear the great Crockett speak.

It was announced in Louisville that he was to address the citizens the succeeding evening. Accordingly he was sent for and taken out to Jeffersonville Springs, Indiana, on the opposite side of the river. A speech was the inevitable consequence; and, as Crockett was now nearing home, he put a good deal of politics in what he said, presenting his charges against the course of General Jackson on several important public measures, with his usual pith and point.

In the evening he was conducted to the State-House yard, where a stand had been erected from which he was to address the assembled people. One of the old citizens said that the gathering was the largest that had been known in the history of Louisville. The backwoodsman must have been stirred at the sight, and he made the best speech of which he was capable.

As he was unable to leave for a day or two, another oration was given in response to clamorous demands. Finally he took his departure on the steamboat Scotland, Captain Buckner, and arrived at Mills' Point on the 22d of July, 1834. He was now upon the soil of Tennessee, and was met by his son William, who drove him to his home thirty-five miles distant.

CHAPTER XVI.

Crockett Returns Home—A Candidate for Re-election to Congress — Defeated — His Bitter Disappointment—Starts for Texas.

THE triumphant tour was at last ended. Colonel Crockett had received honors and recognition in the leading cities of the Union and throughout the North, which would have turned the head of many an abler man than he, and which doubtless awoke longings in him that were destined never to be satisfied. The taste of public office and the expressions of admiration were peculiarly gratifying to him. He had earned the title of an honest man, the "noblest work of God."

But he saw not that this amazing popularity, from its very nature, was short-lived, and that the time must soon come when some other idol would take his place in the eyes of the multitude.

It is a bitter lesson for the man hoisted into public notice by exceptional circumstances to learn,— but it must be learned, and Colonel Davy Crockett was close to the hour when the bitter cup was to be pressed to his own lips.

He rode rapidly along the rough country road with his son for nearly two-score miles, and at last caught sight of his humble home. There stood the rude cabin, with the logs he had helped to hew and put together with his own hands, with the huge deer-antlers and bear's claws nailed over the door, and with the familiar sights upon which he had not looked for months.

They were dearer to him than ever before; and, when he sprang out of the wagon and clasped his wife and children in his arms, he felt that more genuine pleasure was his, than when the thousands were shouting his name and crowding forward to grasp his hand.

As a matter of course, Crockett became a candidate for re-election. He now possessed a national reputation, but he was known as an antagonist of President Jackson. Representing, as the backwoodsman did, a State which posesssed peculiar claims to " Old Hickory," and which fairly idolized him, it can be seen that the congressman had placed himself in an exceedingly dangerous attitude. General Jackson was fiery-tempered, impetuous, and possessed no mercy for a political foe. Nothing could be more assured than that he would use his prodigious power to the utmost to crush the fearless backwoodsman who defied him to his face.

It followed, therefore, that the fight would be a hot one, and none realized the task before him more strongly than did Crockett himself.

He threw all his energies into the canvass, and traveling from one end of his district to the other, made speeches day after day, with all the humor, vim, and argument at his command.

His opponent was Adam Huntsman—a man who

lost a leg in the war of 1812, and who had the tremendous backing of President Jackson in the strife for office.

Crockett had picked up a great deal of political information, during his years in Congress, and aside from his native humor, was much the superior of Huntsman in a fair discussion of the public questions of the day.

He jibed his opponent unmercifully, reminding him that there would soon be a second fall of Adam, for the congressman was never more assured of anything than he was that he would be returned to Congress by the largest majority he had ever received.

The signs everywhere were "auspicious." Wherever he went, the crowds thronged about him, and he told funnier stories than ever, and he had all the arguments against "Old Hickory" at his tongue's end, and when he spoke, he was cheered to the echo. As a candidate for public office hears scarcely anything except from his friends, Colonel Crockett could not understand why it was that Huntsman was so blind as not to see there was not the remotest hope for his success.

In the first place, he could not approach the backwoodsman in his humor, readiness at repartee, and amusing anecdote. He must have known, too, that the skill of the backwoodsman with the rifle is one of the surest passports that any one can possess to the goodwill of a frontier community.

Such was the case, as it presented itself to a

superficial observer, who would have seen that about the only thing left for Huntsman to stand upon was (to use an Hibernicism) the leg he had lost in the war.

But the elements were at work to destroy Crockett. The foundation upon which he had builded his popularity was only sand. Already the insidious current was washing it away, and when he thought his structure stood the firmest, it was on the very eve of falling in irretrievable ruin.

It may have been that many of Crockett's old friends were stirred by a feeling of unworthy envy at the amazing degree of popularity he had attained. They may have concluded that the rough, uneducated woodsman had received all the public honors he was entitled to, and that the time had come for him to be reminded that he was still one of them, and that his proper position was with the people, instead of making triumphant tours through the North as their representative.

But unquestionably the most potent cause was the influence of President Jackson, which was precipitated with irresistible weight into the scale against him.

The canvass was waged with unexampled vigor and bitterness on both sides, and when Colonel Crockett's four weeks of incessant speech-making and travel were ended, he went back to his cabin and sat down to await with serene confidence the tidings of his election by a tremendous majority.

When the news reached him, it was to the effect that he was beaten by nearly three hundred votes.

The result, as may be supposed, astounded Crockett. He was almost staggered into disbelief, but was soon compelled to see that in his joust with President Jackson, he had been unhorsed and overthrown, as was many a greater man than he.

The political career of Colonel David Crockett was ended.

He had rushed to a sudden and unique glory, and, while the central figure of an admiring country, he was suddenly snuffed out, so to speak. Where a brief time before he was a shining luminous light, there was nothing but blank darkness.

The unexpected repulse soured for the time the sunny nature of Crockett. He was beaten unfairly, for money was used lavishly to defeat him, and every trick known to politics was employed to encompass his overthrow.

It mattered not that he was treading in the footsteps of hundreds who had gone before, and who must continue going, so long as our republic shall last. He only knew that he had been defeated in obtaining the dearest wish of his life; that he had put forth his most earnest efforts, and had been ignominiously cast down and trampled upon; that he had been taken by the neck and heels, as may be said, and thrown outside the stockade of politics —thrown so far that he could never clamber over again into the enclosure and mingle in the fray.

And all this, as he believed, was simply because he had chosen to be conscientious while in Congress. He had followed no man's bidding, but had been governed by what he conceived to be right in casting his vote, and in uttering his voice in favor of or against any measure.

It was a bitter reflection, and there were many hours when chagrin, anger, and resentment gnawed at the heart of Colonel Crockett.

What added to his indignation was his unshakable belief that he had been deliberately defrauded out of his election by means put in operation by President Jackson himself. Probably a majority of the defeated candidates throughout the country are equally strong in their belief that an untrammeled ballot would have secured their triumph; but, in Crockett's case, it can scarcely be doubted that a fair test would have returned him to Congress.

But all these reflections only increased the bitterness of the backwoodsman's resentment without bringing any consolation. The days passed, and the dagger-thrust still rankled in his wounds. There is something touching in the following homely words which he wrote in his lonely cabin in Tennessee.

" As my country no longer requires my services, I have made up my mind to go to Texas. My life has been one of danger, toil, and privation; but these difficulties I had to encounter at a time when I considered them nothing. But now I start anew upon my own hook, and God only grant that I may be strong enough to support the weight that may be hung upon it. I have a new row to hoe, a long and rough one, but come what will, *I'll go ahead.*

"When I returned home from making a sort of farewell speech to my friends, I felt cast down at the change that had taken place in my fortunes, and sorrow, it is said, will make even an oyster feel poetical. I never tried my hand at that sort of writing, but on this particular occasion, such was my state of feeling that I began to fancy myself inspired; so I took pen in hand, and, as usual, I went ahead. When I had got fairly through, my poetry looked as zigzag as a worm fence; the lines wouldn't tally; so I showed them to a friend who had a reputation for that kind of writing, having some years ago made a carrier's address for the *Nashville Banner*. He lopped off some lines and stretched out others, but when he was through, I think the words were worse than when I placed them in his hands. It being my first, and no doubt my last piece of poetry, I give it here:

"Farewell to the mountains, whose mazes to me,
Were more beautiful far, than Eden could be:
No fruit was forbidden, but nature had spread
Her bountiful board, and her children were fed.
The hills were our garners—our herds wildly grew,
And nature was shepherd and husbandman too.
I felt like a monarch, yet thought like a man,
As I thanked the Great Giver and worshiped his plan.

"The home I forsake where my offspring arose;
The graves I forsake where my children repose.
The home I redeemed from the savage and wild:
The home I have loved as a father his child;
The corn that I planted, the fields that I cleared,
The flocks that I raised, and the cabin I reared;
The wife of my bosom—farewell to ye all!
In the land of the stranger, I rise or I fall.

" Farewell to my country ! I fought for thee well,
When the savage rushed forth like the demons from hell.
In peace or in war I have stood by thy side—
My country, for thee I have lived—would have died !
But I am cast off—my career is now run,
And I wander abroad like the prodigal son—
Where the wild savage roves, and the broad prairies spread,
The fallen—despised—will again *go ahead !*"

It was a severe trial for Crockett to bid his wife
and children good-by, for at that day Texas was
a far-away land, and the enterprise in which he and
a few hardy spirits had determined to engage was
a desperate one. The vast territory was claimed as
a Mexican province, and Santa Anna, its dictator,
was a merciless tyrant, who would use every means
to crush the rebellion which a handful of invaders,
as he viewed them, were seeking to set on foot.

But the hour for parting came. It was characteristic of Crockett, as we have shown, that, when
he had made up his mind to follow a certain course
of action, he allowed nothing to swerve him from it.

No doubt he shared with others in the dream of
the coming empire, with which he wished and believed it possible to identify himself. It required
no wonderful prescience to forecast the grand
future of that country, when it should secure its
independence from Mexican dominion, and become
one of the States of the Union.

Crockett was not yet fifty years old—an age
which, in his case, was his prime, and he may have
believed that his talents would secure speedy recognition in a new country of that character.

At any rate, whatever may have been his controlling motives, his mind was unalterably set on casting his fortunes with those of the hardy adventurers who had fixed their hopes upon Texas.

So he bade the wife good-by, he kissed her and the children again and again, he pressed them to his heart, he cheered them with the hope of a speedy return, and while the tears trickled down his bronzed cheeks, he hurriedly walked away.

Dressed in his homespun suit, and with the beautiful rifle presented him by his admirers in Philadelphia, he strode off toward Mill's Point, where he was to take the steamboat down the Mississippi.

Wife and children stood in the door of the humble cabin, waving him good-by, while he turned back and answered the signals affectionately, for he was always tenderly attached to his family, until at last the loved form of the hardy hunter disappeared from sight.

He was gone, never to return!

He who went away with such high hopes of success, was nevermore to set foot upon Tennessee soil, nor look in the face of wife and children again.

When Davy Crockett went forth to his fight for the independence of Texas, he went to his death, as did many another gallant patriot.

CHAPTER XVII.

Early History of Texas—The Home of Adventurers—Disreputable Character of many of the Early Settlers—General Antonio Lopez de Santa Anna—Texas begins its way for Independence—Santa Anna, with a large force, invades the Territory.

AT the time Colonel Crockett left his home in Tennessee for the distant State of Texas, there were less than 40,000 white people within its borders. It contained thousands upon thousands of square miles that had never been trod by a Caucasian, and which, from the nature of the circumstances, must remain an unknown region for years to follow.

The area of Texas is enormous. It exceeds that of New York, Pennsylvania, Ohio, Virginia, Maryland, Delaware, and the six New England States together. It is more than thirty-six times as extensive as New Jersey. Great Britain and Ireland are not half as large; France, Holland, Belgium, and Denmark united scarcely approach it in area, and its future grandeur can scarcely be forecast.

The greatest length of Texas is 825, and its greatest breadth 740 miles. Its area is 274,356 square miles, an expanse of territory which almost surpasses imagination.

This State has a most eventful history. In 1685, a number of French emigrants, under the leadership of the Sieur de la Salle, landed in Matagorda Bay, and built Fort St. Louis on the Lavaga. The fort was soon after abandoned, and the garrison dispersed.

Five years later, Captain De Leon, a Spanish officer, established the mission of San Francisco on the site of the deserted fort, and the following year a Spanish governor was appointed. These attempts at settlements, however, were without any permanency in their character, for in 1693, all were abandoned.

A few years later, Spanish missions were founded at different points, but these were like lighthouses erected along the coast of a continent. The whole vast territory stretching beyond remained undeveloped and unknown.

In the year 1715, the name of " The New Phillippines" was given to the country, and the Marquis De Aguayo was made Governor-General of the Colony. For the following twenty years, the Spanish held sole sway, and their settlements multiplied. They penetrated into the interior, and erected their mission-houses, where they were environed by the fierce Comanche and Apache, and shut off for months from communication with others of their own race.

They were sometimes assailed by the wild Indians, who resented this intrusion upon their domains; but the mission-houses were strongly built, and were capable of endless resistance against all the forces the red men could bring against them. Their solid adobe walls have defied the modern artillery more than once; and, to-day, when viewed from a distance, they suggest the old tempest-beaten and war-worn castles of the feudal times that have been the pride of many sections of Europe for hundreds of years.

While the Catholics were engaged in preaching to and seeking to convert the Indians around them, they did not neglect the fertile soil. They put in their crops, and gathered abundant harvests, for they possessed the worldly wisdom to make preparation for the coming of the days when such reserves were likely to prove indispensable.

More than once this provision was the salvation of the little band of settlers gathered about the mission-houses. Some were besieged for three and six months, and there is an apparently trustworthy legend that one of the mission-houses near San Antonio withstood successfully a siege at the hands of the Comanches which lasted a year and a half.

With the primitive weapons at the command of the Indians, it can be understood that the men and women behind the massive walls were safe against harm, so long as they used ordinary prudence. It became simply a question of supplies on the part of the defenders.

As there was sufficient corn and wheat stowed away in the impenetrable vaults, and their supply of water was exhaustless, the Comanches finally raised the siege and departed.

These mission houses, scattered at wide intervals through the Texan wilderness, made little impression on the aboriginal population, and the traveler to-day through the Lone Star State views them with wondering curiosity, scarcely comprehending that they played any appreciable part in the settlement of the section.

In the year 1803, France ceded to the United States the Louisiana territory, which had formerly belonged to Spain, and a controversy as to boundaries immediately arose. Spain claimed the region east of the Sabine, and the United States insisted they were entitled to all the country as far west as the Rio Grande. The dispute was settled three years later, by establishing the territory between the Sabine and Arroya Honda into neutral ground.

This proved anything but the termination of the vexed question. Expeditions for the invasion of Texas were continually formed within the territory of the United States. In 1813, the invaders had a fierce fight with the Spanish army, and defeated it with the loss of more than a thousand men. In the same year a force of 2,500 Americans and Mexicans were cut to pieces, barely a hundred escaping with their lives.

The disturbances continued, much as they have in Cuba, for years. In 1817, Mina, a Spanish refugee, won a number of victories over the Spaniards, and it looked for a time as if he would sweep everything before him. But the usual fate of such adventurers overtook him. His forces were scattered like chaff, and he was captured and shot.

In 1819, the controversy between Spain and the United States was ended by the acceptance of the

Sabine River as the boundary line, but the disturbances in the south-west were in no way affected
by the agreement between the two countries.

During the same year a revolutionary expedition
was organized at Natchez, under the command of
Dr. James Long, a Tennessean. He penetrated
with his followers as far as Nacogdoches, and
established a provisional government. But, while
the leader was absent, his forces were attacked and
destroyed by the royalist troops.

The undaunted Dr. Long speedily organized another expedition, which took possession of La
Bahia. But it came to grief as did the former one.
The entire company and himself were taken prisoners, and carried to the city of Mexico. Unex-
pectedly he was released, for the quality of mercy
is a rare virtue with a Mexican. Dr. Long, however, was assassinated in 1822.

In 1823, Stephen S. Austin, under a grant from
the Mexican government, established a colony in
Southeastern Texas, and other settlers speedily followed. The Mexican Constitution, adopted in
1824, united Coahuila, hitherto a separate province,
with Texas in a single State, and the Congress of
the united state placed a Mexican as commandant of the Department of Texas. He was a tyrant,
and treated the settlers with great severity. .

Lafitte, the noted pirate, established a settlement
at Galveston, but it was broken up in 1821. In-
famous as was the character of this colony of free-
booters, it was no worse than that of hundreds who
flocked to Texas from the United States.

The worst desperadoes, thieves, murderers, and gamblers that were produced in the Union hurried toward the Rio Grande. It became a land of refuge for all manner of criminals fleeing from justice. Probably no country in the world ever received a larger percentage of outlaws as settlers within her borders.

The expression, "Gone to Texas," became proverbial as signifying that the criminal had fled from justice. The probabilities were that if several persons were introduced to each other on the soil of that territory, not a single one was known by his right name.

There was an old couplet, which contained no poetry, but a great deal of truth:

> "When the other States reject us,
> This is the one that always *takes-us*."

Possibly the origin of the name may be traced to these lines, for many a fugitive from justice could testify to the truth of the declaration.

The character of the American emigrants to Texas became so notorious that Bustamante, the Dictator of Mexico, issued a decree forbidding any more Americans coming into the country. This, from the nature of the case, was inoperative except to a limited extent, for all Mexico could not have patrolled the boundary line of the immense territory. But the issuance of the decree is proof of the statement that the majority of Americans who entered Texas were of the most disreputable character.

This decree was revoked four years later, for it amounted to little more than an irritation to the hordes of the North who continually poured over the frontier and scattered through the illimitable territory.

The material congregated on the soil of Texas was of the exact kind from which unsuccessful revolutions are organized. The knife and pistol were a part of every man's wardrobe, and considered more indispensable than boots or hat. Neither weapon was allowed to rust for want of use. Gamblers plied their unholy vocation all night and day; murders were of such common occurrence as scarcely to excite remark. There was no thought of establishing schools or of developing the unbounded resources of the favored country, excepting on the part of a few, who probably felt that Texas must need be burned in the crucible in order to separate the gold from the dross.

Such men, we repeat, while engaged in scenes of violence and outlawry, never forget to consider the matter of revolution.

In the year 1833, the American settlers in Texas numbered about twenty thousand, and they concluded the time had come for establishing their independence. Accordingly they met in convention and decided to separate themselves from Coahuila. They prepared a State constitution and issued an address to the Mexican government, of which Santa Anna was the head.

General Antonio Lopez de Santa Anna was probably one of the most detestable tyrants of all history.

192 LIFE OF COLONEL DAVID CROCKETT.

Treachery was inborn with him, and there was no
vice of which man is personally capable that he was
not personally guilty.

He was born at Xalapa in 1798, and at the out-
set of his career served in the Spanish army, in
which he attained the rank of lieutenant-colonel in
1821. The following year, while stationed at Vera
Cruz, he joined the movement inaugurated by Iturbide, which resulted in the total defeat of the
Spanish forces and the reduction of the whole of
that province.

In accordance with his treacherous nature, Santa
Anna, within a twelvemonth, turned against Iturbide, who had proclaimed himself emperor. Shortly
after this the Mexican " Republic " was formed,
and for ten years Santa Anna was engaged in defending the claims of rival chiefs for the presidency
of this model government.

Iturbide, Pedraza, Guerrero, and Bustamante
were toppled over like so many ten-pins, and, in
1833, Santa Anna himself obtained the president-
ship of the republic. The only wonder is that he
consented to wait so long before seizing the prize.

This tyrant, therefore, was at the head of the
Mexican government at the time of the Declaration of Independence of the 20,000 American settlers, and their address to the Mexican government was laid before him.

It was impossible for one of his nature to return
a frank reply to their request to be admitted as a
separate State into the republic. He was apprehensive of any such movement, for one of his

treacherous nature was always ready to suspect treachery in another.

But the governments of Coahuila and Texas having been overthrown, committees of safety were established, the first being appointed at a meeting held at Mina (now Bastrop), May 17, 1835.

Goliad was captured by the Texans, October 9th, and the battle of Concepcion was fought near San Antonio on the 28th.

Revolution having been set on foot, now moved rapidly forward. On the 3rd of the following November a number of delegates from the Municipalities met at San Felipe de Austin, and gave themselves the name of the " Consultation."

They showed their earnestness in the serious business by proceeding to organize a Provisional government. Henry Smith was elected Governor, and Sam Houston was made Commander-in-Chief. .

San Antonio was taken on December 10th, and the revolution pushed with such vigor that the entire armed force of Mexico was driven shortly after out of Texas.

On the 20th of December a Declaration of Independence was issued at Goliad, and the freedom of the new State might have been considered settled, could Santa Anna have been brought to see the justice of acknowledging it. But justice was not a quality of his nature, and in the single respect of his attempt to subdue the rebellious province, he did not transcend the inalienable right of all rulers.

In the means which he used to subdue the Texans, he showed himself as cruel and treacherous as the Comanches and Apaches around him.

Santa Anna had been engaged in revloution most of his life since reaching manhood, and he knew the mettle of which the Texans were composed. No ordinary means would answer to subdue them. If he attempted it with an inadequate force he would be overthrown, as so many of his incapable soldiers have been in recent years.

He placed himself at the head of 7,500 men, and started for Texas with the determination to " stamp out " the detested Americans who had dared to issue a Declaration of Independence, as their fathers had dared to do sixty years before.

He took with him some of his best lieutenants, who could be trusted to do his terrible work, and left the city of Mexico in the early spring of 1836.

Meanwhile the Americans were straggling into Texas, without any organization or settled plan of procedure. But all were eager to measure swords with the Mexican " Greasers," as they were termed, and whom they held in greater contempt than any other people known on the face of the earth.

Such was the state of affairs when Colonel Davy Crockett left his home in Tennessee to join the patriots in Texas struggling for their independence.

CHAPTER XVIII.

Crockett's Trip to Texas—The Friends whom he Encountered
on the Steamer—His Speech of Advice.

WE have endeavored to trace the course of
Colonel Davy Crockett from the time he left his
home in Tennessee until he reached the fortress of
the Alamo. No authentic account of that journey
has ever been published. What purports to be an
autobiography of his gives a minute account of his
travels with several companions, and the diary is
complete up to within a few days of his death; but
Crockett was a man little accustomed to writing,
and though in the high tide of his popularity, and
when a member of Congress, he may have contributed a truthful narrative of the principal incidents of his life, it is unreasonable to suppose that
he continued it after starting for Texas, and especially that he kept up his full records amid the
sulphurous smoke and horrors of the Alamo, or
that had he done so, they should have been pre-
served intact.

The only survivor who was a companion of
Crockett on the voyage down the Mississippi, so
far as the writer knows, is Jonathan H. Greene, at
that time a young and desperate gambler, but who
reformed in 1842, made restitution of the large for-

tune he had acquired, and with great self-sacrificing energy has devoted himself to humanitarian works since then.

Mr. Greene retains a vivid recollection of those days, including the battle of San Jacinto, in which he was desperately wounded, and where he lay in the tent when Santa Anna was brought in a prisoner.

In a carefully written letter to us, Mr. Greene says: ·

"On my way down the Mississippi, on board the steamer Mediterranean, I met Colonel Crockett at Randolph, Tennessee, sixty miles above Memphis. When he renewed our acquaintance, he reminded me that we had met three years previous at Clarksville, Tennessee, where we went to attend a circus. At the time, we spent an hour or so in trying the range of our rifles; 'I recollect,' said Crockett, 'that you were suffering from a confoundedly bad cold, and I called you a circus rider.'

"It was as Crockett said; I was slowly convalescing from a long attack of fever, and was not in as lively a mood as he, by any means. The few years that had elapsed had made no perceptible difference in the appearance of Crockett. He wore no beard, but was very eccentric in manner, and his face was one of those which always looked older than was really the case. I had seen him several times, while he was in Washington.

"Colonel Crockett had no sooner stepped on the steamer than he found himself among acquaintances and friends. The invasion of Texas from

the United States was the all-absorbing question
of the day, and there were converging streams from
the North in that direction.

"Among those on board the Mediterranean—
one of the largest and best of boats—I recall Samuel and John Carter, William Wood (as I understood of the firm of Yeatman and Wood, the
celebrated bankers), George and James Cheatham,
Samuel Searcy, Blanton McAlpin, Pleasant Wat-
son, George Zollicoffer, Colonel Wharton, Timothy
Gillam, J. Pointdexter, S. Ellis, Abner Ellis, and
many friends from Kentucky.

"Crockett was full of anecdote and fun, and we
all laughed over his stories, of which his fund was
exhaustless. I remember one, which I have told
many times since, but without the droll, entertaining manner of the great Tennessean.

"'A neighbor of mine,' said Crockett, 'found
some animal was making the most destructive kind
of raids upon his hens. He watched for it continually, but couldn't catch sight of it for a long time.
From its tracks he discovered it was a large dog,
which visited his place nightly, and sneaking
among the roosts of the fowls slaughtered them
wholesale.

"'One night the settler caught sight of the dog
and fired, but so quickly, that he missed. Determined that the thief should not escape, he dropped
his gun and rushed upon him with his knife.

"'Well, it was the worst fight in which he was
ever mixed up. He was never handled so roughly
in all his life, and he had been in many desperate

scrimmages. The dog slit one of his ears, chewed his nose, ripped his clothes to tatters, peeled the skin pretty well off his face, and then trotted off.

" ' As he passed out where the moon shone upon him, the amazed settler caught a plainer view of him, and then discovered that instead of being a dog, it was a gigantic she-wolf.

" He went back to the cabin, and when he got within doors, examined himself to see whether he was all there. He then thought over the matter, and finally brightened up, for in telling the story afterward, he said he had one blissful consolation : ' considered strictly as a fight,' said he, ' it was fust class, and I got the wust of it, but I'm cheered by the sartinty that I *fit the biggest fight that was ever fout in Tennessee.'*

" After our boat left Helena, we halted at Montgomery's Point on the Arkansas side, at the mouth of White River. It was here Colonel Crockett met Captain William Cumby, then residing at the mouth of the Arkansas, where he died many years after.

" Colonel' Crockett introduced Cumby to his companions as one of his old Tennessee friends, and the crowd was a merry one indeed. Several years later, Captain Cumby fought a duel with Abe Garrison in a bar-room, on that same spot. It was a desperate one, hand to hand with bowie and pistol, and Garrison was killed.

" Captain Cumby, ' Doc ' Bennett, Crockett and myself, with three Mexicans from Fort Smith, traveled through the Indian nation. We went to

Fort Towson, and thence to Washington, Hempstead County, Arkansas, to call on a mutual friend of Crockett and Cumby. He was Hugh Blevins, of Tennessee.

"We then crossed to Natchitoches, rode on to San Augustine, and finally reached Nacogdoches, where Bowie, Travers, Ricord and others joined us. Shortly after, in company with John Featherston, 'Hoppy' Johnson, Ephraim Tally, and Mat Despallie, we went to Natchitoches, then to New Orleans, and finally returned to Arkansas, whence we did our utmost in forwarding 'war material' to Texas.

"The steamer Mediterranean—to return for a few minutes—proceeded slowly down the river, making many stoppages. We came to at Columbia, Colonel Estill's plantation at Point Chicot, Lake Providence, Lake Washington, the mouth of the Yazoo, and Vicksburg. At the last named city, Colonel Vick, S. S. Prentiss, Governor Foote, and Aleck McClung escorted Crockett to the planter's house. McClung locked arms with Crockett. The weather was so bad that no public speaking was held. When Crockett took the steamer again he spoke a few words of farewell, and was loudly cheered by the crowds on the wharf.

"I remember that many of the voices shouted the name of Texas, and wished us God-speed in its conquest.

"Crockett made several excursions through parts of Texas, the Indian nation, and Arkansas. On one of these he was accompanied by two friends, one of whom was Colonel Sandy Faulkner, known as the 'Arkansas Traveler,' and one of the most genial gentlemen I ever met.

"Faulkner wore military whiskers, which, like his hair, was of a glossy black. Everybody liked Sandy, and he and Crockett were much attached to each other. But Crockett's propensity to joke was so great, that when he came back with Sandy, he had a story to tell about him. It originated with Crockett, but was one of the best I ever heard when told by the eccentric Tennessean. It was rather severe on Faulkner, but he always laughed with the rest and never denied it, though I believe it was pure fiction.

"They were riding through the wildest portion of Arkansas, but the path was known, and as a rule they found a stopping-place at the end of every twenty miles. But there was one stretch of fifty, through the woods, which they were obliged to make before they reached a cabin by the wayside. When they finally struck the latter, it may be judged they were tired and hungry enough to take a good rest and meal.

"'Sandy wore a close-fitting cap,' said Crockett, with a side glance toward the 'Arkansas Traveler,' who was already smiling at what he knew was coming, 'and when he took his seat just a little behind me, he was in such a hurry to get at the eatables that he snatched off his cap, and flung it to the floor.

"'A few minutes after, the son of the landlord, a young man, came in, and was walking toward the table, when he started mighty sudden like. I looked up, and saw he was craning his neck, and peeping behind and over my shoulder; I didn't know what was the matter of him, but he hadn't been gone a minute and a quarter, when he came back and did the same thing. His mouth was wide open, and there was such a look of wonder on his face that he seemed struck dumb. But I was too busy eating to bother my head.

"'Bime by, he snickered, and said to Sandy, 'I say, sir, ain't you bald-headed?'

"'You know how dignified Sandy is, and he straightened up so much at that, that he leaned over backwards. He scowled at the impudent young man, and made no answer. But the fellow stood there snickering and grinning and gaping, and it wasn't long before he asked the question again, 'I say, sir, ain't you bald-headed?'

"'No, sir,' said Sandy, with an awful frown.

"'It wasn't five seconds before the young man out with the question again, and Sandy got mad. He fairly thundered, as he threw his shoulders back, 'No, sir, I am *not* bald-headed, sir!'

"'And then the fellow backed up against the door, and laughed till he dropped to the floor. When he could speak, he climbed to his feet again, and said, ' *Well, all I've got to say then, stranger, is, that you've the longest face I ever seen on a living man!* '

"'And then he roared again. Sandy turned as red as fire, and clapped his hand to the top of his head. Sure enough, he was as bald as your boot.

He had jerked off his cap in such a hurry that he took his wig with it. He scrambled from his chair, and snapped up his cap mighty sudden. His face was redder yet, and he hadn't much appetite after that.'

"Those who knew the genial Sandy Faulkner, can appreciate this story of Crockett. Sandy had natural fine black hair around his ears and neck, but there was a broad path over his forehead and crown which was like a billiard-ball. I have been told that he had this peculiar baldness from infancy, and he wore his wig with such skill that scarcely one person in a thousand would have suspected his hair was not natural.

"It was when the steamer Mediterranean, with Crockett and his friends on board, came to rest off Helena, where the weather was very bad, that the 'Crockett Fund,' as it was called, was formed. A number came on board, and I remember among them, James M. Estill, Archie Wood, R. M. and D. Curl, G. W. White, John Slidell, William R. Preston, Governor White, John R. Grimes, Darius J. Green, A. L. McClung (duelist), Governor Foote, Colonel Vick, Dr. Anderson senior, and his son.

"Judge McAlpin drew up the paper, and I give you the names of those who subscribed ten thousand dollars apiece. I have never seen the list published, but it is to be relied upon:

John Slidell, - - - -	$10,000.
Governor White, - - -	10,000.
John R. Preston, - - -	10,000.

S. S. Prentiss, - - - -		$10,000.
'Doc' Bennett, - - -		10,000.
Robert Wickliffe, - - -		10,000.
Col. J. M. Estill & D. Curl,	-	10,000.
James Guthrie & Purtell,	-	10,000.
Rowan Wooley Wickliffe -	-	10,000.

"The paper signed read as follows:

"'We men, whose names are here set down, obligate our willingness to pay the amount opposite to any person who shall be vouched for by a majority of this committee—Colonel Davy Crockett, James Bowie, Colonel Hawkins, Captain Fanning, and Captain Travers—this money to be used for the purpose of aiding our countrymen now in the field, and to be further used in recruiting five companies of two hundred and fifty men each. And it is understood and agreed upon that these men will immediately march south to Red River, and enter into Texas, and there await orders to join such forces as may be present to co-operate with the United States army, and they are to serve under such officers as may be assigned to their command.'

"The subscription made by 'Doc' Bennett included that of Featherton and myself, and it was understood among us three that it was to be known on the list as Colonel Crockett's personal subscription.

"I saw Crockett sign a paper drawn up by Slidell, Zollicoffer, and Judge McAlpin, which I signed as a witness, without knowing its contents. James

M. Estill and Bennett also put their names to it, and from the latter I learned some months later that it was merely Crockett's acknowledgment of the amount subscribed for him. It should be stated, that some of the large subscriptions were not made personally by the gentlemen named, but by their authorized friends.

"John Slidell, then a lawyer of New Orleans, was given charge of the funds, which were deposited with Slidell, White, & S. S. Prentiss. Every dollar in that large list was paid when called for.

"This, of course, was months before the barbecue at John Bowie's, below Helena.

"I mentioned that Crockett, with several companions, including myself, made a call upon Hugh Blevins at Washington, Arkansas. Hugh was a great hunter from Tennessee, brother of John of Huntsville, Alabama, who was the owner of the celebrated race-horse, 'Wild Will of the Woods'; his brother William was a highly respected planter at Selma, Alabama, and was said to have killed his man; their younger brother Dillon shot and killed Cooley Whitney at the gambling-table in Bell Tavern, Huntsville, in the fall of 1832.

"Mat Despallie, of whom I have spoken as being our companion to Natchitoches was a villainous bully. He drew on me at Alexandria, Red River, in 1833, but I was expecting it, and shot him with a Derringer, when he was no more than six feet distant. I hurried away, supposing he was killed, and was assisted to escape by J. Madison Wells' father, who kept me at his plantation several days, when

I went down the river in the steamer Caspian. I found afterward that the ball which struck Despallie in the stomach was turned aside by a button. Wells did the job more effectually afterwards, but I am not sure whether it was Matt, or his equally bad brother, who was killed by Ex-Governor Wells. They were both as bad as bad could be.

"At Natchez, Crockett was the guest of A. L. Bingham, Colonel Claiborne, Judge L. Fitch and others. From that point, my recollection does not enable me to speak with certainty of the movements of Colonel Crockett, whom I regard as one of the purest patriots and ablest men that ever set foot on Texan soil. He and I separated at Augustine, and never met afterwards."

Crockett was in continual demand as a speaker, and the following is given as a specimen of one of his humorous addresses on political affairs:

"Attend all public meetings, and get some friends to move that you take the chair; if you fail in this attempt, make a push to be appointed secretary; the proceedings of course will be published, and your name is introduced to the public. But should you fail in both undertakings, get two or three acquaintances, over a bottle of whiskey, to pass some resolutions, no matter on what subject; publish them, even if you pay the printer—it will answer the purpose of breaking the ice, which is the main point in these matters. Intrigue until you are elected an officer of the militia; this is the second step toward promotion, and can be accomplished with ease, as I know an instance of an election being advertised, and no one attending, the innkeeper at whose house it was to be held, having a military turn, elected himself colonel of his regiment. You may not accomplish your ends with as little difficulty, but do not be discouraged—Rome wasn't built in a day.

"If your ambition or circumstances compel you to serve your country, and earn three dollars a day, by becoming a member of the Legislature, you must first publicly avow that the Constitution of the State is a shackle upon free and liberal legislation; and is, therefore, of as little use in the present enlightened age, as an old almanac of the year in which it was framed. There is a policy in this measure, for by making the Constitution a mere dead letter, your headlong proceedings will be attributed to a bold and unshackled mind; whereas, otherwise it might be thought they arose from sheer mulish ignorance. 'The Government' has set the example in his attack upon the Constitution of the United States, and who should fear to follow where the Government leads?

"When the day of election approaches, visit your constituents far and wide. Treat liberally, and drink freely, in order to rise in their estimation, though you fall in your own. True, you may be called a drunken dog by some of the clean shirt and silk stocking gentry, but the real rough necks will style you a jovial fellow, their votes are certain, and frequently count double. Do all you can to appear to advantage to the eyes of the women. That's easily done—you have but to kiss and slabber the children, wipe their noses, and pat them on the head; this cannot fail to please the mothers, and you may rely upon your business being done in that quarter.

"Promise all that is asked," said I, "and more, if you can think of anything. Offer to build a bridge, to divide a county, create a batch of new offices, make a turnpike, or anything they like. Promises cost nothing, therefore deny nobody who has a vote, or sufficient influence to obtain one.

"Get up on all occasions, and sometimes on no occasion at all, and make long-winded speeches, though composed of nothing else than wind— talk ¬of your devotion to your country, your modesty, and disinterestedness, or of any such fanciful subject. Rail against taxes of all kinds, office-holders, and bad harvest weather; and wind up with a flourish about the heroes who fought and bled for our liberties in the times that tried men's souls. To be sure, you run the risk of being considered a bladder of wind, or an empty barrel, but never mind that; you will find enough of the same fraternity to keep you in countenance.

"If any charity be going forward, be at the top of it, provided it is to be advertised publicly; if not, it isn't worth your while. None but a fool would place his candle under a bushel on such an occasion.

"These few directions," said I, "if properly attended to, will do your business; and when once elected, why a fig for the dirty children, the promises, the bridges, the churches, the taxes, the offices, and the subscriptions, for it is absolutely necessary to forget all these before you can become a thorough-going politician, and a patriot of the first water."

CHAPTER XIX.

Sketches of General Sam Houston and Colonels James and
Rezin P. Bowie.

THERE are other names beside those of Colonel
David Crockett identified with the conquest of
Texas, and it is appropriate that in this place reference should be made to the most prominent.
The leading figure is that of General Sam Houston, one of the most unique and extraordinary
characters in American history. He was born near
Lexington, Rockbridge County, Virginia, in 1793.
While yet a boy his mother emigrated to Tennessee, and at the age of fifteen he ran away and lived
among the Cherokee Indians for three years. During that singular piece of wilfulness he was utterly
lost sight of by his family, who scarcely expected
ever to see him again.

In 1811, he reappeared as suddenly as he had
departed,·but remained only a short time. The war
of 1812 soon broke out, and he enlisted, serving
against the Indians under General Jackson. He
entered the army as a private, but was appointed
ensign, and displayed such bravery that he won the
lasting friendship of General Jackson.

After the ratification of peace in 1815, he was
made lieutenant, and was stationed near Knoxville,
and afterwards at New Orleans. In November,

1817, he was appointed a subordinate Indian agent to carry out the treaty with the Cherokee Indians which had just been ratified. The succeeding year he began the practice of law in Lebanon, Tennessee. He soon after became adjutant-general of the State, and was recognized as a rising political power —a man with a "future" before him.

In 1823, while yet a young man, he was chosen a Representative in Congress, and was re-elected the succeeding term. In 1827, he became governor of Tennessee, and two years afterward was united in marriage to the daughter of an ex-governor. Almost immediately they separated forever.

A great deal has been made of this singular act, and many have sought to throw a mystery around it, somewhat akin to that which envelopes the case of Lady and Lord Byron; but there seems to be no doubt that the explanation has been given correctly by thousands. Houston was informed by his bride, immediately after marriage, that she loved another irrevocably, and he immediately released all claim upon her, the couple never living together as man and wife.

In accordance with his eccentric and inexplainble character, Houston, in the month of April, 1829, abandoned friends, civilization, and tempting political honors, and made his way to the Cherokee nation in Arkansas, where he was adopted as a son by a chief, and became a chief himself.

He appeared in Washington as a champion of their rights, and secured the removal of several United States agents on the charge of frauds. His vigor and persistency in this matter got him into several difficulties with the friends of these agents.

At this time Texas, as we have shown, was beginning to attract wide attention, and Houston saw in it an inviting field for the exercise of his peculiar genius. He made his appearance in the territory in December, 1832, and immediately became a prominent figure in the revolutionary movement. He was especially active at the constitutional convention the succeeding year; and, when difficulties began, was chosen to the chief command of the military district east of the Trinity. In October, 1835, he led his forces to the camp of General Austin, who was besieging San Antonio.

In was in the year following that Albert Sydney Johnston, who had graduated at West Point in 1826, entered the Texan army as a private, and eventually rose to the chief command.

Sam Houston, therefore, was the most conspicuous figure in Texas, when Colonel Davy Crockett reached the borders of the embryo republic.

There can be no question as to the personal bravery of Houston, who seemed to be the embodiment of many contradictions of character. He was pompous, conceited, careless, and addicted at times to profanity and drink.

When Davy Crockett was presented to Houston at Little Rock, the latter received his callers without the formality of clothing himself, excepting with a newspaper, if that may be termed such, which he held before him. His manner led to the remark by one who was present, that he was envious of the brave Tennessean, but Crockett conducted himself with becoming modesty, even though his chief did not. The only remark the visitor indulged in, by way of reference to the unbecoming conduct of Houston, was the characteristic one, that he was in a bad plight to repel musquitoes.

With all his peculiar personal traits, Houston possessed great courage and ability. A man who can represent one State in Congress for two terms, then become its governor, then become commander-in-chief of a revolutionary army, win a brilliant and decisive victory, attain the presidency of the new republic, be chosen again to Congress, and finally be elected to represent the same as United States Senator, and then as governor,—who unflinchingly opposed the secession lunacy,—such a man, we repeat, is possessed of no ordinary ability, and the State of Texas owes Sam Houston a debt of gratitude which can never be repaid by the coming generations.

REZIN P. AND COLONEL JAMES BOWIE.

Another name associated with the stirring memories of the Texan war of independence is that of Colonel James Bowie, whose history is singularly romantic and eventful.

His name is attached to that of the terrible weapon, so popular in the southwest a generation ago, although it was his brother Rezin P. who caused the weapon first to be made.

Rezin P. and James Bowie were natives of Tennessee, and became residents of Opelousas Parish,
Louisiana, when they were very young. Their
father was in good circumstances, and at his death
left the family independent. The mother of these
remarkable brothers was a woman of Roman stern-
ness and heroism, well fitted to bring forth children
whose personal bravery was probably never excelled by that of any man living or dead.

It is said that when the news reached her of
the death of James at the Alamo, she only remarked that she was sure of one thing—Jim had
not died from a wound in the back; after which she
went about her household duties as usual.

The following sketch is by William H. Sparks,
of Atlanta, Georgia, who was personally intimate
with the famous brothers, and is very accurate in
his statements:

" Rezin P. Bowie was a man of most exalted genius,
wonderful originality and high attainments; was
better educated, perhaps, in the French and Spanish ·
languages than the English. Eminently social and
genial in his nature, fond of adventure, as careless
of the present as indifferent to the future, quick to
serve a friend as to punish an enemy, but never
pursuing a quailing foe; always ready to forgive, as
ready to do justice to an enemy as to a friend—little
in nothing, but noble even in his vices.

" James Bowie was equally brave, equally generous.
There was no malice in his nature. Cool, determined and enterprising, he sought adventure for its
hazards and courted danger as he would the girl he

loved. Tolerant of opposing opinions and always respectful to an adversary, slow to anger, but when aroused as fierce as the hunted tiger, he wanted the social qualities of his brother and was without a particle of his genius.

"Whenever it was possible without dishonor, Rezin P. Bowie avoided difficulties with his fellow-man. James was quicker, but never took offence where he did not feel it was intended, but was always belligerent in the presence of his enemies. In this he differed materially from his brother. No one would ever suppose from the manner or emotion of Rezin P. Bowie that he was in the presence of an enemy, though every man about him was such—always cool, always courteous, never the first to give offence.

"With James the deeper ardor of his nature forbade this equanimity. The flash of his eye, the compression of his thin lips, told in a moment the presence of an enemy. This presence he would not bear. It was his habit promptly to settle all difficulties without regard to time or place, and it was the same whether he met one or many. At the same time he was self-possessed and conspicuously cool. An unyielding enemy, he pursued unrelentingly, but was always willing to forgive his worst foe when properly approached. He was sincere in all he said. No man was ever deceived as to his feelings or conduct. The fiery impulse of his nature was instantly subdued into a cool caution in the immediate presence of real danger. His power of will on such occasions was remarkable, and sometimes subjected him to the imputation of fear, so instantaneous was the change from the fervor of passion to the quiet coolness of apparent trepidation. It was then that he was terribly dangerous to an over-confident foe.

"To this imperturbable coolness, in the memorable conflict upon the sand-bar at Natchez on the 19th of September, 1827, he owed his life. A feud had existed for years between two parties of the parish of Rapides, on Red River. The principals in these parties were Dr. Maddox, Major Wright and the Blanchards on the one part, the Curreys, the Wells and Bowies on the other.

"A challenge had passed between Dr. Maddox and Samuel Wells, and a meeting arranged to take place near Natchez, in the State of Mississippi. Hither the parties repaired with their friends. It was agreed that no person should be present but the combatants, their seconds and surgeons. The place of meeting was a large sand-bar, immediately below the upper bluff, near the city of Natchez. The sand-bar, at low water, is of considerable width, bordered above and below with forest growth; on the opposite side of this bar were stationed the friends of each party; one of these parties was something nearer the combatants than the other. Colonel Crane was the second of Maddox. Between him and James Bowie and General Currey, there had long existed a deadly feud, and some months before this affair General Currey shot Colonel Crane with a shot-gun, on Bayou Rapides, disabling one of his arms.

"The parties to the duel approached the spot

selected for the combat from different directions. The preliminaries were soon arranged. The combatants took their positions and exchanged two shots without effect, and the difficulty was amicably adjusted.

" Bowie was just in the edge of the woods with Generals Wells and Currey, armed with pistols, Bowie carrying a huge knife. As the dueling party started to leave the grounds, Bowie and party started to meet them. The friends of Maddox and Crane on the opposite side of the sand-bar seeing this and being furthest from the party started on a run to meet them as soon as they should reach the retiring combatants. General Currey was the first on the ground, closely followed by Bowie. Currey immediately advanced upon Colonel Crane and remarked, 'Colonel Crane, this is a good time to settle our difficulty,' and commenced drawing his pistol. Bowie did the same. Crane was armed with a brace of dueling pistols, and, standing, awaited the attack of Currey. At this moment Currey was seized by his brother and begged to desist. Bowie and Crane fired at each other, it was said without effect. There were those who said Bowie was wounded.. This latter statement I think the most probable, for Bowie stopped, felt of his hip, and then drawing his knife limped toward Crane, who was watching General Currey. Released from the hold of his brother, Currey was advancing. At this moment Crane leaped across a small ravine, cut through the sand by the rain-water flowing from the acclivities above, and, resting his pistol upon his crippled arm, fired at Currey, wounding him fatally. He fell. Crane was now disarmed, and Bowie advanced cautiously upon him. Clubbing his pistol he struck Bowie over the head, as he avoided his knife adroitly, and felled him to the ground. Crane retreated a step as his friend Major Wright approached. Bowie, in the meantime, had risen and was sustaining himself by holding on to a snag which the river when at flood had left sticking firmly in the sand. Major Wright advanced upon him and with a long, slender spear, drawn from a walking-cane which he carried, and seeing Crane's danger, attacked Bowie, who made a pass to parry the spear with his knife, in which he failed. The spear was of cold iron, and striking the breast-bone bent and went round upon the rib. Bowie at this moment seized Wright and fell, pulling Wright down with and on top of him, and holding him strongly to his person. Wright was a slender and by no means a strong man and was powerless in the hands of Bowie, who coolly said to him : ' Now, Major, you die ! ' and plunging the knife into his heart killed him instantly.

"THE BOWIE KNIFE.

" This knife was made by Rezin P. Bowie out of a blacksmith's rasp, or large file, and was the original of the famous Bowie knife. When James Bowie received this knife from his brother he was told by him that it was ' strong and of admirable temper. It is more trustworthy in the hands of a strong man

10

than a pistol, for it will not snap. Crane and Wright are both your enemies; they are from Maryland, the birth-place of our ancestors, and are as brave as you are, but not so cool. They are both inferior in strength to yourself and therefore not your equal in a close fight. They are both dangerous, but Wright the most so. Keep this knife always with you. It will be your friend in a last resort and may save your life.' After this conflict Rezin P. Bowie carried this knife to Philadelphia, where it was fashioned by a cutler into the form of a model made by him, and I presume the knife is yet in the possession of some member of the family.

"There was no reconciliation between Crane and Bowie after the conflict, though Crane aided personally in carrying Bowie from the ground, and Bowie thanked him and said : ' Colonel Crane, I do not think under the circumstances you ought to have shot me.' Almost immediately upon the attack of Currey upon Crane the fight between their friends became general, in which there were several wounded, but Wright and Currey were the only persons killed. All the men engaged in this terrible affair were men of wealth and high social position, and the two parties included almost every man of fortune in the extensive and wealthy parish of Rapides. All are gone save Maddox and General Wells, both very old and still residing in the same parish. Between these two there has never been any reconciliation. Wells is the brother of J. Madison, of Louisiana. These brothers are hostile

politically and personally to each other, and have
not spoken with each other for more than twenty
years.   Upon a recent occasion the writer met in
the same hotel in New Orleans General Mumford
Wells and Dr. Maddox, who is now, at the age of
eighty-four years, a vigorous and active man.   Wells
is nearly as old and equally vigorous.   We had not
met in many years, and both being personal friends
of fifty years standing, I attempted to effect a reconciliation between them.   This was promptly
declined by both, and, in all probability, they will
die enemies.

"BOWIE AND CRANE.

"It was thought such would be the same with
Bowie and Crane.   But some years after their conflict on the sand-bar Colonel Crane, happening in
New York, discovered a runaway slave belonging
to his father, who resided in Maryland, and had
him arrested.   The negro was brought into court
by writ of habeas corpus.   It was necessary that he
should be identified and proven to be a slave and
the property of Crane.   Colonel Crane was the
only witness present who could prove this.   The
lawyer of the negro asked the witness if he could
swear the negro was born a slave, and being answered in the affirmative, asked Crane ' if he could
swear he himself was born a free man.'

"Indignant at the insulting impertinence, Crane
threw down his glove at the feet of the attorney,
and in words further insulted him.   This caused

some commotion in court from those who crowded
the lobby. It happened that James Bowie was
among that crowd. He had witnessed the entire
proceedings and coolly remarked :

"' Be quiet, gentlemen. The court-room is no
place for a mob. This business will soon be over,
and then is your opportunity if you desire a fight.'

" He then deliberately walked within the bar,
and approaching Colonel Crane, said :

"' Colonel, you are threatened by a mob, now in
the court-room. I am here, sir, and will stand by
you.'

" Crane bowed with the ease and dignity of a
knight of chivalry, saying :

"' I thank you, Colonel Bowie. I could not
have more reliable aid than from your gallant
hand.'

" Bowie bowed respectfully to the presiding
judge, turned, and gave the attorney a look and a
smile he will remember while he lives, and returned
to the lobby.

" Ten days subsequently they met at Niagara.
Crane advanced, tendered his hand to Bowie,
which was accepted politely, and without explanation; amicable relations were restored, which
were never after disturbed.

" James Bowie always dressed with good taste;
his extreme politeness and fascinating manners
were captivating, and he was much esteemed by
his friends, and those who knew him best. His
name, however, was a terror to those who only
knew him from public report. The many daring

and perilous adventures of his early life heralded his name to the whole country, and made him the observed of all, wherever he was seen. This had caused his name to be a synonym for desperate daring and bloody deeds, and the theme of many an imaginary and ridiculous story of doubtful morality.

"If there ever lived a man who never felt the sensation of fear, it was James Bowie. He was by nature fond of adventure—the more hazardous, the most courted. A thousand stories might be told truthfully of these adventures where his life was periled ; of conflicts where the odds against him were so great as to seem overwhelming, and where his coolness, courage and daring triumphed. His bare presence was sufficient to allay anger and quiet the most excited crowd. The same was equally true of his brother, Rezin P. They were much attached to each other, and held all property in common, and there never was any disagreement between them. They were equally enterprising, equally brave. Here the resemblance ceased.

"Rezin P. was careless in dress and equally so about his associates. He could adapt himself to any society, but in all he was the most prominent figure, leading always in conversation, and always suiting this and his manners to his company. No man ever remained in his society one hour that did not carry away something said or done by Bowie that was original or startling. Both brothers were truthful to the extreme. Devoid of dissimulation, frank in manner, sincere in conduct and expression, they held in contempt all little men and all little meannesses. They despised a petty thief, but admircd Lafitte; despised a man who would defraud a neighbor or deceive a friend, but would without hesitation co-operate with a man or party who or which aspired to any stupendous scheme or daring enterprise without inquiring as to its morality. Their minds, their souls and aspirations were all grand, and they rarely failed to achieve whatever they undertook.

"THE SLAVE TRADE.

"About 1817 or 1818 there were imported into Georgia by certain parties a number of African negroes. They were discovered and taken possession of by the State authorities and brought to the seat of government, Milledgeville, and by some process of pretended law were sold into slavery to the number of fifty or sixty. These were carried away and retained by the purchasers when the sale was arrested. The remaining sixty or seventy were retained in custody of the officers of the State. There appeared a claimant by the name of Madraza, from Havana, for these slaves. The slave trade . then was legitimate in all the Spanish-American possessions. It was proven that John Madraza, of Havana, was the owner of the ship, and the slaves captured in Georgia were all that had been saved from the wreck, which had occurred on the coast of Florida; that they had been taken possession of by parties who had no interest in the ship or

slaves, and secretly carried into Georgia. The suit
before the court was to recover the money for the
slaves sold and those remaining in the hands of the
State officers. Madraza appeared with an interpre-
ter, as he could only speak Spanish. At the final
trial, proof of the most unquestionable character
was produced to establish the identity of Madraza,
and that he was a resident merchant of Havana
and the owner of the ship and cargo. A recovery
was had of the money and the negroes, all of which
was paid and delivered to Madraza.

"The prime mover and he who had furnished the
money to buy and ship these negroes resided in
New Orleans. The negroes were purchased in
Cuba from a regular trader and shipped to Apala-
chicola, and sent up to the agency of the Creek
Indians, where they were captured. The New
Orleans owner knew Rezin P. Bowie, and to him
communicated the condition of things and asked
his aid. 'It is easy enough,' said Bowie; 'establish a house in Havana, let it claim the negroes, let
the ship be lost and the negroes stolen and carried
into Georgia, without the consent of the owners.'
It was all left to Bowie, who was to be amply compensated if successful. He established the house,
was himself Madraza, furnished the proof and succeeded, but was never compensated.

"TEXAN INDEPENDENCE.

"For some years the Bowies were planters in the
parish of Lafourche and Terrebonne. This interest

was under the charge of Rezin P. Bowie. James
was only an occasional visitor. Most of his time
was spent in Texas, whose independence he was
scheming to accomplish, in connection with Austin,
Houston, Lamar, Fannin, Travis, and some others.
He had implicit faith in the wisdom and abilities
of his brother. To obtain his counsel he made
sometimes a hasty visit to him. The care of his
family and plantations kept Rezin P. Bowie from
active personal participation in this great enterprise. He frequently complained of the imprudent
impetuosity of his brother. He said: ' James is
too impatient to wait for events; he will hurry
them before matters are ripe for action.' He remarked in my presence: ' Sam Houston is the
master-spirit in this movement. He is a great and
prudent man, despite his vanity and buffoonery.
Lamar is full of genius and is chivalrously brave,
and is truly a noble spirit, but is not practical.
Fannin and Travis are enterprising and brave, but
not calculated to plan or to lead in a desperate
fight. So is Lamar; and if there is wisdom enough
in these men to follow the counsels of Houston and
Austin, their success is certain.'

" James Bowie was among the first to take up
arms in the war for Texas independence. He re-
sisted the counsels of Austin and Houston, and following the impulse of his nature, with Crockett,
Travis and Fannin, who were all equally as impul-
sive and ardent, with an insufficient force, despis-
ing their enemy, they precipitated a conflict with
vastly superior numbers, and when their own small

force was divided—a portion under Fannin at
Goliad, a part at San Antonio—both these divisions
of their little army were attacked and destroyed.
The body of Bowie was found in the Alamo, with
twenty dead Mexicans lying around him, and of
his whole command only two were saved.

"THE DEATH OF THE BOWIES.

"The death of James Bowie was acutely felt by
his brother. From that until his death, which soon
followed, he brooded over his loss, lost much of his
vitality and all that disposition to rove in search
of adventure. He had sold his plantation and removed to a small farm on the Mississippi, in the
parish of Iberville. His two daughters, his only
living children, were growing up to womanhood,
were being educated, and he devoted much of his
time to them. They were sprightly, and possessed
many of the traits prominent in his own character.
They were, like him, fond of rough sports and out-
of-door amusements. They loved a gun and pistol
and excelled in their use. Both of them were ex-
pert marksmen, both rode gracefully on horseback.
The elder of the two, I think, was the most graceful rider I ever saw, man or woman. She grew up
a queenly woman in appearance; was very intelligent, modest, but not diffident, full of energy, with
a quick and cutting wit, and a self-possession which
was never disturbed by any occurrence. She was
so fond of pistol-shooting that she became remarkable for her accuracy, and the press noticed this

frequently and not always as respectfully as her father thought it should.' This called a card from him which contained a delicate warning that it should forbear even the mention of his daughter's name for the future. Never after were they alluded to.

"A thousand anecdotes might be related of the daring intrepidity of Rezin P. Bowie, his coolness in the most trying moments, his indifference to danger and his generous forbearance to a foe once in his power. In him was eminently combined the moral and the physical which constitutes true courage. There was no malice in his nature. He never hated, for he never feared. He held a bully in contempt, because he despised pretensions of every kind.

"The death of his brother affected him more than was apparent to the common observer. His physician remarked to me, a year after the event, that the death of James Bowie was killing Rezin. His daughters married soon after completing their education. They married cousins, men of high position, who were wealthy. This broke up the family. After this he gradually withdrew from the associations of his better days and, in 1838, died, in the fortieth year of his age.

" PERSONAL TRAITS.

"Both these brothers were entirely exempt from every species of dissipation; never drank, never gambled, or indulged in any immoral or debasing habit. Rezin P. Bowie really was a great man ; his intellect was eminently superior; he perceived quickly, and reasoned with great perspicuity and cogency; his language was beautiful, his wit pungent and polished, and his illustrations always apposite and palpable ; his form was perfect, erect, and tall, and perfectly proportioned; his manner always graceful, but never effeminate ; his muscular strength enormous. His most remarkable feature was his eye ; with the exception of S. S. Prentiss, it was the most variant in expression of any I ever met.

"There was a marked similarity in the minds of these two men. Prentiss was the most eloquent as an orator, Bowie was his superior as a conversationalist. They both elucidated their ideas by apposite anecdotes and figures drawn from surrounding objects. Both were coolly brave, and eminently generous. The difference was more in education than in capacity. Prentiss condensed, Bowie amplified. Prentiss used more Saxon words, Bowie more Norman, polishing the asperity of the thought. Prentiss struck with the two-handed sword of 'Richard Cœur de Lion,' Bowie cut with the keenness of the scimeter of Aladdin. Prentiss was ambitious ; Bowie, entirely without ambition, was indifferent to the fascinations of public applause, or the seductions of public office.

"Such was Rezin P. Bowie, as I knew him, and yet the world, away from his acquaintance, but heard of him only as a bold and desperate man, without scruples, and delighting in blood. A more tender and affectionate nature never lived. A more faithful friend, kinder neighbor, loving husband and father in all my long life I have never known.

"It was my good fortune to know all the men who were most prominent as actors in conceiving and carrying through to success the revolution of Texas. All of these were extraordinary men, many of them were highly educated as well as talented; all were honest and earnest of purpose, and, fortunately, none of them were rich. I say fortunately, for rich men never inaugurate or execute a revolution. They come to love their money more than their country, and to better the condition politically of the latter is to struggle against the tyrannies of those who control the government, and to hazard their money. It is the enterprising, liberty-loving poor man, oppressed by tyrannical exactions, who is without the means to control or bribe power, who strikes to be free. Wealth is cautious and conservative, and rather bears those ills it has, than fly to those it knows not of.

"Of the men most conspicuous in this revolution, Houston combined more of the elements of greatness than any other. Lamar had more genius, more chivalry, and was brave to rashness, but he was wanting in practical prudence. The impetuosity of his genius too frequently overrode the cooler dictates of his judgment. Talent seems an inheritance in this family. There has not been a time within the last century that there has not been a great man in it. And now, the first orator, and one of the foremost statesmen of the South, and perhaps, of the nation, is L. Q. C. Lamar, of Mississippi, the nephew of the late Mirabeau B. Lamar.

"Lamar, Houston, and Fannin were Georgians, all of them the schoolmates of my boyhood; Crockett and the Whartons were Tennesseans; Bowie was born in the same State, but was reared in Louisiana; Austin was a Missourian, and Branch Archer from Virginia. Every one of these were men formed by nature to be leaders. Their enterprise was daring, and their intrepidity made it successful. They wrested from Mexico a dominion larger than the kingdom of France, and, though all died poor, they bequeathed to posterity a fame unstained by crime or corruption—a boon worth more than all which fraud and venality can ever bequeath."

The following incident was told by a Methodist preacher some years ago:

"He said he was one of the first Methodist ministers sent to Texas by the Methodist Conference. He traveled on horseback, crossing the Mississippi below Natchez; that the first day after crossing the Mississippi River he was overtaken by a horseman dressed in buckskin, armed with rifle, pistol, and knife. They entered into conversation, and he found him to be intelligent, pleasant, and well acquainted with the geography of the country. Neither one inquired the name or business of each other. Both were aiming at the same destination,

Texas. Finally they reached a new town, filled with
wild, desperate characters from other States. He
posted a notice that he would preach at the Court-
house the first evening of his arrival there. At the
hour named he found the rude structure thronged
to overflowing—with men only. He gave out a
hymn, and all joined in singing, and sung it well,
but when he announced his text and attempted to
preach, one brayed in imitation of an ass, another
hooted like an owl, etc. He disliked to be driven
from his purpose, and attempted again to preach,
but was stopped by the same species of interrup-
tion. He stood silent and still, not knowing
whether to vacate the pulpit or not. Finally, his
traveling companion, whom he did not know was
in the house, arose in the midst, and with stento-
rious voice said :

"'Men, this man has come here to preach to
you. You need preaching to, and I'll be —— if
he sha'n't preach to you ! The next man that dis-
turbs him shall fight me. My name is Jim Bowie.'

" The preacher said that after this announcement
he never had a more attentive and respectful audience, so much influence had Bowie over that reck-
less and dangerous element."

Respecting the invention of the famous bowie-
knife, an intimate lady-friend of the Bowie family,
in a note to the writer, under date of December,
1878, and written in New Orleans, says :

"The knife was invented by Rezin P., brother of
James, for the purpose of hunting wild cattle on
the plains of the Opelousas. The first one was

manufactured by one of his slaves at the private blacksmith-shop on his plantation.   It was never intended for any other use except that of a simple hunting-knife, nor was it ever used otherwise, until in the duel at Natchez, when James Bowie acted as second, and all the seconds were drawn into the fight.   James Bowie married Ursulita de Veramendez, who was the only daughter of the governor of that name, and although born at Monclova, was of Castilian origin.   Santa Anna was her godfather, and it is said that when all the bodies of the brave men slain at the Alamo were burned, Santa Anna caused that of James Bowie to be interred instead, but would allow no mark to be placed on the grave.   This was to prevent his family reclaiming his body.   At that time Mrs. James Bowie and her child were already deceased.

"The State House at Austin contains a large and excellent painting of James Bowie, who has a nephew living in Austin, and another one in Galveston.   Their mother, the daughter of Rezin P. Bowie, resides in Galveston with her son, Major John S. Moore."

CHAPTER XX.

Plans for the Conquest of Texas—Bowie's Barbecue near Helena
—Distinguished People Present—Enthusiasm and Pledges of
Money and Support given the Scheme.

THE conquest of Texas was one of the favorite
schemes throughout a large portion of the Union
during the first third of the present century. Especially in the South and Southwest was this the
case. Men high in the councils of our country were
identified with the movement, contributed liberally
from their means, and did their utmost in forwarding men and supplies to the debated ground.

At the time of which we speak, Andrew Jackson
was President of the United States, and he was an
ardent friend of the project. His faith grasped not
only Texas, but Mexico itself, and there is every
reason to believe that he hoped for a pretext which
would present itself to the United States for securing the "annexation" of that very large, but by
no means desirable country.

But President Jackson appreciated his position
too well to commit himself, or to do or countenance openly any action inconsistent with his exalted station as President. His encouragement
was rather of an indirect character. When Colonel
Davy Crockett went South, he bore with him a letter from the President, introducing him as a "God-

chosen " patriot ; he appointed men to Government positions who were openly committed to the project, and did a still more positive act by which his sympathy was more practically shown.

On the west side of the Nueces River is a strip of territory which our Government claimed as a part of Louisiana, but which the Mexicans refused to surrender. At the time the Texas movement was assuming practical form, and hundreds of adventurers were flocking thither, President Jackson ordered General Gaines to the disputed territory with a force of three thousand men, and the commanding officer was instructed to go into the camp with them on the west side of the Nueces.

The interpretation of this movement was that they were, in short, to support the invaders. In case the latter were repulsed by Santa Anna, they were to fall back upon General Gaines, who was considered powerful enough not only to repulse the Mexican army, but, gathering the swarms of adventurers around him, to march on to the conquest of Texas, and to open the drama or tragedy as it might be called, which was to close with the conquest of Mexico itself.

It never would have done to proceed openly with this fillibustering business, and the leaders resorted to a very ordinary but effective method of giving it its initial impetus.

The leaders of the Texas movement having agreed that the time had come for action, and realizing how necessary it was to hide their intentions from the Mexican authorities, adopted the suggestion of John Bowie, an elder brother of the famed Rezin P. and James Bowie. John was a planter of independent means, living a few miles below Helena, and he caused invitations to be sent for hundreds of miles throughout the surrounding country to attend a grand barbecue to be given at his place a few weeks afterward. These invitations were of the most cordial character, and covered a vast area of territory.

The announcement was that the barbecue was to be given in honor of Berry Hawkins, who was at that time the Land Office Receiver, and a secret partner of John Bowie in all his "outside" schemes.

Probably there was not one man in a hundred of those who received an invitation who suspected its underlying purpose, although many knew that Berry Hawkins was one of the leaders of the Texan scheme, and was expected to take one of the detachments that was to start for Texas, so soon as preparations for the movement could be made.

As the day approached for the barbecue, the horsemen began wending their way toward John Bowie's plantation. They came from the depths of the Arkansas wilderness, and the furthest boundaries of the Choctaw nation. They traversed miles of lonely forests, camping in the woods at night; but they were men who had handled the rifle, the pistol, and the Bowie knife, and who rather courted than avoided danger.

Many of the visitors were from the east. They

knew of the contemplated invasion of Texas, and some of them possibly received a hint of the meaning of Berry Hawkins' barbecue. These men, like the raftsmen on the Mississippi, the White and the St. Francis Rivers, were eager for anything that promised adventure. On the outskirts of this motley multitude, like the bushwhackers of a devastating army, were the professional gamblers and thieves—men who live upon the credulity and verdancy of others, and who always hold themselves in readiness to draw and shoot, on as slight a provocation as do the proverbial Texan cowboys of to-day.

The barbecue marked an epoch in the wild days of Arkansas. Those who were present were numbered by the thousand, and among them were men who were known as the leaders in the important scheme on foot. The entertainments were of the most varied character, as may well be supposed. Numerous sheds and buildings had been erected to accommodate the crowds, and whisky flowed like water. Gambling, horse-racing, cock-fighting, and dancing were the chief amusements, which continued for several days and nights.

Long before its conclusion the real purpose of the gathering became known, and was freely discussed by the thousands of adventurous spirits that had flocked thither. When the smiling Berry Hawkins passed among the crowd—and he did so frequently—he was greeted with applause, and shouts of " Hurrah for Hawkins and Texas!"

Among the prominent men present were General Bill Montgomery of Montgomery's Point; his son-in-law, Major Moss; the brothers Notripp, who lived at Arkansas Post; Colonel Beauford of Mississippi; three of the brothers Cheatham; John Simpson, a well-known land speculator, and many of the leading planters for many miles around.

On the third day, when the barbecue was about to end, its purpose was openly announced, and everything was done to start the momentous enterprise with a vim and flourish. It was industriously circulated that General Quitman, one of the most popular leaders in the South, had resigned his commission in the regular army, for the purpose of taking command of one wing of that which was to conquer Texas from the dominion of Mexico.

The noted gambler who was known as "Doc Bennett," (though that was not his real name) was one of the trusted leaders of the enterprise. He possessed immense wealth, was personally brave, and was a fine officer. His wife and two children had been murdered by the Mexicans near Vera Cruz, when he was traveling through the country. His hatred of the people amounted to a mania, and he threw his whole soul into the enterprise.

He addressed the barbecue, just before it broke up, in terms of impassioned eloquence, calling upon those present, who chose not to fight, to contribute of their means to carry forward the cause. He was a man of brilliant culture, and when he announced that he would contribute five thousand dollars, and called upon the others to join him in the enterprise, the effect was electrical.

More than thirty thousand dollars were subscribed on the spot, a fifth of which was immediately handed in. Then, amid the excitement and
enthusiasm, Berry Hawkins rallied 160 men about
him, and started on a swinging gallop for the
Brazos River, while the other leaders gathered
detachments of equally eager patriots—if the term
is allowable under the circumstances—and headed
toward the plains of Texas.

Davy Crockett and a few personal friends were
already well advanced on their way, and Sam
Houston was on the spot, so to speak, and kin-
dling the fire, which was soon to spread and never
cease till the last hostile Mexican was driven from
the soil.

There was no want of enthusiasm, nor of men
and means; but there was a most deplorable lack
of one essential—that was of military organization
and a clearly defined course of action on the part
of the leaders.

Had a plan of campaign been carefully studied
out and agreed upon by the military authorities
who were at the head, and had something like dis-
cipline been enforced from the beginning, the invasion from the American side would have met
with no serious check from the Mexicans under
their ineffective leaders.

But the defenders of Texas from the Mexicans
were simply a turbulent mob—hordes of adventurers
flocking thither, bristling with Bowie knife and
eagerly grasping gun and pistol, while they craned
their necks forward on the backs of their mustangs,

peering eagerly through the mesquit bush for some glimpse of the despised " Greasers."

They looked upon the conquest of Texas as a sort of huge revelry and gigantic festival—an expansion of Jim Bowie's barbecue into continental dimensions, with the prospect of unlimited plunder looming up in the near background.

It was agreed that the money subscribed should be deposited at Fort Touson, at the mouth of the Kiemitea River, in February following, and nothing can be mentioned as stronger proof of the earnestness of the subscribers than the fact that on the day fixed every dollar was handed in, and not a penny of it clung to any of the numerous hands through which it passed.

Everything seemed in the most auspicious shape that could be expected or wished, and the multitudes assembled at the barbecue were in the highest spirits, when Doc Bennett received alarming news.

He did not let it be known what it was, but he understood at once that it was of the gravest nature, and that it threatened overwhelming disaster to the cause so dear to his heart.

It came directly from Texas, and was in effect that General Houston was grossly mismanaging affairs in that section; that Santa Anna had become fully apprised of the intentions of the Americans, and had set out for Texas at the head of a well-organized army; that the Texan forces were scattered and without competent leaders, and that unless some radical and decisive steps were taken at once the cause would be crushed beyond hope of resurrection for years to come.

Oppressed with the disheartening tidings, Bennett left Helena at once and made all haste to Louisville.

CHAPTER XXI.

Various Motives for Seeking the Conquest of Texas—Colonel Crockett's Patriotic Letter—The Historic Conference at Louisville—Crockett's Last Letter.

THERE were many governing motives on the part of the leaders who were plotting for the conquest of Texas. Some desired it for the extension of slave territory ; others saw in it the indispensable step toward acquiring Mexico itself, while a few, who suspected the hand of President Jackson, were seeking to frustrate his purpose, and to prevent any of the honor being reaped by him. But by far the great majority were simply ardent friends of Texas, and were willing to risk money and life in securing its independence.

Davy Crockett was angered to discover the preponderance of the political among the governing motives of the leaders. It began to look to him as though an arrangement was taking form by which he and a few others were to do the fighting, while the politicians behind were to reap the honors.

Nothing was so distasteful to one of Crockett's open disposition, and with much earnestness he addressed the following letter to Doc Bennett. This missive, as was the habit with Crockett, was signed with his name in large letters directly across the body of the writing:

"All hopes of becoming reconciled to Houston's proposal regarding Jackson's conquest of Mexico through Generals Gaines and Quitman for political speculation are at an end. Sooner than submit we would pass over the line and abandon the cause. If the battle is to be fought by one party and the honor and emoluments are to be enjoyed by another, we as honorable men will not be participators. While Houston has been on the outskirts surrounded by Federal guns and fed at the cost of the Federal Government, 50,000 men who have followed his even song are at the front for the signal for battle. Sooner than submit to be thus treated we will return to our homes or travel beyond the Southwestern border. Santa Anna's army is now marching forward, and hordes of savages are in his advance covering the Western border. Our men are now in constant trouble and may have already been driven from their posts, while hundreds have been murdered. Cabler's command of 200 have scouted one hundred miles direct on the route that Santa Anna was, and by all appearances he will be at San Antonio by March 1. This leaves but one month for us to prepare to fight or run. Cabler's men accompanied the bearer of despatches from Santa Anna which were delivered in our possession. They speak of 40,000 men under command of President Santa Anna, including 6,000 lancers. We make allowance and credit 30,000, every man of which he will require for body-guards after his arrival. Harrington has forwarded me nearly 400 men, all tigers, well armed. He is with them. His head seems to be filled with wild ideas, yet he is well balanced. He professes that Cabler idolizes him. If they keep their men together they will be a strong arm. We have received 800 well-equipped men by way of the Arkansas and they are now being distributed by Cabler, Harrington and Armstrong along the west front. Houston said he would come in time for our defence. We will not rely on him, but march further south and drop to the rear. With a few field-pieces and a good organization we can manage our own men. Lamar, Austin, Fanning, Rush, Travers, Bowie and others are competent military men, but we must organize, issue commissions, and have a President commander-in-chief. The cry is we want no more bell-sheep to lead us. We don't want missionaries of the United States to do our talking and drink our whisky. We can do both for ourselves. Harrington states that he, Cabler and Armstrong are going south after Hawkins, whom I fear is massacred, with all his men, Let us trust in God and our hearts that he is not. Adieu. I am now starting for our outposts, twenty miles west. We look anxiously for the fulfillment of the promise which induced us to hazard our lives and all our prospects.   Yours as ever,

"CROCKETT.

"No news from Sam Houston since 1st, sent me by way of Augustine."

The "Harrington" named in the foregoing letter as forwarding the 400 tigers was J. H. Green, the reformed gambler, from whom we have gathered many of the facts bearing upon the invasion and conquest of Texas.

" Doc " Bennett, as we stated, while attending the barbecue at Helena, received news which caused him to hasten to Louisville without delay.

The conference which he met there was an historical one. Among those present were George D. Prentice, John Rowan, Judge Purtell, C. M. Thurston, William Pilchers, James Blenn, James Guthrie, J. J. Crittenden, Robert Wickliffe, Judge Wooley, Colonel Avis Throckmorton, Dr. Baum, Dr. Pinkerton, and Dudley of Lexington, Kentucky, John Norton of Lexington, General Leslie Combs, R. M. Johnson, General William Butler, Hon. Ben Harding, Judge Buckner, Judge Bullet, J. I. Jacob, J. D. Swift, Hon. Tom Marshall, Humphrey Marshall, Henry C. Pope, Henry Lazarus, George T. Gray, Robert K. White, Penn the well-known editor, and numerous others.

Bennett, after giving his report, addressed this assemblage in terms of passionate eloquence. He confessed that his deadly earnestness in the business was inspired as much by the desire for vengeance upon the race itself for the murder of his wife and children, as by his desire to wrest Texas from Mexico for the sake of Texas itself.

But he had traveled extensively through the country for ten years, and his knowledge was so intimate, that the men who listened to him gave great heed to his words, feeling they were worthy of serious attention.

He assured them that Texas could be taken in three months, and that a small organized army could march to the capital of Mexico itself. Bennett did not hesitate to make known his distrust of Sam Houston's delays and vacillating course, and he presented the following letter from Davy Crockett, which was read amid breathless silence to that historic assemblage.

This letter is believed to be the last letter ever penned by Crockett, who wrote with his large round-hand, his name being signed, as always, in bold characters across the face of the written page.

The latter is dated San Antonio, whither Crockett had gone some time before, with a few of his brother patriots. The letter was addressed to Col. Richard M. Johnson, who handed it to Hon. Ben Harding, the secretary of the meeting, and he read it to his friends:

"I have thoroughly tested the strength of our silent forces, and to-day, were we called upon to draw, the stiletto of three out of every five men would be buried in the heart of the Mexican general or his soldiers. There are now in Texas 100,000 men who understand English, and more than fifty per cent of this number are with us, if not by arms at least by sympathy, and want to win a country that will make a dozen States. Texas will do this. Probably, when once the revolt is made, the Mexican troops will be like runaway horses—the more they run, the more fright they gather, and they will keep on until all are stampeded. There is no more news regarding the 400 men under Hawkins.

We have heard nothing regarding the material (cannon) so long promised by way of R. R. (Red River). We have been thirty miles further south-west, and find many parties who are traveling east-ward. We will not return without the weather (the enemy) requires. Three hundred men have passed on their way to the States by Trammel's Trail (a blazed path through the timbers). They were in squads of ten, fifteen, and twenty, and will return by February 10. Dr. Ricord says we have news from the agent (Sam Houston), but we have heard nothing from the manufacturer (President Jackson). Agent promises large accessions of new stock (men and munitions of war). If it don't arrive on the 15th, we will return and make ship-ment ourselves on our own account.

"LATER.—Hawkins and friends have been put to rout. Hawkins is missing. It is believed by Dr. Ricord that the worst has not been discovered. Dr. Ricord finds that General Gaines has been ordered forward to the west of the Neches River; with what purpose Houston has no intelligence. If you have, communicate swiftly. The army of Santa Anna is marching eastward, and we will have to fight them. Have a more competent man than Houston. Houston has dealt with us in prevarica-tions. Colonel Bowie and Travers and our forces are all ready for an advance.

"D. CROCKETT."

CHAPTER XXII.

San Antonio—Its Fiery History—Its final Capture by the Texans under General Burlison.

THE city of San Antonio de Bexar, as it was
formerly called, is probably the most interesting
and picturesque city in Texas. It is known now as
San Antonio, but is universally pronounced in the
State, *Santone*.

It lies seventy-five miles southwest of Austin,
and may be said to consist of three separate towns:
the old town of San Antonio proper, lying between
the two rivers ; the Alamo, east of the San Antonio, and Chihuahua west of the Pedro. This
portion is also frequently known as Mexico,—not
an inappropriate name, for it is as characteristically
Mexican as any straggling town that can be found
south of the Rio Grande.

The English, Spanish, German, and French are
spoken by many of the inhabitants, and the population is so mixed that public notices in the churches
and at public resorts are generally posted in three
languages.

San Antonio, viewed from a distance, is strikingly
beautiful and impressive. It nestles in a large am-
phitheatre, the mountains and prairies sloping down
to it from all directions.

Through this quaint old town the lovely San Antonio River winds its way. The San Pedro is a smaller stream, and the city itself is intersected by connecting streams, thus supplying San Antonio with pure, refreshing water, which possesses a peculiar and pleasing bluish tint.

Creeping vines, bananas, fig, and shade trees grow luxuriantly in this semi-tropical town, many of the old houses being almost hidden by the wealth of vegetation. In the spring these are one mass of flowers, whose perfume fills the air, while the singing birds give to the whole an enchanting picture as of fairy land.

But where there is so much that is pleasing to the eye, there is a great deal that is the reverse. The streets are narrow and ill-paved, and on the outskirts and in many quarters are found wretched hovels, whose miserable occupants in any less favored climate would perish of exposure.

San Antonio is one of the few ancient cities of our country, having been founded in 1692 by Franciscan friars from France, who established themselves in that remote though lovely spot, with a view of introducing civilization and Christianity among the fierce Comanches and Apaches.

The mission-houses which they erected are still standing as monuments of their labor, which were rewarded with indifferent success. These structures were strongly built, and will doubtless stand for many years to come, though large portions of them are in ruins.

They were built in enclosures of thick, powerful

adobe walls, with embrasures for defensive weapons, against which the vengeful red man hurled his spears and arrows in vain. Some of these mission-houses have the candles burning on their altars, which have never been extinguished since first lighted hundreds of years ago, and the devout worshipers still gather within the massive and partly fallen walls, just as they did when the shout of the wild Indian was heard without, while the outside world scarcely knew of the existence of these friars buried in the remote wilderness.

The mission-houses stand on either side of the San Antonio, at varying distances from each other, below the city. Their names are La Purissima, Concepcion, La Espada, San Jose, and San Juan.

San Antonio has had a fiery history. The name "Espada," signifying "The Sword," of one of the missions, is typical of its experience.

San Antonio became the focus of the war caused by the revolt against Spain. Only after a hot fight was the city captured on the 4th of March, 1813. Precisely three months later, 8,500 Spaniards and Mexicans attacked the town with great fierceness but they suffered a disastrous and bloody repulse.

The purpose of retaking the city, however, was not given over, and on the 18th of August, the Spaniards once more marched against it. Instead of remaining within the city and awaiting their attack, the revolutionists filed out on the open plain to fight them. The defenders in turn suffered a terrible defeat, nearly six hundred American ad-

venturers losing their lives, and San Antonio again
fell into the hands of the Spaniards.

Besides these crucial experiences, the Comanches
and Apaches have greatly harassed the place, more
than once threatening its very existence and frequently destroying the crops at the very doors of
the settlers.

One of the most memorable struggles witnessed
by the battle-scarred town, was its capture from
the Mexicans by General Burlison on the 10th of
December 1835. The particulars of this fight mark
it as a most extraordinary one in every respect.
There were fully fifteen hundred men in the town,
while the attacking forces were only one-eighth as
numerous.

Every advantage seemed to be on the side of
General Cos and his Mexicans. They had walled
up the streets leading from the public square, with
the intention of " dying in the last ditch." The
attack of the Texans, however, proved irresistbile.
They drove the Mexicans from house to house, the
assailants themselves sometimes clambering the
roofs, in their eagerness to reach the " Greasers."

General Cos found it impossible to hold his
ground, and his demoralized forces slowly gave way,
fighting as they retreated before the impetuous
Texans, who kept up the attack unintermittingly,
for five days and nights, at the end of which time
General Cos, who had gathered his forces in the
Alamo, hoisted the white flag in token of surrender.

It is important to mention at this point the terms
upon which the Mexican General Cos surrendered

to General Burlison, for they have a bearing upon the events that follow.

The Mexican leader agreed to retire within six days, with his officers, arms and private property, on parole of honor, and he pledged himself not to oppose the re-establishment of the constitution of 1824. The infantry and the cavalry, the remnants of Morale's battalion, and the convicts, were to return, taking with them ten rounds of cartridges as a precaution against attacks from the Indians.

All public property, money, arms and ammunition were to be delivered to General Burlison, with some other stipulations respecting the prisoners, of such a liberal character that the Texans would not have accepted them but for the astonishing fact that not a single round of ammunition was left them after the incessant five days' fighting.

General Ugartechea had arrived only the day before with several hundred convicts, but they were of no account in a fight, and were probably accepted at their true value by the Mexicans, who were not much better. .

The latter lost some three hundred during the five days' fight, while the Texans had less than a half dozen killed, with perhaps twice as many wounded, There must have been an amazing amount of poor marksmanship during the prolonged fusillade.

CHAPTER XXIII.

Within the Alamo.

WHEN Colonel Crockett and his friends reached San Antonio there were 1200 citizens in the town, who seemed very indifferent as to the fate of the garrison. The building was built in —1774, but the walls once surrounding it, have long since disappeared. The structure itself is in a fine state of preservation, and is used as a storehouse by one of the leading merchants of the city.

The garrison at the Alamo, at the date of which we speak, consisted of 183 men, under the command of Colonel William Barrett Travis, while the famous Colonels Jim Bowie and Crockett were associated with him. Probably no more desperate men were ever brought together in a single enterprise.

Among them were desperadoes from all parts of the Union, each " armed to the teeth." Many of them carried the terrible weapon known as the Bowie knife, while the majority possessed several pistols and rifles. There was an abundance of ammunition. All the conditions were such as to insure one of the most memorable contests of American history.

The arrival of Colonel Crockett delighted the

small garrison. He was known to the leaders as one of the bravest of men, and his addition to their forces was equivalent to that of a dozen persons. Colonels Travis and Bowie greeted him warmly, and Crockett felt that he was among kindred spirits.

The particulars of the memorable siege and fall of the Alamo, cannot be known with certainty, inasmuch as no defender ever lived to tell the history, but from the legends gathered from some of the Mexicans concerned and from a few of the cowardly inhabitants of San Antonio itself, the following account has been collated, though it must be remembered that no one can vouch for its entire accuracy.

At the time Colonel Crockett joined the garrison, there was no immediate force in the vicinity. Santa Anna was infuriated over the capture and parole of his brother-in-law, General Cos, and was in the mood to show no mercy to the insurgents, who were equally eager to meet him in combat.

A lookout was established at the Alamo, and the scouts were sent through the surrounding country, so as to prevent anything like a surprise. From the battlements streamed a blood-red flag, on which were the letters in large characters, " T-E-X-A-S."

On the 22d of February, 1836, trustworthy news was brought the Texans that Santa Anna was within a few miles of the town. At sunrise, the whole Mexican army was descried, marching in regular order and making in their showy uniforms a most brilliant display. No doubt they intended to strike awe into the hearts of the little band of insurgents by their marching and appearance, but the defenders felt anything but fear at the sight of the force, large as it was.

The banner borne at the head of the Mexican force was of a crimson color and was accepted by the Texans as signifying that no quarter would be shown excepting upon unconditional surrender.

Up to this time there had been no regular occupation of the Alamo, though most of the Texans slept there. It was now decided, in order to prevent themselves being surrounded, to take up their quarters in the massive structure.

This was scarcely done, the defenders carrying with them their guns, ammunition and provisions, when Santa Anna marched in and assumed possession of the town.

On the same afternoon he sent Colonel Travis a formal demand to surrender the garrison, threatening, in case of refusal, to put every man to the sword. The reply to this was a cannon-shot, and the Mexican commander immediately began preparations to bring the defiant rebels to terms.

At dusk, Colonel Travis sent an express to Colonel Fannin at Goliad, four days' march distant, notifying him of the peril of himself and little band and asking him to send assistance without an hour's delay.

The messenger employed to carry this important despatch was a sailor who had once been under Lafitte, the notorious pirate.

The following morning, the Mexicans began erecting a battery on the banks of the San Antonio, three hundred yards distant, and at intervals during the day, they practiced so as to get the exact range of the Alamo.

The marksmanship was poor, and no damage was inflicted. The same day some thirty re-enforcements from Gonzales managed to join the garrison, and they were right royally welcomed.

The following proclamation had been issued by Colonel Travis, and displayed in San Antonio:

"FEBRUARY 24.

"I am besieged by a thousand Mexicans, with Santa Anna at their head. On their arrival, they sent and demanded an unconditional surrender of the garrison under my command, or we would all be put to the sword indiscriminately. I answered their demand with a cannon-shot. I have sustained a bombardment and heavy cannonade for the last twenty-four hours. I have not lost a man. Fellow-citizens, assist me now, for the good of all; for, if they are flushed with one victory, they will be much harder to conquer. I shall defend myself to the last extremity, and die as becomes a soldier. I never intend to retreat or surrender. Victory or death!

"WILLIAM B. TRAVIS, Col. Commanding."

This stirring appeal was thrown away. Not a solitary response was made, and Colonel Travis, who had sought personally to enlist some recruits, went back to his devoted band, feeling that, in all probability, he, like the rest, were soon to meet their doom.

The intrepid Colonel Jim Bowie, whose very presence was a host of itself, had been indisposed for several days, and was at last compelled to take to his bed. He occasionally roused himself, and crept forth to cheer his friends, but he continued to fail, and it was a most dispiriting sight to see him growing more and more helpless as the need of his matchless services became hourly greater.

On the 27th of February, the cannonading was renewed, and ten bombs fell into the fort, exploding without doing injury.

Some alarm was created by discovering that the provisions were running low, and the Mexicans were making efforts to cut off the supply of water. The settlers were rapidly fleeing, to avoid the outrages which the enemy was committing.

The following morning, it was seen that the Mexicans had planted a piece of ordnance within gunshot of the Alamo, and they commenced a hot cannonade of the very spot where Crockett was sleeping.

He sprang out, ascended the rampart, and saw the gunner in the act of firing the piece. Before he could do so, Crockett shot him dead.

A second Mexican caught up the match, but another rifle was passed to Crockett, who picked him off; a third, fourth, and fifth followed, while the hunter killed every one with the rifles which were immediately passed him by the group of Texans that had followed him to the roof.

That silenced the gun, for the time at least.

On the 3d of March, all hope of receiving assistance from Goliad or Refugio was given over. Colonel Travis addressed his men, and exhorted them, in case the enemy should carry the fort, to fight to the last breath, and make the victory a disaster to their enemies.

The brave Texans replied with three cheers.

The bombardment continued all this day and the succeeding, producing no appreciable effect, while full three hundred of the Mexicans had been shot by the unerring rifles of the garrison.

For eleven days the little band of Texans kept twenty times their own number at bay, under Santa Anna, who became so exasperated that he determined the Alamo should be carried, if it cost him every man.

On Sunday morning, March 6, at daylight, the sound of the Mexican bugle notified the Texans that the crisis had come, and they hurried to their posts.

In the gray light, the four thousand Mexicans were descried pouring tumultuously forward, all shouting, while their band played the *Dequelo*, which signifies no quarter.

Santa Anna, caring nothing for the lives of his soldiers, divided his infantry into columns, and surrounded them by cavalry, who with their sabres drove them to the work of carnage.

The Texans were cool and silent.

The terrible hour, they knew, had come at last!

CHAPTER XXIV.

The Texan Thermopylæ.

At three o'clock Sunday morning March 6, 1836, the Matamoras battalion was moved to a point nearer the river and above the Alamo. They were supported by two thousand men under General Cos. The sound of the bugle was heard at four o'clock, and after two hours of desperate fighting, repulses and frightful losses, General Castrillon's division succeeded in effecting an entrance in the upper part 'of the Alamo, in a sort of outwork, now a courtyard. The columns attacking the north, west and east sides, were hurled back by the first fire of the defenders, and all three of them concentrated on the north front, because the houses on the west and east gave the garrison great advantage.

The bugle again sounded the charge, and a second time they were repulsed in confusion, before reaching the foot of the wall, against which they strove to place their scaling ladders. As we have stated the Mexican bands were playing the *Dequelo*, signifying that no quarter would be given the garrison, who were fighting with a bravery beyond description.

The windows and doors were barricaded and guarded by bags of dirt, heaped five feet high, and along the roof were other piles.   Behind these the Texans fought muzzle to muzzle and hand to hand.

Santa Anna gave the signals of battle from a battery near the Commerce street bridge.   At the third charge he encouraged his men in person.   It was this last charge which enabled the Mexicans to reach the foot of the wall, where they were so close that the Texans could not fire down upon them. The ladders were hastily placed in position and the cowardly assailants were forced to ascend them by the officers in the rear, sword in hand.   As they reached the tops, they were tumbled back and the ladders overturned.   The places of the dead and wounded were instantly filled by others, and the attempt was repeated again and again, until the garrison were worn out by the terrific struggle.   The latter were supplied with several rifles apiece, and from behind the dirt bags they fired at random, for there could be no misses, when the foe were huddled like sheep before the muzzles of their guns. With no time to reload their discharged pieces, they used them as clubs.

The continual crash of fire-arms, the shouts of the defiant Texans, the shrieks of the dying, the yells of the Mexicans, the frantic commands of the officers, and the martial music of the bands, made the scene indescribable in its very sublimity of terror.

When the outer walls were gained the garrison took refuge in the chapel, while the cannon beside which Travis fought, was turned on the Mexicans and swept the court-yard below.   Each room in the Alamo was the scene of a fierce struggle between the small band of patriots and the horde of Mexicans, who poured upon them like a resistless mountain torrent.   In the long room, used as a hospital, the sick and the wounded fired rifles and pistols from their pallets.

A cannon was shotted with grape and canister and turned upon these sufferers.   It was aimed all too well, and, after the fire the bodies of fourteen defenders, torn, black and mangled, told the dreadful story.   At the entrance of the room, it is said more than forty Mexicans were stretched in death.

Colonel Jim Bowie was sick and helpless in bed, when two Mexicans approached the door of the apartment raised their guns and fired at him. Then one of the Mexicans ran forward to complete the work of the rifles.   The Louisianan was dying then, but rousing himself by a last effort, he caught his assailant by the hair of the head and plunged his knife into his body.   Both fell back dead.

At last only six of the garrison were left alive. They were surrounded by General Castrillon and his soldiers.   The officer shouted to them to surrender, promising that their lives should be spared. In the little group of Spartans were Davy Crockett and Travis, so exhausted they were scarcely able to stand.   Crockett stood in an angle of the fort, the barrel of his shattered rifle in his right hand, while the massive Bowie in his left was dripping with blood.   His face was crimson from a gash in his forehead, and nearly a score of Mexicans were stretched around him, either dead or dying from his fearful blows.

There were a few brave and humane officers, and among them were General Castrillon and Burdillon. They spoke sympathizingly to Crockett and Travis, and with several other officers walked to where the scowling Santa Anna stood and asked that the surrender of the few survivors might be received.

The reply was an order that all should be shot. Seeing his treachery, the enraged Crockett roused himself, and swinging his Bowie aloft, made a furious rush for the Mexican Nana Sahib. The intrepid Tennessean was riddled with bullets before he could pass half the intervening distance.

Almost at the same moment, the other five were shot down. Only a few minutes before, Evans, according to previous agreement, started with a torch for the magazine, but was killed before he could reach it.

The Alamo had fallen!

Over one thousand Mexicans were slain, and the one hundred and eighty three Texans who did it, were slaughtered in turn.

When the awful tumult had subsided, Santa Anna sent for the Alcalde, ordered the clothing stripped from the dead, who were then hauled in ox-carts to an open field northeast of the church, where they were thrown upon a pile and burned to ashes.

Obviously, there can be no certainty concerning the details of the fall of the Alamo. J. H. Greene is positive that one of the survivors was a servant named Nassau, a native of Natchitoches, Louisiana, who told Greene he was asleep outside the Alamo, when it fell. Nassau was known as " Little Nas, or Nat." The other survivors were a babe and its mother, Mary Britton, who christened it Emily. The mother and child were well cared for by the State of Texas.

A gossipy sketch of an interview with a character in New York, known as " Old Uncle Bogardus," was recently published in the *N. Y. Sun*, to which this reply was written.

WASHINGTON, D. C., Nov. 27, 1883.

I see in *The Sun* to-day, an article entitled " He Knew Davy Crockett," in which "Old Uncle Bogardus " is made to tell some anecdotes of the Tennessee hunter. These may all be true, but the closing sentence, which tells of Crockett's life and death in Texas, is not true.

" Uncle Bogardus " says: "Crockett went to Texas, where, after a series of daring military exploits, he was finally killed at Fort Alamo, in San Antonio De Bexar. He was one of the six survivors who, under promise of being spared, at last surrendered, and were afterward treacherously put to death by Santa Anna's orders."

This is all a mistake. Crockett never had the opportunity to perform any " daring military exploits " in Texas, because there was no force of

Mexicans east of San Antonio, and Crockett arrived there from the East just before the Mexican army, under Gen. Cos. arrived from the West.

The Texas forces undertook to defend the Alamo, solely to enable Houston to collect an army that could meet the two Mexican armies advancing into the country. Every man who went into the Alamo knew it would be his tomb. No one surrendered. Crockett was killed inside the walls while defending himself to the last, with his trusty rifle used as a club.

The only persons who "surrendered," or were taken alive in the Alamo, were Mrs. Dickinson, and her infant girl Angelina, afterward known as "The Child of the Alamo," and a negro servant, who belonged to or waited upon Col. Travis.

I was one of the children in the Mission Refugio when it was taken, just previous to the fall of the Alamo, by the other Mexican army under General Urrea, and saw the brave defenders of that place shot down and lanced after they had surrendered as prisoners of war.

The stubborn defence of the Alamo enabled Houston to collect the forces with which he met and defeated the united armies of Cos and Urrea, under Santa Anna, at San Jacinto.

The monument to the heroes of the Alamo, a plain shaft that stood in the old State House at Austin, has inscribed on it the most expressive sentence in the English language: "Thermopylæ had three messengers of defeat; the Alamo had none."

I have often talked with all three of the survivors of the Alamo, and your "Uncle Bogardus" is the first person I ever heard of who said Crockett surrendered. He is mistaken.

E. N. H.

The following letter is also given. It will be· noticed that it differs in some slight particulars from the other accounts. These differences, it is not probable, will ever be authoritatively settled.

WASHINGTON, Feb. 5, 1884.

Captain Reuben M. Potter, in his criticism of my sketch of Colonel David Crockett in the December number of the Magazine of American History, takes issue with me on the statement that the garrison of the Alamo surrendered. I was fully aware at the time of writing the sketch that this had been a mooted question, but from the research that I gave the subject, I was satisfied that the weight of authority favored the affirmative view. Captain Potter may be assured that no part of that article was written on the evidence of extravagant story-tellers, by whom he thinks the author may have been misled. The writer was born and passed the greater part of his life in the district of Tennessee which Colonel Crockett represented in Congress, has known him, and heard him make stump speeches, and is familiar with many of his comrades, and his descendants now living. In the preparation of the article, all known authorities were consulted. It is true that in the work called "Texas and Texans," written and published in 1841, by Hon. Henry S. Foote, the author relies upon a newspaper article to contradict the theory of the surrender. Edwards, also, in his " History of Texas," evidently copying from Foote, asserts that there was no surrender.

Other authorities, and the tradition sustained by the survivors, go to prove to the contrary. The weight of authorities show, I think, that when the combined attack on the fort was made by the Mexicans on the morning of the 6th of March with 4,000 men—infantry and artillery—in which they were twice repulsed with heavy loss, that they at last succeeded in entering the fort, and after some desperate hand-to-hand fighting with the clubs of guns and bowie-knives, but six of the garrison remained alive. Being surrounded on all sides by overpowering numbers, and unable to load their guns, that they surrendered to General Castrillon under a solemn promise that they would be treated as prisoners of war. Santa Anna, however, ordered them put to death. This was evidently what the victorious army at San Jacinto believed of the affair of the Alamo, for their war-cry in that memorable battle was, " Remember the Alamo!"

Captain Potter's comments on the statement "that there were around Crockett a complete barrier of about twenty Mexicans lying pell-mell, dead and dying," is, to say the least of it, disingenuous. The claim is not made that Crockett slew or wounded all of these men, or that it was done in a "minute." On the entrance of the Mexicans into the fort, the six survivors fought with their knives and the butts of their guns in a body, and it is not only not unlikely that they wounded and killed about twenty of the enemy, but it is probable that the number was far greater than stated. There is no evidence in any authentic account of this memorable engagement that there was any "group of skulkers" in the garrison, as stated by Captain Potter. It is told, but on somewhat doubtful authority, that one of the garrison, named Warner, asked for quarter, which was denied him.

There were, according to the best authorities, four persons who escaped : Mrs. Dickinson, wife of Lieutenant Dickinson, who fell fighting in the fort, her child, and two negro servants—one the servant of Colonel Travis, and the other of Colonel Bowie. It has been stated also that two Mexican women of Bexar escaped from the fort on the morning of the 6th of March. One of the known survivors, Mrs. Hanning, is now living in Austin, Texas. She was at the time of the siege of the Alamo about eighteen years old. During the siege she received a wound from a bullet which pierced one of her legs. MARCUS J. WRIGHT.

CHAPTER XXV.

Conclusion.

THUS died Colonel David Crockett, and the one hundred and eighty-two immortal defenders of the Alamo, whose name recalls one of the most thrilling episodes of the world's history. But as is often the case, the blood of the martyrs proved the seed that bore the independence of Texas as its fruit.

After the capture of San Antonio, Santa Anna made a feint on Gonzales, where General Sam Houston lay with an inferior force. Houston at once fell back to the Colorado, believing the whole Mexican army was on the point of attacking him. A similar feint was made on Bastrop, a town on the Colorado, northeast of San Antonio.

This done Santa Anna marched directly for Goliad, which is something less than a hundred miles southeast of San Antonio, on the Colorado. The fort there was very strong and was defended by Colonel Fanning with a small force of volunteers. About the middle of March, General Houston ordered Fanning to evacuate and blow up the fort and join him on the Colorado. With 260 men and several field-pieces, Fanning set out across the country to unite with his commander-in-chief.

At the close of the first day, the Mexicans appeared in the rear and Colonel Fanning halted and opened fire, with his artillery, instead of hastening forward and availing himself of the shelter of the wood a short distance in advance. A fierce fight was maintained for hours, but the Texans repulsed the Mexicans, losing themselves only seven men while the Mexicans admitted a loss nearly two hundred.

Colonel Fanning, finding he was not only cut off from the shelter of the wood, but that the enemy had interposed between him and his advanced guard, spent the night in throwing up intrenchments.

At daylight the Texans saw that the Mexicans were receiving large re-enforcements, and there was no more hope of success in contending against the overwhelming forces than the garrison of the Alamo had in fighting the Mexican army.

At this opportune moment, Santa Anna sent forward a white flag demanding the surrender of Colonel Fanning, promising in the most solemn manner that they should retain all their private property; that they might return by the first opportunity as prisoners of war to the United States, or remain until they were regularly exchanged; and that they should be treated in a humane manner while in confinement.

Under these assurances, Colonel Fanning and his men surrendered. The Mexicans succeeded in capturing a number of stragglers until they had about four hundred prisoners, who were confined for several days in an old church within the fort at Goliad. They were finally marched out, and conducted along a high brush fence, some distance away, where the Mexicans opened fire upon and shot them down as though they were dogs. Nearly all fell dead or mortally wounded at the first fire, but a few escaped by dropping at the instant of the flash, and these instantly sprang to their feet and made off to the woods.

The Mexicans having emptied their guns, bayoneted all who showed any signs of life. The authorities of Texas gathered the blackened remains on the 4th of June following, and bestowed solemn obsequies upon them.

About the middle of April, Santa Anna marched one division of his army in the direction of Lynch's Ferry on the San Jacinto, burning Harrisburg as he passed through it. On the 21st they were re-enforced by General Cos who thus broke his parole with five hundred of their best troops. This increased their effective force to 1500 men, while that of the Texans is given as 783.

The Texan army was tired of retreating, and eager for the battle to open. The disparity in numbers intensified their courage and a few fiery words from Houston rendered them almost irrestrainable.

Having perfected their arrangements, and making sure the enemy were scattered and unprepared, the Texans made their attack upon the "Greasers," cheering each other on by the war-cry, "Remember the Alamo!"

So fierce was the assault that in less than twenty minutes the Mexicans were utterly routed. The patriots not having bayonets, clubbed their rifles, and scores were splintered in crushing the skulls of the panic-stricken Mexicans.

The Bowie knife did frightful execution at San Jacinto. It is said on good authority, that the Texans soon turned the fight into a wild amusement, feeling that they were in little personal danger.

The simple results tell the story of the indescribable scene. The Texans had two killed and twenty-three wounded, six of whom died. The enemy had 630 killed and 730 were taken prisoners. Among the plunder captured were 600 muskets, 300 sabres, several hundred horses and mules, and over a thousand dollars in specie.

Among the wounded Texans was J. H. Green, to whom we have already alluded. He received a bad bayonet thrust and was struck by a glancing ball in the forehead, which passed around and imbedded itself in his neck.

He lay in the tent of Sam Houston, at dusk, suffering much from his hurts. Houston himself was sound asleep, his slumber being profound, from something besides natural causes. His negro servant was also asleep, when a couple of the guards brought in a prisoner whom they had found in a swamp, and who begged so piteously for his life that they could not refuse his prayer. As he kept continually asking for General Houston, he was taken to his tent.

Houston with difficulty was aroused, but he preferred to sleep, and, turning upon his side with an impatient exclamation, did not stir until the next morning.

All the night through, the prisoner, pale and and trembling, sat in the tent, refusing to eat a mouthful or even to touch a drop of water. He seemed to be in mortal dread of losing his life.

When Houston awoke at sunrise, the frightened prisoner addressed him in Spanish and then Italian, announcing that he was Santa Anna and begging to be protected from the fury of the soldiers.

Houston at once ordered Santa Anna's sword to be returned to him; but he had none on when taken, so the order could not be obeyed.

General Cos was also among the captured, and he too was in mortal terror lest he should be made to suffer the just penalty of violating his parole; but General Almonte, another captive, was as brave and cool as he had been all through the battle.

Santa Anna offered to acknowledge the independence of and to evacuate Texas, on condition that his life should be spared. The terms were accepted, as a matter of course. He was held a prisoner until the succeeding year, although Mexico repudiated his treaty with the insurgent Texans.

But the battle of San Jacinto secured the independence of Texas. It became an independent republic, acknowledged as such by the United States in 1837, and in 1840, by England, France and Belgium. It was admitted into the Union in December, 1845, but Mexico, which had never recognized its independence, invaded the territory, and the Mexican war was the result.

To day Texas is one of the most brilliant stars in the grand constellation of the Union. With an area of more than a quarter of a million square miles, with an unlimited variety of soil, climate and productions, with a capacity for growth and prosperity beyond calculation, with a steady stream of immigration converging from all parts of the world, with her vast prairies, her rivers, her streams, her enterprise, her history, her sacred memories and her teeming future, Texas is indeed the *Coming Empire.*

STANDARD AND POPULAR BOOKS

PUBLISHED BY

PORTER & COATES, PHILADELPHIA, PA.

WAVERLEY NOVELS. By SIR WALTER SCOTT.

*Waverley.	The Fortunes of Nigel.
*Guy Mannering.	Peveril of the Peak.
The Antiquary.	Quentin Durward.
Rob Roy.	St. Ronan's Well.
Black Dwarf; and Old Mortality.	Redgauntlet.
The Heart of Mid-Lothian.	The Betrothed; and The Talisman.
The Bride of Lammermoor; and A Legend of Montrose.	Woodstock.
	The Fair Maid of Perth.
*Ivanhoe.	Anne of Geierstein.
The Monastery.	Count Robert of Paris; and Castle Dangerous.
The Abbott.	
Kenilworth.	Chronicles of the Canongate.
The Pirate.	

Household Edition. 23 vols. Illustrated. 12mo. Cloth, extra, black and gold, per vol., $1.00; sheep, marbled edges, per vol., $1.50; half calf, gilt, marbled edges, per vol., $3.00. Sold separately in cloth binding only.

Universe Edition. 25 vols. Printed on thin paper, and containing one illustration to the volume. 12mo. Cloth, extra, black and gold, per vol., 75 cts.

World Edition. 12 vols. Thick 12mo. (Sold in sets only.) Cloth, extra, black and gold, $18.00; half imt. Russia, marbled edges, $24.00.

This is the best edition for the library or for general use published. Its convenient size. the extreme legibility of the type, which is larger than is used in any other 12mo edition, either English or American.

TALES OF A GRANDFATHER. By SIR WALTER SCOTT, Bart. 4 vols. Uniform with the Waverley Novels. Household Edition. Illustrated. 12mo. Cloth, extra, black and gold, per vol., $1.00; sheep, marbled edges, per vol., $1.50; half calf, gilt, marbled edges, per vol., $3.00.

This edition contains the Fourth Series—Tales from French history—and is the only complete edition published in this country.

CHARLES DICKENS' COMPLETE WORKS. Author's Edition.
14 vols., with a portrait of the author on steel, and eight
illustrations by F. O. C. Darley, Cruikshank, Fildes, Eytinge,
and others, in each volume. 12mo. Cloth, extra, black and
gold, per vol., $1.00; sheep, marbled edges, per vol., $1.50; half
int. Russia, marbled edges, per vol., $1.50: half calf, gilt,
marbled edges, per vol., $2.75.

*Pickwick Papers.
*Oliver Twist, Pictures of Italy, and
   American Notes.
*Nicholas Nickleby.
Old Curiosity Shop, and Reprinted
   Pieces.
Barnaby Rudge, and Hard Times.
*Martin Chuzzlewit.
Dombey and Son.
*David Copperfield.

Christmas Books, Uncommercial
   Traveller, and Additional
   Christmas Stories.
Bleak House.
Little Dorrit.
Tale of Two Cities, and Great Ex-
   pectations.
Our Mutual Friend.
Edwin Drood, Sketches, Master
   Humphrey's Clock, etc., etc.

Sold separately in cloth binding only.
*Also in Alta Edition, one illustration, 75 cents.
The same. Universe Edition. Printed on thin paper and containing one illustration to the volume. 14 vols., 12mo. Cloth,
extra, black and gold, per vol., 75 cents.
The same. World Edition. 7 vols., thick 12mo., $12.25. (Sold
in sets only.)

CHILD'S HISTORY OF ENGLAND. By CHARLES DICKENS.
Popular 12mo. edition; from new electrotype plates. Large
clear type. Beautifully illustrated with 8 engravings on wood.
12mo. Cloth, extra, black and gold, $1.00.
Alta Edition. One illustration, 75 cents.
"Dickens as a novelist and prose poet is to be classed in the front rank of
the noble company to which he belongs. He has revived the novel of genuine practical life, as it existed in the works of Fielding, Smollett, and Gold-
smith; but at the same time has given to his material an individual coloring
and expression peculiarly his own. His characters, like those of his great
exemplars, constitute a world of their own, whose truth to nature every
reader instinctively recognizes in connection with their truth to darkness."
—E. P. Whipple.

MACAULAY'S HISTORY OF ENGLAND. From the accession
of James II. By THOMAS BABINGTON MACAULAY. With a
steel portrait of the author. Printed from new electrotype
plates from the last English Edition. Being by far the most
correct edition in the American market. 5 volumes, 12mo.
Cloth, extra, black and gold, per set, $5.00; sheep, marbled
edges, per set, $7.50; half imitation Russia, $7.50; half calf,
gilt, marbled edges, per set, $15.00.
Popular Edition. 5 vols., cloth, plain, $5.00.
8vo. Edition. 5 volumes in one, with portrait. Cloth, extra,
black and gold, $3.00; sheep, marbled edges, $3.50.

MARTINEAU'S HISTORY OF ENGLAND. From the beginning
of the 19th Century to the Crimean War. By HARRIET MAR-
TINEAU. Complete in 4 vols., with full Index. Cloth, extra,
black and gold, per set, $4.00; sheep, marbled edges, $6.00; half
calf, gilt, marbled edges, $12.00.

HUME'S HISTORY OF ENGLAND. From the invasion of
Julius Cæsar to the abdication of James II, 1688. By DAVID
HUME. Standard Edition. With the author's last corrections
and improvements; to which is prefixed a short account of
his life, written by himself. With a portrait on steel. A new
edition from entirely new stereotype plates. 5 vols., 12mo.
Cloth, extra, black and gold, per set, $5.00; sheep, marbled
edges, per set, $7.50; half imitation Russia, $7.50; half calf,
gilt, marbled edges, per set, $15.00.
Popular Edition. 5 vols. Cloth, plain, $5.00.

GIBBON'S DECLINE AND FALL OF THE ROMAN EMPIRE.
By EDWARD GIBBON. With Notes, by Rev. H. H. MILMAN.
Standard Edition. To which is added a complete Index of
the work. A new edition from entirely new stereotype plates.
With portrait on steel. 5 vols., 12mo. Cloth, extra, black and
gold, per set, $5.00; sheep, marbled edges, per set, $7.50; half
imitation Russia, $7.50; half calf, gilt, marbled edges, per set,
$15.00.
Popular Edition. 5 vols. Cloth, plain, $5.00.

ENGLAND, PICTURESQUE AND DESCRIPTIVE. By JOEL
COOK, author of "A Holiday Tour in Europe," etc. With 487
finely engraved illustrations, descriptive of the most famous
and attractive places, as well as of the historic scenes and
rural life of England and Wales. With Mr. Cook's admirable
descriptions of the places and the country, and the splendid illustrations, this is the most valuable and attractive book of the
season, and the sale will doubtless be very large. 4to. Cloth,
extra, gilt side and edges, $7.50; half calf, gilt, marbled edges,
$10.00; half morocco, full gilt edges, $10.00; full Turkey morocco, gilt edges, $15.00; tree calf, gilt edges, $18.00.

This work, which is prepared in elegant style, and profusely illustrated,
is a comprehensive description of England and Wales, arranged in convenient form for the tourist, and at the same time providing an illustrated
gu de-book to a country which Americans always view with interest. There
are few satisfactory works about this land which is so generously gifted by
Nature and so full of memorials of the past. Such books as there are, either
cover a few counties or are devoted to special localities, or are merely guide-
books. The present work is believed to be the first attempt to give in attractive form a description of the stately homes, renowned castles, ivy-clad ruins
of abbeys, churches, and ancient fortresses, delicious scenery, rock-bound
coasts, and celebrated places of England and Wales. It is written by an
author fully competent from travel and reading, and in position to properly
describe his very interesting subject; and the artist's pencil has been called
into requisition to graphically illustrate its well-written pages. There are
487 illustrations, prepared in the highest style of the engraver's art, while
the book itself is one of the most attractive ever presented to the American
public.
It's method of construction is systematic, following the most convenient
routes taken by tourists, and the letter-press includes enough of the history
and legend of each of the places described to make the story highly interesting. Its pages fairly overflow with picture and description, telling of
everything attractive that is presented by England and Wales. Executed
in the highest style of the printer's and engraver's art, "England, Picturesque and Descriptive," is one of the best American books of the year.

HISTORY OF THE CIVIL WAR IN AMERICA. By the COMTE
DE PARIS. With Maps faithfully Engraved from the Origin-
als, and Printed in Three Colors. 8vo. Cloth, per volume,
$3.50; red cloth, extra, Roxburgh style, uncut edges, $3.50;
sheep, library style, $4.50; half Turkey morocco, $6.00. Vols.
I, II, and III now ready.

The third volume embraces, without abridgment, the fifth and sixth
volumes of the French edition, and covers one of the most interesting as
well as the most anxious periods of the war, describing the operations of the
Army of the Potomac in the East, and the Army of the Cumberland and
Tennessee in the West.
It contains full accounts of the battle of Chancellorsville, the attack of the
monitors on Fort Sumter, the sieges and fall of Vicksburg and Port Hudson;
the battles of Port Gibson and Champion's Hill, and the fullest and most
authentic account of the battle of Gettysburg ever written.

"The head of the Orleans family has put pen to paper with excellent
result. . . . . Our present impression is that it will form by far the best
history of the American war."—*Athenæum, London.*

"We advise all Americans to read it carefully, and judge for themselves
if 'the future historian of our war,' of whom we have heard so much, be not
already arrived in the Comte de Paris."—*Nation, New York.*

"This is incomparably the best account of our great second revolution
that has yet been even attempted. It is so calm, so di-passionate, so accurate
in detail, and at the same time so philosophical in general, that its reader
counts confidently on finding the complete work thoroughly satisfactory."—
Evening Bulletin, Philadelphia.

"The work expresses the calm, deliberate judgment of an experienced
military observer and a highly intelligent man. Many of its statements
will excite discussion, but we much mistake if it does not take high and
permanent rank among the standard histories of the civil war. Indeed
that place has been assigned it by the most competent critics both of this
country and abroad."—*Times, Cincinnati.*

"Messrs. Porter & Coates, of Philadelphia, will publish in a few days the
authorized translation of the new volume of the Comte de Paris' History of
Our Civil War. The two volumes in French—the fifth and sixth—are bound
together in the translation in one volume. Our readers already know,
through a table of contents of these volumes, published in the cable columns
of the *Herald*, the period covered by this new installment of a work remarkable in several ways. It includes the most important and decisive period of
the war, and the two great campaigns of Gettysburg and Vicksburg.
"The great civil war has had no better, no abler historian than the French
prince who, emulating the example of Lafayette, took part in this new
struggle for freedom, and who now writes of events, in many of which he
participated, as an accomplished officer, and one who, by his independent
position, his high character and eminent talents, was placed in circumstances and relations which gave him almost unequalled opportunities to
gain correct information and form impartial judgments.
"The new installment of a work which has already become a classic will
be read with increased interest by Americans because of the importance of
the period it covers and the stirring events it describes. In advance of a
careful review we present to-day some extracts from the advance sheets sent
us by Messrs. Porter & Coates, which will give our readers a foretaste of
chapters which bring back to memory so many half-forgotten and not a few
hitherto unvalued details of a time which Americans of this generation at
least cannot read of without a fresh thrill of excitement."

HALF-HOURS WITH THE BEST AUTHORS. With short Biographical and Critical Notes. By CHARLES KNIGHT.
New Household Edition. With six portraits on steel. 3 vols.,
thick 12mo. Cloth, extra, black and gold, per set, $4.50; half imt.
Russia, marbled edges, $6.00; half calf, gilt, marbled edges, $12.00.
Library Edition. Printed on fine laid and tinted paper. With
twenty-four portraits on steel. 6 vols., 12mo. Cloth, extra, per
set, $7.50; half calf, gilt, marbled edges, per set, $18.00; half Russia, gilt top, $21.00; full French morocco, limp, per set, $12.00;
full smooth Russia, limp, round corners, in Russia case, per set,
$25.00; full seal grained Russia, limp, round corners, in Russia
case to match, $25.00.

The excellent idea of the editor of these choice volumes has been most
admirably carried out, as will be seen by the list of authors upon all subjects. Selecting some choice passages of the best standard authors, each of sufficient length to occupy half an hour in its perusal, there is here food for
thought for every day in the year: so that if the purchaser will devote but
one-half hour each day to its appropriate selection he will read through
these six volumes in one year, and in such a leisurely manner that the
noblest thoughts of many of the greatest minds will be firmly in his mind
forever. For every Sunday there is a suitable selection from some of the
most eminent writers in sacred literature. We venture to say if the editor's
idea is carried out the reader will possess more and better knowledge of the
English classics at the end of the year than he would by five years of desul-
tory reading.

They can be commenced at any day in the year. The variety of reading
is so great that no one will ever tire of these volumes. It is a library in
itself.

THE POETRY OF OTHER LANDS. A Collection of Translations into English Verse of the Poetry of Other Languages,
Ancient and Modern. Compiled by N. CLEMMONS HUNT.
Containing translations from the Greek, Latin, Persian, Arabian, Japanese, Turkish, Servian, Russian, Bohemian, Polish,
Dutch, German, Italian, French, Spanish, and Portuguese
languages. 12mo. Cloth, extra, gilt edges, $2.50; half calf, gilt,
marbled edges, $4.00; Turkey morocco, gilt edges, $6.00.

"Another of the publications of Porter & Coates, called 'The Poetry of
Other Lands,' compiled by N. Clemmons Hunt, we most warmly commend.
It is one of the best collections we have seen, containing many exquisite
poems and fragments of verse which have not before been put into book
form in English words. We find many of the old favorites, which appear
in every well-selected collection of sonnets and songs, and we miss others,
which seem a necessity to complete the bouquet of grasses and flowers,
some of which, from time to time, we hope to republish in the 'Courier.'"—
Cincinnati Courier.

"A book of rare excellence, because it gives a collection of choice gems in
many languages not available to the general lover of poetry. It contains
translations from the Greek, Latin, Persian, Arabian, Japanese, Turkish,
Servian, Russian, Bohemian, Polish, Dutch, German, Italian, French,
Spanish, and Portuguese languages. The book will be an admirable companion volume to any one of the collections of English poetry that are now
published. With the full index of authors immediately preceding the collection, and the arrangement of the poems under headings, the reader will
find it convenient for reference. It is a gift that will be more valued by
very many than some of the transitory ones at these holiday times."—
Philadelphia Methodist.

THE FIRESIDE ENCYCLOPÆDIA OF POETRY. Edited by
HENRY T. COATES. This is the latest, and beyond doubt the
best collection of poetry published. Printed on fine paper and
illustrated with thirteen steel engravings and fifteen title
pages, containing portraits of prominent American poets and
fac-similes of their handwriting, made expressly for this book.
8vo. Cloth, extra, black and gold, gilt edges, $5.00; half calf,
gilt, marbled edges, $7.50; half morocco, full gilt edges, $7.50;
full Turkey morocco, gilt edges, $10.00; tree calf, gilt edges,
$12.00; plush, padded side, nickel lettering, $14.00.

"The editor shows a wide acquaintance with the most precious treasures
of English verse, and has gathered the most admirable specimens of their
ample wealth. Many pieces which have been passed by in previous collections hold a place of honor in the present volume, and will be heartily welcomed by the lovers of poetry as a delightful addition to their sources of
enjoyment. It is a volume rich in solace, in entertainment, in inspiration,
of which the possession may well be coveted by every lover of poetry. The
pictorial illustrations of the work are in keeping with its poetical contents,
and the beauty of the typographical execution entitles it to a place among
the choicest ornaments of the library."—New York Tribune.
"Lovers of good poetry will find this one of the richest collections ever
made. All the best singers in our language are r presented, and the selec-
tions are generally those which reveal their highest qualities. . . . . The
lights and shades, the finer play of thought and imagination belonging to
individual authors, are brought out in this way (by the arrangement of
poems under subject-headings) as they would not be under any other system. . . . . We are deeply impressed with the keen appreciation of poetical
worth, and also with the good taste manifested by the compiler."—Church-
man.
"Cyclopædias of poetry are numerous, but for sterling value of its contents
for the library, or as a book of reference, no work of the kind will compare
with this admirable volume of Mr. Coates It takes the gems from many
volumes, culling with rare skill and judgment."—Chicago Inter-Ocean.

THE CHILDREN'S BOOK OF POETRY. Compiled by HENRY
T. COATES. Containing over 500 poems carefully selected
from the works of the best and most popular writers for children; with nearly 200 illustrations. The most complete collection of poetry for children ever published. 4to. Cloth,
extra, black and gold, gilt side and edges, $3.00; full Turkey
morocco, gilt edges, $7.50.

"This seems to us the best book of poetry for children in existence. We
have examined many other collections, but we cannot name another that
deserves to be compared with this admirable compilation."—Worcester Spy.
"The special value of the book lies in the fact that it nearly or quite
covers the entire field. There is not a great deal of good poetry which has
been written for children that cannot be found in this book. The collection
is particularly strong in ballads and tales, which are apt to interest children
more than poems of other kinds; and Mr. Coates has shown good judgment
in supplementing this department with some of the best poems of that class
that have been written for grown people. A surer method of forming the
taste of children for good and pure literature than by reading to them from
any portion of this book can hardly be imagined. The volume is richly
illustrated and beautifully bound."—Philadelphia Evening Bulletin.
"A more excellent volume cannot be found. We have found within the
covers of this handsome volume, and upon its fair pages, many of the most
exquisite poems which our language contains. It must become a standard
volume, and can never grow old or obsolete."—Episcopal Recorder.

THE COMPLETE WORKS OF THOS. HOOD. With engravings on steel. 4 vols., 12mo., tinted paper. Poetical Works; Up the Rhine; Miscellanies and Hood's Own; Whimsicalities, Whims, and Oddities. Cloth, extra, black and gold, $6.00; red cloth, paper label, gilt top, uncut edges, $6.00; half calf, gilt, marbled edges, $14.00; half Russia, gilt top, $18.00.

Hood's verse, whether serious or comic—whether serene like a cloudless autumn evening or sparkling with puns like a frosty January midnight with stars—was ever pregnant with materials for the thought. Like every author distinguished for true comic humor, there was a deep vein of melancholy pathos running through his mirth, and even when his sun shone brightly its light seemed often reflected as if only over the rim of a cloud. Well may we say, in the words of Tennyson, "Would he could have stayed with us," for never could it be more truly recorded of any one—in the words of Hamlet characterizing Yorick—that "he was a fellow of infinite jest, of most excellent fancy."   D. M. MOIR.

THE ILIAD OF HOMER RENDERED INTO ENGLISH BLANK VERSE. By EDWARD, EARL OF DERBY. From the latest London edition, with all the author's last revisions and corrections, and with a Biographical Sketch of Lord Derby, by R. SHELTON MACKENZIE, D.C.L. With twelve steel engravings from Flaxman's celebrated designs. 2 vols., 12mo. Cloth, extra, bev. boards, gilt top, $3.50; half calf, gilt, marbled edges, $7.00; half Turkey morocco, gilt top, $7.00.

The same. Popular edition. Two vols. in one. 12mo. Cloth, extra, $1 50.

"It must equally be considered a splendid performance; and for the present we have no hesitation in saying that it is by far the best representation of Homer's Iliad in the English language."—*London Times.*

"The merits of Lord Derby's translation may be summed up in one word. It is eminently attractive; it is instinct with life; it may be read with fervent interest; it is immeasurably nearer than Pope to the text of the original . . . . Lord Derby has given a version far more closely allied to the original, and superior to any that has yet been attempted in the blank verse of our language."—*Edinburg Review.*

THE WORKS OF FLAVIUS JOSEPHUS. Comprising the Antiquities of the Jews; a History of the Jewish Wars, and a Life of Flavius Josephus, written by himself. Translated from the original Greek, by WILLIAM WHISTON, A.M. Together with numerous explanatory Notes and seven Dissertations concerning Jesus Christ, John the Baptist, James the Just, God's command to Abraham, etc., with an Introductory Essay by Rev. H. STEBBING, D.D. 8vo. Cloth, extra, black and gold, plain edges, $3.00; cloth, red, black and gold, gilt edges, $1.50; sheep, marbled edges, $3.50; Turkey morocco, gilt edges, $8.00.

This is the largest type one volume edition published.

THE ANCIENT HISTORY OF THE EGYPTIANS, CARTHAGINIANS, ASSYRIANS, BABYLONIANS, MEDES AND PERSIANS, GRECIANS AND MACEDONIANS. Including a History of the Arts and Sciences of the Ancients. By CHARLES ROLLIN. With a Life of the Author, by JAMES BELL. 2 vols., royal 8vo. Sheep, marbled edges, per set, $6.00.

COOKERY FROM EXPERIENCE. A Practical Guide for House-keepers in the Preparation of Every-day Meals, containing more than One Thousand Domestic Recipes, mostly tested by Personal Experience, with Suggestions for Meals, Lists of Meats and Vegetables in Season, etc. By Mrs. SARA T. PAUL. 12mo. Cloth, extra, black and gold, $1.50. Interleaved Edition. Cloth, extra, black and gold, $1.75.

THE COMPARATIVE EDITION OF THE NEW TESTAMENT. Both Versions in One Book.

The proof readings of our Comparative Edition have been gone over by so many competent proof readers, that we believe the text is absolutely correct.

Large 12mo., 700 pp. Cloth, extra, plain edges, $1.50; cloth, extra, bevelled boards and carmine edges, $1.75; imitation panelled calf, yellow edges, $2.00; arabesque, gilt edges, $2.50; French morocco, limp, gilt edges, $4.00; Turkey morocco, limp, gilt edges, $6.00.

The Comparative New Testament has been published by Porter & Coates. In parallel columns on each page are given the old and new versions of the Testament, divided also as far as practicable into comparative verses, so that it is almost impossible for the slightest new word to escape the notice of either the ordinary reader or the analytical student. It is decidedly the best edition yet published of the most interest-exciting literary production of the day. No more convenient form for comparison could be devised either for economizing time or labor. Another feature is the foot-notes, and there is also given in an appendix the various words and expressions preferred by the American members of the Revising Commission. The work is handsomely printed on excellent paper with clear, legible type. It contains nearly 700 pages.

THE COUNT OF MONTE CRISTO. By ALEXANDRE DUMAS. Complete in one volume, with two illustrations by George G. White. 12mo. Cloth, extra, black and gold, $1.25.

THE THREE GUARDSMEN. By ALEXANDRE DUMAS. Complete in one volume, with two illustrations by George G. White. 12mo. Cloth, extra, black and gold, $1.25.

There is a magic influence in his pen, a magnetic attraction in his descriptions, a fertility in his literary resources which are characteristic of Dumas alone, and the seal of the master of light literature is set upon all his works. Even when not strictly historical, his romances give an insight into the habits and modes of thought and action of the people of the time described, which are not offered in any other author's productions.

THE LAST DAYS OF POMPEII. By Sir EDWARD BULWER LYTTON, Bart. Illustrated. 12mo. Cloth, extra, black and gold, $1.00. Alta edition, one illustration, 75 cts.

JANE EYRE. By CHARLOTTE BRONTÉ (Currer Bell). New Library Edition. With five illustrations by E. M. WIMPERIS. 12mo. Cloth, extra, black and gold, $1.00.

SHIRLEY. By CHARLOTTE BRONTÉ (Currer Bell). New Library Edition. With five illustrations by E. M. WIMPERIS. 12mo. Cloth, extra, black and gold, $1.00.

VILLETTE. By CHARLOTTE BRONTÉ (Currer Bell). New Library Edition. With five illustrations by E. M. WIMPERIS. 12mo. Cloth, extra, black and gold, $1.00.

THE PROFESSOR, EMMA and POEMS. By CHARLOTTE BRONTÉ (Currer Bell). New Library Edition. With five illustrations by E. M. WIMPERIS. 12mo. Cloth, extra, black and gold, $1.00. Cloth, extra, black and gold, per set, $4.00; red cloth, paper label, gilt top, uncut edges, per set, $5.00; half calf, gilt, per set, $12.00. The four volumes forming the complete works of Charlotte Bronté (Currer Bell).

The wondrous power of Currer Bell's stories consists in their fiery insight into the human heart, their merciless dissection of passion, and their stern analysis of character and motive. The style of these productions possesses incredible force, sometimes almost grim in its bare severity, then relapsing into passages of melting pathos—always direct, natural, and effective in its unpretending strength. They exhibit the identity which always belongs to works of genius by the same author, though without the slightest approach to monotony. The characters portrayed by Currer Bell all have a strongly marked individuality. Once brought before the imagination, they haunt the memory like a strange dream. The sinewy, muscular strength of her writings guarantees their permanent duration, and thus far they have lost nothing of their intensity of interest since the period of their composition.

CAPTAIN JACK THE SCOUT; or, The Indian Wars about Old Fort Duquesne. An Historical Novel, with copious notes. By CHARLES McKNIGHT. Illustrated with eight engravings. 12mo. Cloth, extra, black and gold, $1.50.

A work of such rare merit and thrilling interest as to have been republished both in England and Germany. This genuine American historical work has been received with extraordinary popular favor, and has "won golden opinions" from all sorts of people" for its freshness, its forest life, and its fidelity to truth. In many instances it even corrects History and uses the drapery of fiction simply to enliven and illustrate the fact.

It is a universal favorite with both sexes, and with all ages and conditions, and is not only proving a marked and notable success in this country, but has been eagerly taken up abroad and republished in London, England, and issued in two volumes in the far-famed "Tauchnetz Edition" of Leipsic, Germany.

ORANGE BLOSSOMS, FRESH AND FADED. By T. S. ARTHUR. Illustrated. 12mo. Cloth, extra, black and gold, $1.50.

"Orange Blossoms" contains a number of short stories of society. Like all of Mr. Arthur's works, it has a special moral purpose, and is especially addressed to the young who have just entered the marital experience, whom it pleasantly warns against those social and moral pitfalls into which they may almost innocently plunge.

THE BAR ROOMS AT BRANTLEY; or, The Great Hotel Speculation. By T. S. ARTHUR. Illustrated. 12mo. Cloth, extra, black and gold, $1.50.

"One of the best temperance stories recently issued."—N. Y. Commercial Advertiser.

"Although it is in the form of a novel, its truthful delineation of characters is such that in every village in the land you meet the broken manhood it pictures upon the streets, and look upon sad, tear-dimmed eyes of women and children. The characters are not overdrawn, but are as truthful as an artist's pencil could make them."—Inter-Ocean, Chicago.

EMMA. By JANE AUSTEN. Illustrated. 12mo. Cloth, extra, $1.25.

MANSFIELD PARK. By JANE AUSTEN. Illustrated. 12mo. Cloth, extra, $1.25.

PRIDE AND PREJUDICE; and Northanger Abbey. By JANE AUSTEN. Illustrated. 12mo. Cloth, extra, $1.25.

SENSE AND SENSIBILITY; and Persuasion. By JANE AUSTEN. Illustrated. 12mo. Cloth, extra, $1.25.

The four volumes, forming the complete works of Jane Austen, in a neat box: Cloth, extra, per set, $5.00; red cloth, paper label, gilt top, uncut edges, $5.00; half calf, gilt, per set, $12.00.

"Jane Austen, a woman of whom England is justly proud. In her novels she has given us a multitude of characters, all, in a certain sense, commonplace, all such as we meet every day. Yet they are all as perfectly discriminated from each other as if they were the most eccentric of human beings. . . . . And almost all this is done by touches so delicate that they elude analysis, that they defy the powers of description, and that we know them to exist only by the general effect to which they have contributed."—*Macaulay's Essays.*

ART AT HOME. Containing in one volume House Decoration, by RHODA and AGNES GARRETT; Plea for Art in the House, by W. J. LOFTIE; Music, by JOHN HULLAH; and Dress, by Mrs. OLIPHANT. 12mo. Cloth, extra, black and gold, $1.50.

TOM BROWN'S SCHOOL DAYS AT RUGBY. By THOMAS HUGHES. New Edition, large clear type. With 36 illustrations after Caldecott and others. 12mo., 400 pp. Cloth, extra, black and gold, $1.25; half calf, gilt, $2.75.
Alta Edition. One illustration, 75 cents.

"It is difficult to estimate the amount of good which may be done by 'Tom Brown's School Days.' It gives, in the main, a most faithful and interesting picture of our public schools, the most English institutions of England, and which educate the best and most powerful elements in our upper classes. But it is more than this; it is an attempt, a very noble and successful attempt, to Christianize the society of our youth, through the only practicable channel—hearty and brotherly sympathy with their feelings; a book, in short, which a father might well wish to see in the hands of his son."—*London Times.*

TOM BROWN AT OXFORD. By THOMAS HUGHES. Illustrated. 12mo. Cloth, extra, black and gold, $1.50; half calf, gilt, $3.00.

"Fairly entitled to the rank and dignity of an English classic. Plot, style and truthfulness are of the soundest British character. Racy, idiomatic, mirror-like, always interesting, suggesting thought on the knottiest social and religious questions, now deeply moving by its unconscious pathos, and anon inspiring uproarious laughter, it is a work the world will not willingly let die."—*N. Y. Christian Advocate.*

SENSIBLE ETIQUETTE OF THE BEST SOCIETY. By Mrs. H. O. WARD. Customs, manners, morals, and home culture, with suggestions how to word notes and letters of invitations, acceptances, and regrets, and general instructions as to calls, rules for watering places, lunches, kettle drums, dinners, receptions, weddings, parties, dress, toilet and manners, salutations, introductions, social reforms, etc., etc. Bound in cloth, with gilt edge, and sent by mail, postage paid, on receipt of $2.00.

LADIES' AND GENTLEMEN'S ETIQUETTE: A Complete Manual of the Manners and Dress of American Society. Containing forms of Letters, Invitations, Acceptances, and Regrets. With a copious index. By E. B. DUFFEY. 12mo. Cloth, extra, black and gold, $1.50.

"It is peculiarly an American book, especially adapted to our people, and its greatest beauty is found in the fact that in every line and precept it inculcates the principles of true politeness, instead of those formal rules that serve only to gild the surface without affecting the substance. It is admirably written, the style being clear, terse, and forcible."—*St. Louis Times.*

THE UNDERGROUND CITY; or, The Child of the Cavern. By JULES VERNE. Translated from the French by W. H. KINGSTON. With 43 illustrations. Standard Edition. 12mo. Cloth, extra, black and gold, $1.50.

AROUND THE WORLD IN EIGHTY DAYS. By JULES VERNE. Translated by GEO. M. TOWLE. With 12 full-page illustrations. 12mo. Cloth, extra, black and gold, $1.25.

AT THE NORTH POLE; or, The Voyages and Adventures of Captain Hatteras. By JULES VERNE. With 130 illustrations by RIOU. Standard Edition. 12mo. Cloth, extra, black and gold, $1.25.

THE DESERT OF ICE; or, The Further Adventures of Captain Hatteras. By JULES VERNE. With 126 illustrations by RIOU. Standard Edition. 12mo. Cloth, extra, black and gold, $1.25.

TWENTY THOUSAND LEAGUES UNDER THE SEAS; or, The Marvellous and Exciting Adventures of Pierre Aronnax, Conseil his servant, and Ned Land, a Canadian Harpooner. By JULES VERNE. Standard Edition. Illustrated. 12mo. Cloth, extra, black and gold, $1.25.

THE WRECK OF THE CHANCELLOR. Diary of J. R. Kazallon, Passenger, and Martin Paz. By JULES VERNE. Translated from the French by ELLEN FREWER. With 10 illustrations. Standard Edition. 12mo. Cloth, extra, black and gold, $1.25.

Jules Verne is so well known that the mere announcement of anything from his pen is sufficient to create a demand for it. One of his chief merits is the wonderful art with which he lays under contribution every branch of science and natural history, while he vividly describes with minute exactness all parts of the world and its inhabitants.

THE INGOLDSBY LEGENDS; or, Mirth and Marvels. By RICHARD HARRIS BARHAM (Thomas Ingoldsby, Esq.). New edition, printed from entirely new stereotype plates. Illustrated. 12mo. Cloth, extra, black and gold, $1.50; half calf, gilt, marbled edges, $3.00.

"Of his poetical powers it is not too much to say that, for originality of design and diction, for grand illustration and musical verse, they are not surpassed in the English language. The Witches' Frolic is second only to Tam O'Shanter. But why recapitulate the titles of either prose or verse—since they have been confessed by every judgment to be singularly rich in classic allusion and modern illustration. From the days of Hudibras to our time the drollery invested in rhymes has never been so amply or felicitously exemplified."—*Bentley's Miscellany.*

TEN THOUSAND A YEAR. By SAMUEL C. WARREN, author of "The Diary of a London Physician." A new edition, carefully revised, with three illustrations by GEORGE G. WHITE. 12mo. Cloth, extra, black and gold, $1 50.

"Mr. Warren has taken a lasting place among the imaginative writers of this period of English history. He possesses, in a remarkable manner, the tenderness of heart and vividness of feeling, as well as powers of description, which are essential to the delineation of the pathetic, and which, when existing in the degree in which he enjoys them, fill his pages with scenes which can never be forgotten."—*Sir Archibald Alison.*

THOMPSON'S POLITICAL ECONOMY; With Especial Reference to the Industrial History of Nations. By Prof. R. E. THOMPSON, of the University of Pennsylvania. 12mo. Cloth, extra, $1.50.

This book possesses an especial interest at the present moment. The questions of Free Trade and Protection are before the country more directly than at any earlier period of our history. As a rule the works and textbooks used in our American colleges are either of English origin or teach Doctrines of a political economy which, as Walter Bagehot says, was made for England. Prof. Thompson belongs to the Nationalist School of Economists, to which Alexander Hamilton, Tench Coxe, Henry Clay, Matthew Carey, and his greater son, Henry C. Carey, Stephen Colwell, and James Abram Garfield were adherents. He believes in that policy of Protection to American industry which has had the sanction of every great American statesman, not excepting Thomas Jefferson and John C. Calhoun. He makes his appeal to history in defence of that policy, showing that wherever a weaker or less advanced country has practiced Free Trade with one more powerful or richer, the former has lost its industries as well as its money, and has become economically dependent on the latter. Those who wish to learn what is the real source of Irish poverty and discontent will find it here stated fully.

The method of the book is historical. It is therefore no series of dry and abstract reasonings, such as repel readers from books of this class. The writer does not ride the *a priori* nag, and say "this must be so," and "that must be conceded." He shows what has been true, and seeks to elicit the laws of the science from the experience of the world. The book overflows with facts told in an interesting manner.

THE ENGLISH PEOPLE IN ITS THREE HOMES, and the Practical Bearings of general European History. By EDWARD A. FREEMAN, LL.D., Author of the "Norman Conquest of England." 12mo. Cloth, extra, $1.75.

HANDY ANDY. A Tale of Irish Life. By SAMUEL LOVER. New Library Edition, with two original illustrations by GEORGE G. WHITE. 12mo. Cloth, extra, black and gold, $1.25.

"Decidedly the best story of the day, full of frolic, genuine fun, and exquisite touches of Irish humor."—*Dublin Monitor.*

CHARLES O'MALLEY, The Irish Dragoon. By CHARLES LEVER. New Library Edition, with two original illustrations by F. O. C. DARLEY. 12mo. Cloth, extra, black and gold, $1.25.

HARRY LORREQUER. By CHARLES LEVER. New Library Edition, with two original illustrations by GEO. G. WHITE. 12mo. Cloth, extra, black and gold, $1.25.

"The intense spirit and frolic of the author's sketches have made him one of the most successful writers of the day."—*London Literary Gazette.*

"The author is pre-eminent for his mirth-moving powers, for his acute sense of the ridiculous, for the breadth of his humor, and his powers of dramatic writing which render his boldest conceptions with the happiest facility."—*London Athenæum.*

"We hardly know how to convey an adequate notion of the exuberant whim and drollery by which this writer is characterized. His works are a perpetual feast of gayety."—*John Bull, London.*

POPULAR NATURAL HISTORY. By the Rev. J. G. WOOD, M.A. From entirely new electrotype plates, with five hundred illustrations by eminent artists. Crown 8vo. Cloth, extra, black and gold, $1.75.

Mr. Wood is an amusing, instructive, and sensible writer—always doing good work in a good way—and his work on Natural History is without doubt his masterpiece.

THE ODES OF HORACE. Translated into English verse, with Life and Notes, by THEODORE MARTIN. With a fine portrait of Horace. 16mo. Cloth, extra, $1.00.

Mr. Martin's translation has been commended as preserving—more than any other—the spirit and grace of the original. It is the most successful attempt ever made to render into English the inimitable odes of Horace. The memoir prefixed to the volume is a most charming piece of biography.

GREEK MYTHOLOGY SYSTEMATIZED. With complete Tables based on Hesiod's Theogony; Tables showing the relation of Greek Mythology and History, arranged from Grote's History of Greece; and Gladstone's Homeric Tables. With a full Index. By S. A. SCULL. Profusely illustrated. 12mo. Cloth, black and gold, $1.50.

"A book which will prove very useful to the student and man of letters, and of incalculable benefit as a hand-book."—*Republic, Washington.*

"A real want is supplied by this book, which is, in fact, a cyclopædia of Greek Mythology, so far as that is possible in a single volume of reasonable size and moderate cost."—*Evening Mail, New York.*

"This text-book on Mythology presents the subject in a more practical and more attractive style than any other work on the subject with which we are familiar, and we feel assured that it will at once take a leading position among books of its class."—*The Teacher, Philadelphia.*

THE IMITATION OF CHRIST. By Thomas a Kempis. New
and best edition, from entirely new electrotype plates, single
column, large, clear type. 18mo.
Plain Edition, round corners. Cloth, extra, red edges, 50 cents;
French morocco, gilt cross, 75 cents; limp Russia, inlaid cross, red
under gold edges, $2.00.
Red Line Edition, round corners. Cloth, black and gold, red
edges, 75 cents; cloth, black and gold, gilt edges, $1.00; French
morocco, red under gold edges, $1.50; limp Russia, inlaid cross, red
under gold edges, $2.50; limp Russia, solid gilt edges, box circuit,
$3.00; limp calf, red under gold edges, $2.50; limp calf, solid gilt
edges, box circuit, $3.00.

THE WORDS AND MIND OF JESUS AND FAITHFUL PROM-
ISER. By Rev. J. R. Macduff, D.D., author of "Morning and
Night Watches." New and best edition, from entirely new
electrotype plates. single column, large, clear type. 18mo.
Plain Edition, round corners. Cloth, extra, red edges, 50 cents;
French morocco, gilt cross, 75 cents; limp Russia, inlaid cross, red
under gold edges, $2.00.
Red Line Edition, round corners. Cloth, black and gold, red
edges, 75 cents; cloth, black and gold, gilt edges, $1.00; limp calf
or Russia, red under gold edges, $2.50.

A DICTIONARY OF THE BIBLE. Comprising its Antiquities,
Biography, Geography, Natural History, and Literature.
Edited by William Smith, LL.D. Revised and adapted to
the present use of Sunday-school Teachers and Bible Students
by Rev. F. N. and M. A. Peloubet. With eight colored maps
and over 350 engravings on wood. 8vo. Cloth, extra, black
and gold, $2.00; sheep, marbled edges, $3.00; half morocco,
gilt top, $3 50.
"No similar work in our own or in any other language is for a moment to
be compared with Dr. Smith's Dictionary of the Bible. The Christian and
the scholar have a treasure-house on every subject connected with the
Bible, full to overflowing, and minute even to the telling of mint and cum-
min."—*London Quarterly Review.*

COMPREHENSIVE BIOGRAPHICAL DICTIONARY. Embra-
cing accounts of the most eminent persons of all ages, nations,
and professions. By E. A. Thomas. Crown 8vo. Cloth, extra,
gilt top, $2.50; sheep, marbled edges, $3.00; half morocco, gilt
top, $3.50; half Russia, gilt top, $4.50.
The aim of the publishers in issuing this work is to present in convenient
size and at moderate price a comprehensive dictionary of biography, em-
bracing accounts of the most eminent personages in all ages, countries, and
professions.
During the last quarter of a century so many important events have been
enacted, such as the Civil War in America and the Franco-Prussian War of
1870, and such great advances have been made in the line of invention and
scientific investigation, that within that period many persons have risen by
superior merit to conspicuous positions; and as the plan of this work embraces accounts of the living as well as of the dead, many names are included that are not to be found in other dictionaries of biography.

THE HORSE IN THE STABLE AND THE FIELD. His Management in Health and Disease. By J. H. WALSH, F.R.C.S.
(Stonehenge.)   From the last London edition.   Illustrated
with over 80 engravings, and full-page engravings from photo-
graphs. 12mo. Cloth, extra, bev. boards, black and gold, $2.00.

"It sustains its claim to be the only work which has brought together in
a single volume, and in clear, concise, and comprehensive language, adequate
information on the various subjects on which it treats."—*Harper's Magazine.*
"This is the best English book on the horse, revised and improved by
competent persons for publication in this country. It is the most complete
work on the subject, probably, in the English language, and that, of course,
means the most complete in existence. Everything relating to a horse that
history, science, observation, or practical knowledge can furnish, has a place
in it."—*Worcester Daily Spy.*

THE HORSE. By WILLIAM YOUATT, together with a General
History of the Horse; a dissertation on the American Trotting
Horse, and an essay on the Ass and the Mule. By J. S. SKIN-
NER. With a beautiful engraving on steel of the famous
"West Australian," and 58 illustrations on wood. 8vo. Cloth,
extra, black and gold, $1.75.

BOOK OF THE FARM. The Handy-book of Husbandry. Containing Practical Information in Regard to Buying or Leasing
a Farm; Fences and Farm Buildings, Farming Implements,
Drainage, Plowing, Subsoiling, Manuring, Rotation of Crops,
Care and Medical Treatment of the Cattle, Sheep, and Poul-
try; Management of the Dairy; Useful Tables, etc. By
GEORGE E. WARING, JR., of Ogden Farm, author of "Drain-
ing for Profit and for Health," etc. New edition, thoroughly
revised by the author. With 100 illustrations. 12mo. Cloth,
extra, black and gold, $2.00.

AMERICAN ORNITHOLOGY; or, The Natural History of the
Birds of the United States. By ALEXANDER WILSON and
CHARLES LUCIEN BONAPARTE. Popular Edition, complete in
one volume imperial octavo. 1200 pages and nearly 400 illustrations of birds. Formerly published at $100; now published
at the low price: Cloth, extra, black and gold, $7.50; half
morocco, marbled edges, $12.50.

This large and handsome volume, printed in a superior manner on good
paper from the original stereotype plates of the larger edition, contains the
Life of Wilson, occupying 132 pages; a full Catalogue of North American
Birds, furnished by Professor Spencer F. Baird, of the Smithsonian Institution; Complete Index, with the names of over 900 birds described in the
text, and is illustrated with nearly 400 figures of birds engraved on wood.
It is exactly the same size as the larger edition, with the exception that the
engravings are reduced in size and are not colored, reproducing every line
of the original edition. It is one of the best books of permanent value
(strictly an American book) ever published, noted for its beauty of diction
and power of description, pre-eminent as the ablest work on Ornithology,
and now published at a moderate price, that places it within the reach of
all. Every lover of birds, every school, public or family library should
have this book. We know of no other way in which so much pleasure, so
much information, and so much usefulness can be had for the price.

AMERICAN CHESS PLAYER'S HAND-BOOK. Teaching the
Rudiments of the Game, and giving an Analysis of all the
recognized openings. Exemplified by appropriate Games act-
ually played by Paul Morphy, Harrwitz, Anderssen, Staunton,
Paulsen, Montgomery, Meek, and others. From the works of
Staunton and others. Illustrated. 16mo. Cloth, extra, $1.25.

AMERICAN GARDENER'S ASSISTANT. Containing complete
Practical Directions for the Cultivation of Vegetables, Flowers,
Fruit Trees, and Grape Vines. By THOMAS BRIDGMAN. New
edition, revised and enlarged, by S. EDWARDS TODD. With
70 illustrations. 12mo. Cloth, extra, black and gold, $2.00.

DISEASES OF THE HORSE, AND HOW TO TREAT THEM.
A concise Manual of Special Pathology, for the use of Horsemen, Farmers, Stock Raisers, and Students in Agricultural
Colleges. By ROBERT CHAWNER. Illustrated. 12mo. Cloth,
extra, black and gold, $1.25.

JERSEY, ALDERNEY, AND GUERNSEY COWS. Their History, Nature, and Management. Edited from the writings of
Edward P. Fowler, George E. Waring, Jr., Charles L. Sharp-
less, Prof. John Gamgee, C. P. Le Cornu, Col. Le Couteur,
Prof. Magne, Fr. Guenon, Dr. Twaddell, and others, by
WILLIS P. HAZARD. 8vo. Illustrated with about 30 engravings, diagrams, etc. Cloth, extra, black and gold, $1.50.

THE TROTTING HORSE OF AMERICA. How to Train and
Drive him, with Reminiscences of the Trotting Turf. By
HIRAM WOODRUFF. Edited by CHARLES J. FOSTER. Including an Introductory Notice by GEORGE WILKES, and a Biographical Sketch by the Editor. 20th edition, revised and
brought down to 1878, and containing a full account of the
famous "Rarus." With a steel portrait of the author, and six
engravings on wood of celebrated trotters. 12mo. Cloth,
extra, black and gold, $2.50.

PORTER & COATES' INTEREST TABLES. Containing accurate
calculations of interest at ½, 1, 2, 3, 3½, 4, 4½, 5, 6, 7, 8 and 10 per
cent. per annum, on all sums from $1.00 to $10,000, and from
one day to six years. Also some very valuable tables, calculated by John E. Coffin. 8vo. Cloth, extra, $1.00.

READY RECKONER (The Improved,) FORM AND LOGBOOK.
The Trader's, Farmer's and Merchant's useful assistant. Con-
taining Tables of Values, Wages, Interest, Scantling, Board,
Plank and Log Measurements, Business Forms, etc. 18mo.
Boards, cloth back, illustrated cover, 25 cents.